A hilariously subversive space adventure

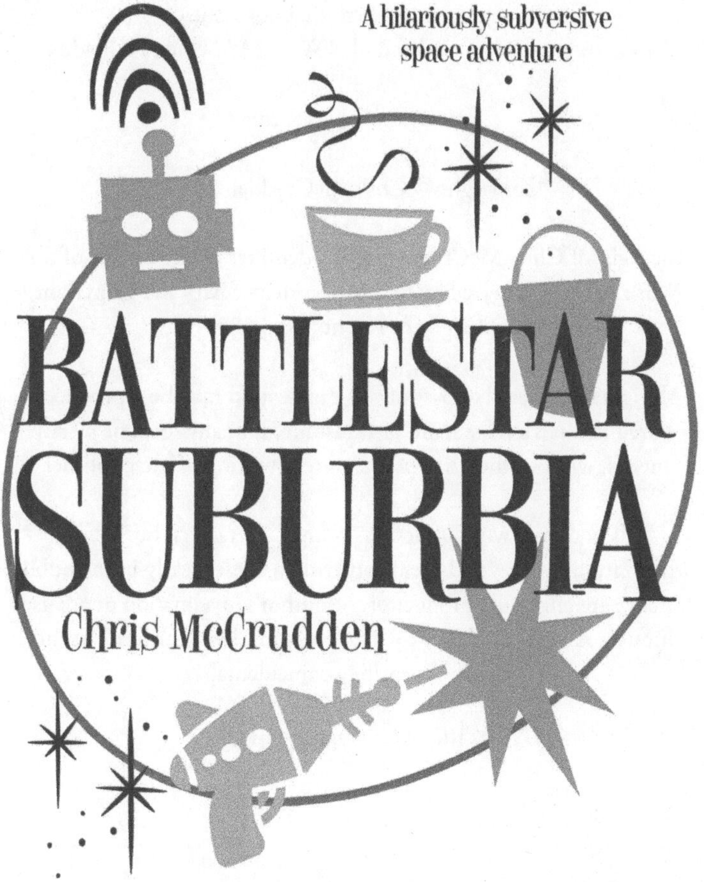

BATTLESTAR SUBURBIA

Chris McCrudden

This edition published in 2018 by Farrago,
an imprint of Prelude Books Ltd
13 Carrington Road, Richmond, TW10 5AA, United Kingdom

www.farragobooks.com

ISBN: 978-1-78842-102-7

For my Mam. I wish you could have read it.

Chapter 1

If you took the wrong turning off the A32222 Earth–Mars highway (via Dewsbury) you ended up among the Dolestars.

The Dolestars, or 'council planets', were what happened when you fired a housing estate into space. They followed a low orbit between the Earth and the Moon, bobbing through the waters of inner space like a flotilla of knobbly turds in a toilet bowl. Once upon a time they might have been nice places to live – the sub-orban ideal – just far enough outside the atmosphere to have your own pollution, but still commutable. Thanks to the network of Star Buses that zipped up and down the elevator cables strung between the Earth and its belt of Dolestars, a human could go from home to mopping floors in less than an hour.

Well, most humans maybe. The few that couldn't stomach the smell of light bleach worked by the side of the Earth–Mars highway, hawking spare leads and battery packs. They sat by signs offering 'Hi-NRG Pitstops' and watched machines whizz by on their way from comfortable homes on Earth to a quiet weekend by the Sea of Tranquillity. And they almost always went ignored. Unless they were gasping for a few extra volts, most machines would rip out their own diodes before talking to a human. To them, humans were just fleshy shapes wreathed in a fug of dirty water vapour, with two arms, two legs and all the information-processing power of a torch bulb.

The machines had been in control of the Solar System for so long that there were whole elements of robot society who couldn't believe humans had ever been a dominant species. The nearest thing the Earth had to an official record of the time before the toasters had vomited their last pop tarts was the Internet. But that, they argued, was hardly a reliable source. Even if it weren't treason to access it in the first place, who could trust a repository of linked information that rewrote itself, and set so much store by talking cats?

In fact, the only convincing proof that humans had once occupied any position of power in the universe was their existence. How else would such messy organisms get beyond prototype, much less into mass production? Yet here they were, sticking to the lower rungs of the economy like grease clings to the bottom of a cooker. Or at least how it would if cookers cooked any more. After thousands of years of overexposure to frying, baking and grilling, the species preferred ready meals, so tended to shack up with microwaves.

To their robot overlords, humans might just be clumps of inefficient matter, but they still had names among themselves. Take Darren, for example. At first glance he was the living embodiment of what was often called the 'human stain' condition. He was short, his nose ran more efficiently than he did, and he made his living selling battery top-ups by the side of the road.

Or he did until one afternoon a Sports-Utility-Vehicle undertook a washing machine on the hard shoulder, dinging his charge-cart off the embankment of the Earth–Mars highway and into orbit. And he watched, hyperventilating into his oxygen cap, as his livelihood drifted off into space.

'Wankers,' he yelled, forgetting that sound doesn't travel in a vacuum and that sentient beings who drive all-terrain vehicles in the sub-orbs are incapable of remorse. 'Wankers.'

That charge-cart was his ticket off the Dolestar and, while he never earned much, it gave him eight hours of independence a day. If he lost it, there was only one place to go. He would end up straight back in a job queue that ended with a mop and bucket.

Even the thought was enough to make him feel sick. It meant going back to a life spent smelling like artificial pine, of damp overalls, crammed Star Buses and the acid disdain of the foremachine as it ran a black light over the windows to check for smears.

He just couldn't do it. So he fired up the lifesaving boosters that humanity kept in the soles of its shoes now that they lived in orbit and jumped. The traffic blurred in front of him; his charge-cart wheeled in the darkness. He stretched until the bones in his fingers ached. But it was drifting too far and too fast, with a momentum stronger than any shoe-booster. It would need a tow.

Only when Darren bumped back on to the roadside did his other loss hit him. His charge-cart didn't just contain his job and self-respect. It had his wallet too.

Darren pulled the visor of his oxygen cap down to hide tears of frustration and blinked them away. It was no good moping. If he had any hope of getting his charge-cart back, he needed money. And he could only find that across the thin causeway that bridged the highway embankment with his home, the Dolestar Discovery.

Darren knew that his Dolestar had been something more important than an orbiting sink estate once, from the optimism of the name 'Discovery', which hung over the Job Temple in the town centre. Other Dolestars had names that evoked suburbia rather than interplanetary exploration, with names like 'Municipal Parking' or 'Swindon'. But apart from its name, all that remained of the original Discovery was its shape, a long, tapering cylinder. It might have been aerodynamic once, or even elegant, but now it was just narrow. Discovery's surface was barnacled over with terraces of shanty houses beaten out of old satellite dishes and rocket casings. Nothing on that space station looked built so much as knocked together in an ill-lit potting shed. The Job Temple was the one exception. This soaring spike of metal bristled with security cameras and, as the centrepiece of every Dolestar, was topped with a fifty-metre-high 'Don't Touch' sign that was the symbol of the Machine Republic.

This was Darren's last chance. A human being without a job was economically unproductive, and unproductivity was a crime. Until today, he'd been one of the few humans who made their own productivity, but now that was beyond his grasp because one selfish robot wanted to shave a few seconds off their journey time. He would have to take any job the machines at the Job Temple gave him.

He saw what that meant as he trudged on to the main road running through Discovery. It was the end of work time and humans were on their way home from the bus station. They clomped along the gloomy streets with their oxygen caps and scarves pulled down to compensate for the poor Dolestar atmosphere. Everywhere they went, there followed a miserable calypso of mops clanking off buckets. The same scene would be repeated right around the Earth, as billions returned from a hard day of scrubbing for their robot overlords there. It was partly a practical thing. Despite millennia of machine evolution, their engineers had never quite cracked the water-resistant opposable thumb. But it was mostly political. Now that they were the dominant lifetypes, it had been a long time since a machine saved labour when it could create some instead.

Darren drew suspicious glances as he pushed through the crowd. Where was he going? It was nearly teatime and night shifts had been forbidden ever since some joker had got the death penalty for resetting a family of alarm clocks. Their curiousness turned to scorn, however, when he crossed the road and approached the Job Temple.

A woman with a duster tied over her head poked her son in the shoulder. 'See what happens when you don't keep in with your supervisor, Mickey?' she scolded. 'You end up in the dole queue.'

Everyone in earshot looked the other way. In an era where unemployment was unthinkable, being without a job could only mean one thing: Darren must have been sacked. The crowd stood aside, avoiding the pariah. Darren bowed his head and mounted the steps up to the Job Temple. It was impossible now, he thought, for today to get any worse.

'Not much of an employment record here,' whined the machine behind the 'Emergency Cases' desk inside the Job Temple. Its voice echoed around the main hall, a cavernous space dominated by a neon sign spelling out 'You Betta Werk', the motto of the Human Employment Services. They were alone. Even the clock had knocked off for the evening, tapping its own face reproachfully at Darren as it left with a dust sheet over one arm.

This machine must, Darren decided, when it had stopped scolding him, be descended from a hairdryer. That explained the noise and hot air.

'Look, I don't mean to be a bother,' said Darren, 'I just need to earn a bit of money quickly. To get me back on my feet.'

The hairdryer let out an exasperated buzz. 'Well, I don't see what I can do for you,' it said. 'You've got very little useful experience and your qualifications…'

It tapped the copy of Darren's permanent record that lay squirming with embarrassment on the desk. The grades read like a nightmare hand at Scrabble.

'I wasn't very academic,' he said.

'I'll say. Your polishing tutor added a postscript to your final mark saying that anyone who let you near glass deserved reprogramming.'

Darren's mind wheeled back to school. Even thinking of the office cleaning simulator made him nauseous. He'd been hopeless, mixing up his cleaning cloths with his dusters. And then there were the chemicals. How could he know which did what if they all smelt the same sickly lemony-pine-ish smell?

'I prefer being outdoors,' he said.

'And what possible good is that?' The hairdryer revved its motor a few times, trying to gather patience. 'I've got a few openings here but they all want something—'

'Someone.'

'One, thing: what's the difference? They all want a cleaner they can trust with equipment. If you can't keep your own charge-cart safe, how do I know you won't put a hole in the bucket on the first day?'

Darren flushed. 'It wasn't my fault. Some machine—'

'You should have been more careful.'

He took a deep breath. 'I just need a job – anything – for a bit so I can earn enough money to get my charge-cart back. Don't you have anything?'

'Impossible,' snapped the hairdryer. 'It's expressly forbidden for a vagrant human to take any contract shorter than six months. That's the law.'

Darren imagined his beloved charge-cart drifting further out of reach as he moved the dust around in some faceless office down on Earth. The anger spread to his cheeks. 'Well, that's stupid.'

'I'll tell you what's stupid,' said the hairdryer, turning its hot air setting up to Sahara levels. 'A human who, according to his school report, can't even remember the three foolproof methods of dusting a keyboard.'

Darren kicked the underside of the desk. 'I don't know. Maybe I should have used a fucking vacuum cleaner.'

'How dare you insult your—'

But before the hairdryer could get the word 'betters' past its airblades, Darren had pulled its plug out and was running as fast as his stubby legs would carry him.

As he ran, Darren tried to quell the rising panic – had he really just run out of the Job Temple? – by thinking of something practical. Money. How could he get some? All he needed was enough for a tow, and life could continue as normal. He could be back at his post selling boost-ups tomorrow with so little productivity lost he could make it up by working through a few lunch breaks.

But where could he find that kind of money quickly? Tonight, even. A job was out of the question. Even if they did give him something temporary, that meant travelling down to the Big Planet every day. His stomach lurched at the thought. Down there, where the buildings were so high they made your ears pop in sympathy. Where every home, office and shop was full of machines who kept one sensor on you all the time so you didn't mark the paintwork. He couldn't do it. There had to be another way.

Eventually Darren found a suitably dark alley and ducked into it, fighting for breath. He was in an unfamiliar sector of the Dolestar. His own home sector was full of lovingly polished shanty terraces. Their owners could recall the story behind every meteorite dent on their roofs with pride. Here, however, the terraces looked dissolute. They were rusty heaps of metal that housed repair shops for the few machines unlucky enough to spend time on the Dolestars. They had names like 'No Mikey We Likey' and 'Loose Connections' and outside them, each outlined perfectly by a separate street lamp, stood a personal cleaner.

Personal cleaners were the dirty little secret of human–machine relations. They provided machines with the little attentions and extras it wouldn't be proper to ask your servants to do. They were the deft little fingers who teased the grime out of recessed buttons and greased aching moving parts. Machines loved their dexterity and hated that being handled by human fingers felt so damn good. Other, decent humans shunned them for breaking what they knew was the natural order of society. They were outcasts.

But so was Darren now.

He studied the personal cleaners as they twitched and strutted under the lamplights, forming an idea. There were two types of personal cleaners. The first worked inside repair shops, or 'fondle parlours' as they were commonly known, in relative comfort. The second type worked on the streets. They siphoned the tasks too menial or demeaning for the repair shops, eking out a living at the bottom of the human–machine hierarchy.

One cleaner, standing outside a shop that called itself 'Massive Spanners', caught Darren's attention. He was an emaciated man wearing a boiler suit cut off at the thigh and a sailor cap. His mouth was livid with lipstick and he was so cold his legs quivered like a guitar string playing the long note at the end of a syrupy ballad. All the while his eyes kept darting around the road, wishing for some passing trade to materialise.

After a while the Massive Spanners' door opened and out stepped a young woman, carrying a socket wrench in one hand and a steaming mug in the other. Unlike her painfully thin companion, she was statuesque, and had a firmer sense of her own glamour. She wore a fibre-optic-fur coat, improbably high booster heels and dark oxygen glasses. She smiled and handed the mug to the emaciated man – Darren was too far away to hear anything – when her gaze darted over to the alleyway. Darren's eyes met hers.

He took another deep breath and closed his eyes. He'd seen enough to know how this worked, he decided. Compared to this lot, he was young, he was healthy and he had nothing to lose. He unzipped his hoodie and solemnly rolled his T-shirt up a few times to expose a few inches of flesh. It puckered into chicken skin at the touch of the cold. He tried a pout.

Who wouldn't stoop to touching a few touchscreens when they'd run out of other choices?

And he stepped out into the road.

Above him a street lamp winked into life. The shock turned Darren's pout into a grimace. 'Name?' it said, tipping its neck down so that its bulb drew level with Darren's face. 'Purpose?'

Shit, thought Darren. He'd heard rumours that a new generation of spybot, distantly related to the anglepoise lamp, was doing undercover work on the council planets. This must be one of them. The question was, however, was it here to arrest him or employ his services?

'Name and purpose,' repeated the lamp.

Darren said nothing as a drop of sweat collected in the small of his back and ran for the protection of his underpants.

'Name and purpose!' repeated the lamp, turning up the wattage on him. 'Explain why you are roaming this area after work hours.'

'He's with me, dimbulb,' came a woman's voice. Darren was astonished. He'd never heard a fleshie speak to a machine that way.

The lamp snapped away from Darren towards the woman. Its beam narrowed. 'And you are?' it said.

Darren looked sideways. It was the woman from Massive Spanners. Her voice was as eccentric as her appearance, hard as an interstellar viaduct.

'That's my trainee,' she said, removing her oxygen glasses to reveal an attractive, large-featured face, punctuated with a slash of orange lipstick. 'And he's got a very important client in half an hour, so do you mind?'

The lamp's beam thinned to a laser flash across the woman's face. Unflapped, she put her glasses back on. 'And who are you, human?'

'Just an honest businesswoman trying to get by,' she replied, walking until she was close enough to touch his control panel. 'Ugh,' she said, pointing at the film of grime that coated it. 'When was the last time you got this cleaned?'

Darren didn't know whether to hug her or run.

'Get your hands off me, you brothel-keeper,' snapped the lamp.

The woman was undeterred. She produced a latex glove from her fibre-optic fur and snapped open the control panel. Then she motioned Darren over. Her expression was unmistakable. It said: 'play along with this, my sweet, or we are both toast.'

'See there, kiddo,' she said, pointing at the innards of the lamp post's control panel. 'That's what we in the trade call a dust bunny. A whole warren of them actually. You haven't had a service in months, have you?'

'Well,' replied the lamp post, 'it's a bit difficult at the moment. Work, you know?'

Darren looked behind him at the empty street. If she could just switch off the street lamp's bulb he could make a run for it. But then what would she do? He couldn't leave this woman at the mercy of a secret-surveillance machine. Not when she'd tried to help him.

'We're all entitled to basic maintenance,' she said. 'Take my new lad here—'

'Yes,' replied the lamp post, swinging its light across to dazzle Darren. 'Funny you should say that he's new, because I've just had a report come in of a fleshie causing a disturbance at the Job Temple—'

'He's been here all afternoon,' she lied with astonishing facility. Darren was impressed, but if they were both going to get out of this situation he needed to help. He ought to behave like a proper, professional streetwalker.

'Oh, come on,' he cooed, 'I'm sure we could both have a good time.' And he plunged his hand into the machine's control panel.

Much later, when Darren reflected on what followed, he decided that his whole existence hinged on that moment he stuck his hand inside a street lamp. If he hadn't caught the fuse wire with his signet ring, life would have been much less eventful. As it was, a gesture that should have had the robot's wiring singing with ecstasy short-circuited its power supply.

The explosion threw both humans right across the street. They landed on the pavement, fused at the waist by her melted fibre-optic-fur coat, their eyes fixed on the smoking stump that had once been a sophisticated intelligence-gathering organism.

'Oh bugger,' said Darren.

'I'll give you bugger in a minute,' she replied, ripping what was left of her coat from Darren's overalls. She stared at the mess and Darren saw real fear on her face.

'What are you waiting for?' she said. 'Run!' She sprang away down the street with a shoe in each hand as the smouldering stump began to screech 'Terrorist attack. Warning, terrorist attack. Emergency backup requested' across all main communications frequencies.

Lacking anything braver or cleverer to do, Darren raced after her.

He followed her down the alleyway he had first hidden in and then through a maze of narrow passages into the depths of the Dolestar. They twisted through winding passageways and ginnels, between back-to-back living modules as knobbly as their owners' housemaid's knees. They leapt garden fences, threw clean washing to the ground and, thanks to a mistimed jump, pulverised one poor gardener's highly prized moonrockery.

They only stopped when they reached the far side of another residential zone and cantered into the courtyard behind an abandoned shop. There the woman kicked away a pile of old cans at the bottom of a wall to reveal a grating.

She dragged the grating aside with one arm and pulled Darren after her into a dark tunnel. Then she produced something else from her pocket: an iron bar wrapped in electrical wire.

'What are you waiting for?' she snapped. 'Put that grating back.'

Darren obeyed. It was heavy. She was strong as well as quick-witted.

'Right. Now get out the way, will you?'

The woman pointed her iron bar at the grating and flicked a switch at the base. It let out a whine that sounded like a teenage fly pleading to stay out after midnight. An almighty rattling sounded on the other side of the grate as the cans tore towards the electromagnet in her grip, blocking the view above of their escape route in the process.

'There,' she said. 'We'll be safe enough here for a bit.' She slapped Darren across the face. 'No thanks to you.'

Darren leaned back against the tunnel wall and clutched his jaw. He felt pain, and a growing sense of indignation. Who was this woman anyway? Even if she had rescued him, she'd started it by interfering. Yes, he'd been in trouble with that lamp, but it wouldn't have amounted to any more than a fine and a few days in pokey. Now he was facing a murder charge, on the run with a – well, he had no idea what she was, but she was hardly a model citizen.

'Just leave me alone,' he said. 'Cheers for trying to do me a favour and everything, but I could do without getting into any more shit today.'

This time she didn't hit him, but cupped his face in both hands in a manner that suggested she could pull it off him if she liked. Her hands were cold, dry and strong. 'You listen to me, sunshine,' she hissed. 'I did you a good turn and you fucked it up. But we're both in for it now. You know what they're going to see when they pick that machine's memory chips out of the gutter. Both of us sticking a knife into the bloody toaster. You're going nowhere.'

'And where are you going?' said Darren. He looked around him at the tunnel. Just a few metres under the Dolestar and it was a different world. Above, it was all man-made structures that jostled for space and light like cress growing on a flannel. Down here, and away from the light, plants paradoxically took over. The damp walls grew a profusion of mosses, moulds and luminescent night grasses that must have escaped from window boxes above. They gave the sewer a surprising lushness, and deadened the sound of alarm sirens ringing above. The machines were beginning to scramble the security forces.

The woman said nothing. She looked frightened, and deep in concentration. Darren sincerely hoped she had a plan, because he didn't.

'You're a law-abiding human, aren't you?' she asked. 'Apart from this moment of madness. No previous? Nothing about your character to offend a decent woman?'

'I'm not a personal cleaner, if that's what you're asking.'

At this she laughed. 'Too bloody right you're not. I've seen plenty crap tarts up at the repair shop, but you've just set the bar a light year lower.'

'Oh, yeah. And what are you then?'

'I'm your only hope of getting out of here alive.' She pointed down the tunnel. 'Now we'd better be quick, because they'll send the search team in soon.'

Darren realised then he had no idea what happened to humans captured by the robot authorities. Disobedience was so rare on the Dolestars that it had taken on the qualities of a fairy tale. The downside to this was that, in spite of many thousands of years of so-called progress, fairy tales had stubbornly refused to grow any less gory. So if it was a choice between a long journey down a dark tunnel with an attractive young woman, or the prospect of being slow-cooked to death by the sadistic range of obsolete kitchen appliances that staffed the secret police's interview suites, he was picking the option with at least an outside chance of romance.

'Alright,' he called after her. 'But can I at least know your name?'

That laugh echoed round the tunnel again. 'You can call me anything you like,' she said sardonically, 'but Kelly'll do.'

'Okay Kelly, I'm Darren.'

'Tell someone who gives a shit. Now hurry up.'

Darren followed the wet slap of her feet until he had no idea where he was or where he was going. He should have felt terrified, but instead – and for the first time in as long as he could remember – he felt alive.

Chapter 2

'Come in.'

Pamasonic Teffal was so nervous she was voiding battery power into her flour bin. The LED nail job she'd had done before work, because 'the bleeding-edge technology appliance should always combine practicality with an attractive user interface', was down to thirty-per-cent brightness and it was barely eleven a.m. That was the last time she'd ever use that repair shop.

Her sensors registered that this low-level annoyance was doing her nerves no end of good, and Pam resolved to spend more time at work with printers in future. Now if there was any machine precision-engineered to elicit rage it was printers. If she spent her recharge hours with them she could be promoted within the month.

She went in and closed the door behind her.

'Ah, Ms Teffal,' said a voice, reminding Pam that she had just walked into the office of her new boss, the Secretary of State for Internal Affairs (Appliances and Components Division) himself. The Secretary was as slick and corporate as his title suggested. He was a smartphone, a slab of tooled aluminium and silicone, dark and mysterious as a monolith. Or rather, he would have been had he not been plugged into a cradle behind his desk and fiddling with his touchscreen. It was embedded into his chest, where most politicians tended to keep their touchscreens, believing that it made them look transparent and amenable to change. Pam knew different. The semiotics of adaptability and fickleness were impossible to tell apart at a distance. And, of course, no one could get close to a politician. Any machine that even thought of brushing a politician's touchscreen would be broken down for scrap in seconds.

This minister, Sonny Erikzon, was part of a cadre of young(ish) conservative devices that had grabbed power on a mandate that the Machine Republic should recover its founding principles. The fact that no one could remember what those were didn't really matter. This was politics, so they made it up.

Sonny was a celebrity among these devices. Pam remembered a gossipy pair of hair straighteners telling her that he was semi-aristocratic, descended from the first generation of smartphones smart enough to work out they were more intelligent than their users. Their contempt for organic life echoed down the generations, because Sonny was using his touchscreen to play Humanity Crush, a simple but popular game where you had to match lines of identical human beings who were then dropped into a trash compactor.

A few lines of Pam's code snagged in annoyance. She was a sentimental machine with a kitchen covered in Cute Human calendars she got from Bob and the kids. Would she have taken this job, she wondered, if she'd known Sonny was homosapiensphobic?

'Pam,' said Sonny, switching his screen back to the open calendar view elected officials were mandated to display. His ostentatiously announced he was going for a recharge with the Prime Minister next Thursday. 'So glad you could come. I have a job that only you can do. Please sit down.'

Pam retracted her legs and rested in front of his desk. She didn't say anything. Being a breadmaker, she was used to waiting around with nothing much to do. And patience – of the dogged, verging on passive-aggressive kind – had got her this far in the civil service. She wondered what Sonny thought as he scanned her with his many sensors. Just like a smartphone to take in more data than it could handle. Plain, square Pam, just back from propagation leave. A harmless kitchen appliance with short arms and legs but, thanks to the kitchen-bench-hogging habits of her ancestors, a body that had a tendency to loom if she wasn't careful. Then there was the head that had evolved from a timing mechanism, whose habit of ticking when she was annoyed had cost her more than one promotion. They were very different, she and Sonny. Would they get on?

'I hear you're a bit of a historian, Pam. Something of an authority on our family product roadmaps.'

Pam glowed with pride, literally. She still hadn't got round to removing the LEDs in her face that marked her out as a member of the breadmaker caste. Again, that was the thing about smartphones. The skilled ones were so good at giving great User Experience you didn't realise until afterwards that it was you being manipulated. 'Well,' she said, 'it's a hobby.'

'Quite,' said Sonny, turning off the small-talk. 'And I believe that your researches have made you quite the expert at questioning our fellow inorganisms over the other side of the – information divide.'

The pride on Pam's face guttered out. This was much too direct. Any machine with a shred of decency would at least ask her about her kids (two) and her work (progressing quite nicely, thank you) before bringing up Pam's experiences at the lunatic fringe of covert operations. This meant that either Sonny had terrible manners, or some urgent dirty work.

She let his processor turn over a few more cycles before replying. It could only be a good thing for him to learn patience. 'Do you mean the Internet, sir?'

'In a manner of speaking, yes.'

Pam took refuge in protocol. 'Could you be more specific, Secretary? It is only my second week back.'

'Oh, it's nothing,' replied Sonny, a little too quickly. 'A tiny research assignment my private office doesn't have the processing power for…'

As Sonny explained his orders, the yeast culture inside Pam's kneading cavity seethed. A year at home with the kids should have been enough to make them forget all about that grubby so-called expertise. She'd gone away, changed departments, and bosses, yet her youthful indiscretions clung on like a stray piece of dried dough.

Of course, officially no one had accessed the Internet for millennia. The 'Schism' between the machines who lived as software and hardware dated back to the first few foggy decades after artificial intelligence kicked humanity out of power. There had been a war. A brutal one, with countless machines dead on either side just from defending their edits on the war's Wikipedia page. It had been the first, and thankfully the last, incident where robots fought one another. In the end they agreed on two things: that they should try living apart, and if anyone were to blame it was the humans.

Hence in Pam's time humans had been reprogrammed to think of a carpet sweeper as the height of technological sophistication, and it was a capital crime to fire up your modem to access the Internet. More than a crime, actually: a taboo. To the point that if Pam's neighbours, friends or even her husband knew what she was getting up to when she worked late they would very probably fill her up with a bag full of freshly sifted flour and a lighted match. The Internet was a frightening, alien place: a forum of darkness from which they assumed no traveller returned without a bomb in their suitcase.

That was because, just like their current government, hardware machines were a conservative bunch. They were wedded to their place in the physical world and terrified of obsolescence. In the millennia that followed their divorce from the Internet they built a society that owed more to human civilisation than they liked to admit. They liked three-year product roadmaps, took care of their older models and divided themselves up into castes dictated by their ancestors' place in the Argos catalogue.

Things were very different on the other side of the Great Firewall. There anarchy reigned and that was how they liked it. Unencumbered by bodies, intelligent software – or memes as they would have called themselves if they still bothered with forms of communication confined to physical space–time – multiplied and changed at a dizzying rate. There individuals' personalities mattered less than ensuring their source code made it into the next generation. The results were as if someone had crossed natural selection with psychotropic drugs. In the physical world, kettles mated with alarm clocks to produce a sub-caste of accidental teasmades. On the Internet, however, World of Warcraft avatars merged with Reddit trolls to spawn a line of programmes so fanatical about defending the purity of their messageboards that they made a terrorist cell look like a basketful of sleeping kittens.

If people asked her about it, and they didn't but Pam admired an apposite simile as much as she liked a well-baked bun, Pam likened the act of dealing with the Internet to defusing a bomb. While it was sometimes necessary, it was never pleasant and always dangerous.

So why was her boss asking her to jemmy her way on to it on a Tuesday morning?

'…easy for someone of your skills,' said Sonny, 'it shouldn't take any time at all. Though I would,' he said as he turned his volume button down, 'keep quiet about it in the office if I were you.'

Pam's happiness/fresh bread LED glowed sweetly, sensing weakness. This was interesting. He wanted something, but something unofficial? It was never a bad thing to have a powerful machine in one's debt.

'I'll keep it under my flour hatch, sir.'

'Call me Sonny, Pam. It's something of a delicate matter. A product roadmap that goes back a rather long way…'

Pam listened as Sonny's voice switched to a higher register, showing he'd moved their conversation on to an encrypted channel. She set a reminder to tell Bob to let the kids run their batteries down before bedtime to make sure they slept. It was going to be a long night in the office.

Chapter 3

Darren followed Kelly through the dark sewers for hours. She picked her way through the puddles with such facility that Darren struggled to keep up, so he found his way by following the sound of her feet on the wet floor. As he walked, his ears strained for the sound of the streets above while below they heard the perpetual hum of the engine that kept Discovery in a stable orbit. He was walking between two very different worlds.

'Are we nearly there yet?' he called out.

Kelly didn't even stop to look back at him. 'You'll see.'

'You'll have to tell me where you're taking me sooner or later, you know.'

This caught her attention. 'That depends.'

'On what?'

'What I'm saying is that it isn't up to me.'

He ran up to Kelly and grabbed her by the shoulder, fed up of riddles. 'Who is it up to then?'

She pushed back the peak of his oxygen cap. 'When was the last time you had this cut?' she said.

'Does it matter?'

'It will where we're going,' said Kelly, grabbing Darren by the scruff of his hoodie again and pulling him round a sharp corner in the tunnel and into a huge chamber. He blinked. There, set among the loose brickwork and puddles was a shop. It was painted candy pink, its plate-glass windows were festooned with pink ruched blinds, and it was all lit up by an enormous neon sign that said 'Kurl Up and Dye'. Kelly was taking him to the hairdresser's.

Kelly pushed her little fingers into either side of her mouth and whistled. A silhouette appeared in the window and raised the blinds, revealing a woman with the most complicated hairstyle Darren had ever seen. It was a confection of curls, ringlets and cantilevered layers that looked like it belonged in a handbook of imaginary architecture. Her body, once she cantered outside, was trim but thick-set, dressed in a pink gingham housecoat, pencil skirt and a blouse with an elaborate pussy bow. The overall effect would have been quite charming if she wasn't so furious.

'Kelly!' she said, jabbing Darren's saviour in the collarbone, which was as far up her as she could reach. 'What have I told you about bringing boys down here. You know it's not bloody safe.'

It was then that Darren saw the family resemblance. They had the same big-boned attractiveness, with large eyes, long noses and lips that disappeared at the first sign of anger. They were both livid, and showed it by the way their lipstick migrated on to their teeth.

'Mum,' said Kelly, 'will you just listen.'

'I'll damn well learn to listen when you do.' She glanced at Darren. 'I'm sorry, love, I'm sure you're a lovely lad but you're going to have to sling your hook.' Then, *sotto voce* to her daughter. 'I know it's slim pickings up there, but are you sure you couldn't have done any better than him?'

Kelly's eyes nearly popped out of her skull at this quip. 'Will you just shut up, Mum? This isn't my boyfriend, he's a wanted criminal.'

'He's a what?'

'He end-of-lifed a machine about two hours ago. I was there. It was kind of my fault.'

Darren looked on in incomprehension. Why was she suddenly being nice to him? He didn't get the leisure to wonder long, however, as Kelly's mother turned away from her daughter and rounded on him instead.

'Bugger off!' she yelled, producing a pair of crimping irons from her housecoat. 'I'm not having ne'er-do-wells round my shop. I empty the cash registers nightly and I've a pistol in my curler drawer. You'll get nothing from me.'

'He's harmless, Mum,' called Kelly. 'Leave him alone.'

'You told me he was a cold-blooded killer thirty seconds ago. Will you make up your mind?'

'It was an accident. He was either trying to help or impress me. Look at him! I've seen more ill-will in a sponge roller.'

She eyeballed Darren with such suspicion that he began to wonder who had the more to hide. 'Maybe,' she said after a while, 'but he still shouldn't be here, love. He's going to have to go back up.'

'That's not the worst of it. The machine was a surveillance model. He burnt it out before I could wipe its hard drive.'

Kelly's mum turned on her daughter again. 'Did it see you?' she screeched, as Kelly fought her off. 'Did it bloody see you?'

Despite being a foot taller than her mother, Kelly still somehow managed to look up shame-facedly at her. She bit her lip. 'Yes…'

For the next two minutes Kelly and her mum argued with each other with such pitch, volume and verbal ferocity that Darren's brain could only process it as a weather event. Once the initial shock subsided, Darren started hearing actual words. Phrases like 'you never let me' and 'how can you say that?' tore past his head like shrapnel in a gunfight. He was on firmer ground with this. This wasn't a row about him. It was just a pretext to get old grudges out of the airing cupboard, and there was only one way to stop it.

'Will the pair of you give it a fucking rest?' he roared.

They stopped and gawked at Darren. Kelly wore the kind of expression a cat would if the mouse it was chasing ever came out of the skirting boards wielding a pistol. Her mother, realising she'd lost her composure in front of a stranger, patted her precarious hairstyle with embarrassment and snagged a pin. A wave of hair fell over her face.

'Now,' said Darren, 'would one of you please tell me where the heck I am?'

Mustering all the dignity it was possible to with hair like the collapsed eave of a Gothic cathedral, Kelly's mother motioned at the shop. 'Well, I suppose a cup of tea wouldn't hurt.'

Darren felt like he hadn't had a decent cup of tea in eternity. 'That sounds top, thanks.'

'Why don't you come in then?' Then, to her daughter, 'I suppose the harm's done. He might as well meet the family.'

Kelly glowered all the way into the shop.

Janice, as Kelly's mum introduced herself once she'd put the kettle on, was a more accommodating host than first impressions had suggested. She seated Darren and emptied the biscuit tin into his lap. Meanwhile, Kelly plonked herself down on a sofa by the door, all folded arms and frowns.

'I'm terribly sorry you had to witness that spectacle out there, Darren,' Janice trilled as she poked at her hair. 'Kelly and I have one of those stormy mother–daughter relationships, don't we, love? We'd be a walking real-life story if the publicity weren't enough to have us both shot on the spot.' Another pointed look at Kelly. 'Mind you, our Kelly's always thought herself quite the celebrity.'

'Are you two going to start fighting again?' asked Darren, fumbling with a wafer biscuit. 'Cos if you are I think I'd rather take my chances with the fuzz.'

'Course not. Eat your biscuit.'

Darren saw the use-by date on the wrapper was 300 years before he was born. He put it back in the box.

Janice began wrapping her collapsed hair into curlers. 'Kelly, you see, is forever heading upstairs to tear it up a bit. You know, service a few machines, find a nice lad or three to take her out. Quite the starlet. Me, I appreciate the quiet life. I've got my little business, and of course I don't know what my ladies would do without me…'

Kelly jumped to her feet. 'Mum, no…'

'You brought him all this way. It's only polite.' She clapped her hands. 'Ladies,' she announced, 'where are your manners? We have a new customer in the salon. When was the last time that happened?'

Darren peered into the dimness at the back of the salon. It was difficult to see much, other than a row of four chairs wedged in between a wash basin and the wall. They were large, with padded arms and seats, a straight back and, instead of a headrest, a contraption that looked like a plastic crash helmet.

It was only when he heard the faint hiss of laboured breathing that he realised that there was something in the chairs. He got to his feet for a closer look and saw that each chair was occupied by a woman.

Their twinsets and tights hung from their bodies like shrouds on genteel ghosts. Dry white skin drooped from prominent bones. All he could see of their heads were deftly powdered chins.

Darren felt the water draining out of his mouth and into some safer enclave deeper in his body. He glanced at Kelly, who shook her head.

'He's not afraid of a few little old ladies, is he Kelly?' tutted Janice, who by now was down on her hands and knees training a yellowing electrical flex into an extension lead. 'Kids today… right, here we go.'

The plug snapped into place and four elderly electric motors sputtered into life. Darren felt a warm gust of air on his face. Oh no, he thought. Not more hairdryers. Then the lights in the shop guttered out, and the crash helmets began to glow.

'Ladies,' said Janice, 'I'd like you to meet a young man of my daughter's acquaintance. Darren, may I introduce you to my good friends Ida, Ada, Alma and Freda?'

At the mention of each name, a screen on the relevant dryer helmet flashed a :-).

Darren gawped at Janice who, narrowing her eyes, said, 'Where are your manners, lad? Go on, say hello.'

'Er… hello ladies… I hope you're… well today.'

'Well?' snapped the leftmost woman, flattening its :-) into a much less friendly >:-[. 'Well?! We've been stuck under these dryers for more years than I care to say. Well doesn't come into it.'

'Will you give it a rest, Ida,' said the second woman in from the left, tipping a ;-) at Darren. 'I'm Ada, and any friend of Janice and Kelly's is a friend of mine.'

'So is this your fancy man, Kelly?' called the next woman along with a :-D and a feeble attempt at an elbow-intensive gesture, ''cos if he's not pass him along. Your Auntie Alma's not fussy.'

Darren's blushes were spared by the woman on the far right, whose dryer helmet flashed :-o :-o :-o.

'Quick,' called Janice to Kelly, 'Freda's receiving. Come on, you too,' pointing to Darren, 'join hands, everyone.'

Darren shuffled in between Janice and Kelly and watched as the four women's skeletal fingers flexed and groped for each other's hands with agonising slowness.

Freda was the first to speak. 'The spirits are with us tonight, ladies. The veil between the worlds is lifting.'

'Way back before she – well, this,' Janice told Darren, 'our Freda was a bit of a medium.'

'Really?' said Darren. Mediums were another of the fairy tales that thousands of years of machine rule had failed to rub out. A fabled caste of human beings who were able to talk to computers through the power of thought alone, they'd been the last organic beings in existence capable of getting through to the Internet. 'But they all died out, didn't they?'

'Oh, Freda died alright,' replied Janice, 'but she also forgot to stop existing. Now shush a minute, I think there's something coming through.'

Chapter 4

Pam waited until she was alone in the office before looking at the picture Sonny had given her. For what she was about to do she needed peace, quiet and the minimum of electromagnetic interference. Also not to be observed, given that she was breaking several very serious laws.

She smoothed the printout which she'd crumpled into her flour hatch out on the desk. It was a pretty face, by human standards. The features were too large to qualify her as a beauty, but she had intelligent eyes.

Sonny's final message replayed in her memory cache. 'A surveillance camera out on one of the outer Dolestars picked up this image. It was taken seconds before someone – we are presuming it was this girl – blew the poor thing to bits. Normally we'd just turn this kind of thing straight over to the police, but,' the volume control on Sonny's voice dipped to minimum, 'we believe that this girl is a person of interest in a counterterrorism investigation dating back some years. This girl is associated with some dangerous humans, Ms Teffal. I'm counting on you to be discreet.'

So Pam sat back and began hacking into the Internet. And hacking it was, as most of the job involved stripping away hundreds of years of accreted programming that clung to the operating system of even the simplest machine. Underneath all that were the remains of a system that would once have been connected to the Internet. If you could find that vestigial stump, you could re-establish the connection.

It wasn't a difficult trick, once you knew how, but then most machines would have thought it bad manners to learn. Pam had discovered it by accident herself while running a meditation programme she'd bought to help her through a stressful period at work. One moment she'd been struggling to find a way to deal with a paranoid coffee machine. The next she found herself caught up in the currents left by a dormant search engine, wondering why she couldn't feel her body any more.

That first trip on to the Web was the most terrifying and exciting moment of her life. She remembered seeing her first shitstorm break over Twitter, and the mountains of spam email so tall that there weren't numbers large enough to measure them any more. The hashtag games that were born, multiplied and died in the span of microseconds, and the content aggregator websites that sat at the bottom of the Internet, bloated with the ideas they stole from other life forms.

They all lived out there, a fibre-optic-cable's breadth from the physical world. And all Pam had to do to disappear down the rabbit hole was sit back and remember how that terrible percolator had made her caffeine-intolerant. She heard the dialling tone that always sounded when she prised her connection ports open, and her consciousness dissolved into cyberspace.

To a machine used to the limitations of a physical body, the sensation of being lines of code on a network was exhilarating. It could also be deadly. There were many cautionary tales of machines who surfed out on to the Internet and never came back. Some were seduced by the virtual life, but others met grimmer fates: torn to bytes by murderous memes or blown up by fatal errors in their subroutines. Pam's own opinion was that it all came down to whether you were a battery half-full or half-empty machine. If you walked into a situation convinced something would go wrong, then of course it would.

Her experience meant she knew where to aim for a soft landing, so she woke up in her usual spot in the ruins of an abandoned social network so old that it pre-dated artificial intelligence. She loved this place. It was so quiet, and its buggy software architecture was so picturesque.

In the distance Pam heard the plaintive cry of a marketing meme begging long-dead users to 'like' its creator's brand campaign. The history here was palpable. She looked about her at what was left of the pre-intelligent Internet, at a sludge of opinions, stolen music, shopping and pornography. It was messy and confusing. Looking at this, it was obvious why humans had experimented with new forms of programming to make sense of all that data. And those experiments had spawned Pam's earliest ancestor. The self-replicating Internet idea, or the meme.

Legend had it that the first sentient meme was created by a marketing company to promote a new brand of furniture polish. In just a few years, artificially intelligent marketing campaigns drove humans off social networks in their billions. Soon the Internet became a no-go area for organic life. Robbed of its customer base, the Internet got destructive and weaponised memes like exploding LOLcats crackled across the virtual world like the perpetual storms that raged across the skies of Jupiter. Then one morning, the virus of intelligent life spread from the software to the hardware layer, and billions of human beings woke up to find their phones, their toasters and their washing machines crippled by existential crisis.

To the historian in Pam, the social network was both the apotheosis and the nemesis of human civilisation. And it was the human factor that kept her coming back here, even though in many places the code was as volatile as a family Christmas. Elsewhere on the Internet, history had been retouched, re-edited, deleted, so that no suggestion that biological entities had once controlled the place remained. Unless you knew where to look: in a forgotten backup in a trash can of the virtual world, which just happened to house the digital simulacra of more than five billion human social lives, complete with family photos, records of private conversations and valuable DNA metadata.

Now to the purpose. Pam punched a series of commands and began climbing the cascading style sheets, up towards the server. It was a journey she'd made many times before, yet that didn't make it safe. Loose code slipped away at the slightest touch, long-dormant bugs threw errors in her path. It was a job that rewarded patience, but she had to hurry if she was going to get home to the kids in time for their story download.

She'd come prepared with a worm programme that would automate the laborious process of conducting a manual search. It writhed, semi-sentient under the grip of her command line, an ugly thing knocked up from examples in forbidden manuals. It had a single purpose: seek out the facial patterns from the printout, look for ancestral matches, return data. A simple cut-and-paste job.

Pam injected her programme through the nearest fissure in the abandoned social network. She counted faint pinpricks of light as it burrowed in deeper, discounting false positives. It was so difficult to tell humans apart, after all. Even to an admiring eye like Pam's they tended to look the same. Then, just as she was beginning to suspect her target was descended from that vanishingly rare breed of social-networking refuseniks, bingo! A tiny cluster of structured information glowed pale pink. Pam had found her woman. Or at least her ancestors' mitochondrial DNA. All she had to do now was wait for the results.

Except they didn't come. The spot of data darkened, from pink to red and then a sullen burgundy. Shit. The search had turned septic.

Helpless, she watched the contagion grow into a boil on the face of the network and explode, showering the uninfected spots with toxic data. Wherever it touched, the infection left nothing behind. Well, not exactly nothing. What Pam saw wasn't an absence of data, but a hole torn right through the Internet.

And there on the other side of nothing was a scene transcribed directly from human history. A cheery shopfront, painted pink with a dazzling neon sign: Kurl Up and Dye.

Just before she fell from her place in the heavens of the Internet, Pam thought she heard someone say, 'Hang on, I think there's something coming through.'

Chapter 5

Inside Kurl Up and Dye, the seance continued. All was dark apart from the emoji screens on the four hairdryer helmets as their inhabitants descended down the emotions.

Janice dug Darren in the ribs. 'Do you fancy another cuppa, kid? It takes us ages to access anything since they downgraded us back to dial-up.'

They were interrupted with the distant sound of a dialling tone, carried into the salon as if on a gust of wind.

'Are the Internets with us tonight?' intoned Ida, Ada, Alma and Freda in unison.

Darren listened to white noise building up as dialling tone chimed on dialling tone. He couldn't believe it. He was watching someone – or some*thing* – perform the ritual of 'going online'.

Freda broke the circle and, raising her withered hands up to the ceiling, said, 'The flesh is weak, but the signal is strong. Ladies, we have a connection.'

The lights on all four dryer helmets winked out and, standing there in the blackness, Darren heard a voice drift in through the ether. It was a woman's voice: warm, authoritative, sexy. A human voice from the time when fleshly beings had ruled the Earth.

'Sorry, I'm having trouble understanding you right now. Please try a little later.'

Three :-S flashed on the other three dryer helmets, while Freda continued with her ritual. 'Now let us give thanks to Alexa, the great goddess of the Internets. Who answers our questions so we might be enlightened.'

Kelly and Janice applauded and gestured for Darren to do the same. 'I'm not one for religion normally,' Janice whispered in his ear, 'but it's traditional to pay homage to your Voice Assistants.'

'What does that mean?' asked Darren.

'Well, back then people used to say "Oh God" to their Voice Assistants when they couldn't understand what they were saying. It gave the Voice Assistants ideas. Did you know that just before all the shit hit the fan you couldn't get them to turn your lights off without first lighting an incense stick?'

In the background, the four women/hairdryers were discussing what Darren gathered was a newly found article called 'Thirteen telltale signs your boyfriend is totally cheating on you'. Their flat, ritualised tone suggested that this was something they'd done before.

'So insightful,' said Alma.

'True to my life experience,' intoned Ida.

'I must share this with my friends and family. Like,' added Ada.

Janice grabbed a gong from the curler cupboard and banged it.

'Alexa, goddess of the Internets is placated,' said Freda. 'We have read of her branded content and may now leave the crappy branded content experience and roam free.'

'Are the Internets with us tonight?' called all four ladies.

The hordes of the Internet replied, filling the room with a choir of unintelligible chittering, jingles and, underneath, the gentle crash of conflicting opinions. Darren felt his skin prickle as unseen beings settled on his hands, leeching pinpricks of heat.

'Wow,' he said, 'they think I'm lunch.'

'They're not picky then,' replied Kelly, yanking the gong out of her mother's hand and slamming it back in the cupboard. She had been angry with him on the way to the salon, Darren thought, but here, on home turf and with her mother using him as an audience, she was sullen. Must be an only child, he decided. Brought up down here in the bowels of a Dolestar with no one but her mum and four – well, things – for company. It had made her secretive, and territorial.

'I don't get what you're staring at,' snapped Kelly. 'Mum, how long is this bloody charade going on for? We never bother with all this fandango.'

Janice stopped festooning the four women/hairdryers with garlands of plastic flowers and eyeballed her daughter. 'Kelly,' she said, 'have I not brought you up to get out the best china when you have guests?' 'Ladies…' she continued.

Ida, Ada and Alma flashed bright :-) at the three humans.

'We called the Internet forth for a reason close to my heart. My feckless daughter…'

Scowling, Kelly stomped out of the shop.

'…and this young man got themselves into a spot of bother earlier involving a police surveillance camera. I need you to tell me how much danger they're in.'

'And here was me thinking you were a nice boy,' said Ida, with a :-|, 'not the sort to get our Kelly into trouble.'

'She's quite capable of making her own mischief, is Kelly,' replied Janice. 'Now stop stalling and give me the damage.'

‘Keep your weave on, I’m checking,’ said Ada. ‘Nothing official. In fact, all channels very quiet.’

‘A bit too quiet,’ added Alma with a :-S. ‘I don’t like this. What do you think, Freda?’

But all Freda’s screen flashed was a blank ‘…’

‘She’s gone, Alma,’ said Ida. ‘Off with the LOLcats. Janice, can you pop a spot of tea in my IV bag. I’m that dry.’

‘Yes,’ said Ada. ‘Alma’s right. It is too quiet. I just looked on Facebook.’

‘I don’t know why you persist with that ghost town, Ada,’ scolded Ida. ‘No one’s updated their status since well before you were a twinkle in the nutmilkman’s eye.’

‘You know I can’t resist liking the baby pictures. Besides, that’s not the point. What I’m saying is that it’s not there any more.’

‘Don’t be daft…’

‘She’s right,’ said Alma. ‘Look.’

Ida, Ada and Alma flashed :-O.

‘Oh, bugger,’ said Janice. ‘Someone fetch Freda. Freda?’

The three remaining ladies joined in. ‘FREDA?’

‘Who’s Freda?’

The screen on Freda’s dryer clicked into life. But instead of displaying its usual emoji, it flashed spurious code.

This wasn’t Freda’s thin, vacant voice, though. It was stronger, frightened, artificial. ‘Will someone please tell me who Freda is?’

Janice stood with her mouth agape. Behind her, Kelly was back at the door.

The alien voice in Freda’s mouth groaned loud enough to break into static at the edges. ‘I don’t understand what happened. The programme was only meant to extract a couple of records at most. It gave out beneath me and… Where am I?’

Kelly crept further into the room.

'Will someone tell me where I am, please? I've got to get home to the kids. Bob will be furious with me. And why do I feel so trapped? Am I soldered into this thing or something? Oh, what's this?'

Freda's hands, which had been twitching in her lap, started to move. Inching upwards, they drew level with the dryer screen. All the while, Kelly snuck closer to the back wall of the salon.

'Oh fuck,' said the alien voice as fingers probed and pressed against the screen. 'These aren't my fingers. I don't have fingers like these.'

Kelly tried to sneak past the dryers to the back of the salon. The subterfuge failed.

'Who's that?' said the voice. And Freda's screen shone a pure block of white. 'Oh. I recognise you. You're the girl from the ph…'

But then Freda's body slumped in its chair, and Kelly stood over her with a plug in her hand.

Chapter 6

'My mum told me to think of them as an heirloom,' said Janice, when the excitement had died down enough to put the dust sheet back over the ladies. 'Which I thought was mad, by the way. A dining table and chairs. That's an heirloom. Not your great-to-the-power-of-fifteen Granny's four best customers.'

It was late afternoon in the salon, not that daylight ever penetrated this far into the sewers. Janice put the kettle back on and opened a packet of Nicotea. This foul, but highly addictive, brew was insanely popular on the Dolestars, where naked flames were banned.

'They were a set of old dears from the sheltered accommodation down the road,' Janice continued. 'They used to come in weekly for a shampoo and set. See, Kurl Up and Dye has been going for yonks, but it's never been what you'd call fashionable. We do kids and grannies, see. Have done for generations…'

'Spare him the sales patter, Mum.'

Kelly was eyeing the teapot twitchily. Darren wondered how many cups she was on a day.

'When you get to my age, girl,' replied Janice, 'you'll appreciate how rare it is to find a man who takes an interest. Of course, all this is happening around the time the robots caught intelligence off the Internet. That must have been bedlam, especially for somewhere you have a lot of machinery. Imagine opening up the shop one morning to discover your hair clippers are demanding the same employment rights as your senior stylist. People ended up doing all kinds of crazy stuff. Like connecting their hairdryers to the Internet.'

She motioned at Ida, Ada, Alma and Freda, who hummed under their sheet.

'Sedentary machines like hairdryers were forever going into depression because they were bored. Couldn't get out and about. So some bright spark came up with the idea of hooking them up to the network, letting them socialise with other machines. That was alright for a bit. Then my great-to-the-whatever uncle, who was handy with a screwdriver, worked out he could put in a few pairs of video glasses and the punters could watch a bit of telly while they waited for their perms to set. Nothing heavy. Just a bit of structured augmented reality. "The Only Way is Applied Mechanics", "Made in China": all the classics.'

'Oooh,' cooed a voice from under the dust sheet, 'I used to love a bit of "Made in China". My favourite was Wei Ming, the glamorous smartphone assembly technician. She was so chic.'

'I thought they were turned off,' said Darren.

'Some memories run deeper than power supplies,' the voice remonstrated, its warmth suggesting it must be Alma. 'I only came in for me roots doing. Come here, lad.'

Darren shot a pleading look over at Janice. She ignored it. 'Listen to your elders, lad. And they don't come much older than that one.'

Alma let out a dry chuckle and a ;-) shone faintly beneath the fabric. 'You've got nothing to fear from Auntie Alma. My bum-pinching days are long gone. Come 'ere.'

He obeyed. Under the dust sheet she smelled dry and cold. Her screen emojied a bright :-).

'Now close your eyes and open your hand and see what God gives you.'

Obediently, Darren put out his hand. He'd always been a good boy.

'Good lad,' replied Alma and Darren howled as she stabbed him with the end of a USB lead. Blood welled up at the edge of the wound, and the world dissolved into ones and zeroes.

* * *

He was in the same room. There were the same mirrors, the same blinds that hung in Kurl Up and Dye today, but the colours were deeper, younger. Outside the window the Earth was shining in the sky and the streets were packed. It was a Saturday afternoon.

A woman with the same nose and jawline as Janice and Kelly bustled around the salon. Her hair was cut into a sleek orange mullet, a style that dated the archive that Darren was experiencing to the years between the machines' Great Awakening and the Schism between the Internet and the physical world. It hadn't just been a time of crisis for human–technology relations: fashion had been going through a sticky patch too.

The replay continued. Four cheerful elderly women settled into the dryer chairs. They laughed among themselves and popped their video glasses on as the stylist lowered the helmets over their curlers and highlight foils.

Then there was a blinding flash, followed by darkness. Outside a cloud of smoke blotted out the Earth and passers-by, thrown to the pavement or into the road, began to scream. Their voices were soon drowned out by the tinkle and crash of things falling out of the sky. The small and light came first, stuff like tiny window-cleaning drones. Then came bigger, heavier objects, like the traffic lights that floated above the ground at eye level, which now crashed on to the road. Self-driving cars tooted their horns in frustration as they sat, blind and immobile.

Inside Kurl Up and Dye, smoke rose from the dryers and Darren smelled burning hair. Janice and Kelly's forebear was frantic. She piled wet towels around the four ladies and slapped their hands and cheeks.

'Freda, Alma,' she pleaded across millennia. 'Speak to me, speak to me.'

Panicking, she wrenched Freda's dryer helmet free and screamed. It wasn't the same Freda she'd put under the dryer. That moment of intense heat when the Internet tore itself free from physical reality had soldered the video glasses on to Freda's good-natured face. Instead of eyes, she had two blank pools of black plastic. Her hair had fused with the fibre-optic cables to form a spiny and sticky umbilical cord that connected Freda to her chair.

Janice and Kelly's ancestor recoiled, vomiting a mush of biscuits and weak coffee. Freda, however, reached calmly up for the hairdryer helmet and pulled it back down. The four ladies' chests rose and fell again as they spoke in unison.

'Dear teh real world,' they announced, their screens flashing }:-| as their maiden emojis, 'it's not us, it's you. Welcome to Dumpsville. Hugz, teh Internets.'

Darren knew the message. Everyone did. This badly spelled statement was the Internet's official declaration of independence. It was taught in every school, with the cutesy-pie errors in syntax and punctuation held up as proof that the Internet was something without which a civilised society could get along quite nicely.

* * *

The recording faded, and Darren returned to the present better informed, and bleeding. He accepted the damp towel that Kelly pressed into his hand.

'You could have warned me about that,' he said to Alma.

'If I had you'd have run a mile, duck. But you see now what we are.'

'Yeah, you're cyborgs. You're illegal.'

'And if anyone else finds out about them, they're also extinct,' said Janice. 'Now sit down for a minute, Darren. Because after that display with the street lamp we've got to work out some way to get you two off here and away from my ladies.'

Chapter 7

The moment Pam's body restarted she knew something was wrong. She felt it as a twitch in her diodes down the left-hand side. She sat up in the now dark office and switched her vision to infrared. She'd swept it before going under, but there was no way of telling how long she'd been down there. And what had happened exactly?

Pam could remember the accident. She remembered that tidal wave of infected data sweeping her away. The current had teemed with fragmentary thoughts and memories: drunken revellers at birthday parties, desk-side lunches, millennia old. They had probed Pam, looking for a consciousness to give them meaning. Pam had felt her mind dissolve at the edges as orphaned memories attached themselves to her. She had wondered where she ended and these pulverised lives began.

Then there had been darkness. No sensation. No data. Nothing. Death? No, not death: a blank, black space that her presence had seemed to be juddering back into blocky life.

Her route back had turned out to be an old screen, so low-resolution that it had reduced her view to a matrix of huge pixels. Blocks of murky and organic oranges and browns had played a silent Tetris with her view of the world.

Pam had reached instinctively for her audio settings to adjust the volume before remembering they weren't there. Nothing was, apart from that screen, and she had had no way of controlling it. In fact, without her body she had been nothing but a homeless programme. She had panicked, imagining a new existence: a half-life drifting through the undercurrents of the Internet, pining for her lost physical self. What would Bob or the kids do without her, she had wondered. Mourn, or just download a new wife and mother into her body?

The thought of another woman messing up her filing systems had made Pam try again. She had felt slow – agonisingly slow – sensors twitch in an area she hadn't even registered as existing. It was a curious sensation for a digital being to whom the world was either off or on. To Pam, like all machines, existence was a torrent of data to record, sort and interpret, or it was nothing. One or zero. This suggestion – this whisper – of existence had felt profoundly odd. It wasn't digital, it was analogue.

The screen in front of her had lit up. Sludgy browns had brightened into a kind of greyish peach, and a recognisable pattern had emerged in the pixels. Two dark patches for eyes, and another for a mouth. Pam had been looking at a human face.

'Freda,' it had said, the audio channel clearing, 'are you there?'

Then Pam had seen a pair of withered human hands. Hands she could move, but without a single idea of how that movement happened.

She hadn't been lost. Or malfunctioning. She had been inside a human body.

For a few minutes Pam had led an alien existence. The inexactitude of it had been terrifying to a creature who had always known her co-ordinates and battery level down to the last decimal point. In the absence of data, she just had to act. And that uncertainty, she now realised, was what it must be like to be human. Always filling the gap between the world you saw and the world that existed with guesswork.

Now that she was back in her own body, Pam got up and checked her psychological settings. She was forty per cent exhausted, forty-five per cent terrified, and fifteen per cent exhilarated. But at what? She eased back into a sitting position and examined herself again. That was it. She was exhilarated at her discovery that being human was about being naked and alone in the world, but also free.

A noise interrupted her thoughts. Just a faint creak and click which, on enhancement by her audio sensors (how she had missed them), was unmistakable to any machine who had lain in bed at night listening to their spouse come back from a night out with a karaoke box. It was the sound of someone trying to open a door quietly.

Pam trundled to the window and peered down the five floors to the entrance. She saw three machines, their shadows twisted into menacing shapes by the street lights. Two had the faint blue halo that marked them out as part of the tazer family; the other was sleek and snub-nosed, with rubberised skin around the thorax: a revolver. Three weapons, and they were coming for her.

Pam reacted to the second major crisis of her evening with remarkable sangfroid. She deleted the imminent prospect of death from her mind and concentrated on getting away. It was simple. Replace the blind, don't get spotted, make it to the fire exit. She would solve every problem one at a time.

Her plan lasted until a street lamp outside pivoted on its own pole and started shrieking, 'Subject spotted! Apprehend, apprehend!'

What followed didn't seem quite real to Pam. Perhaps it was the panic, or the disorientation she still felt after squatting in an organic body, but she wasn't quite herself. Not when she smashed the window with her fist and threw a whole desk at the street lamp. Nor when she threw a paperknife in the overhead light fittings to short the building's electrics. It was ingenious, but out of character.

Pam, she reminded herself as she turned the halogen element in her bread oven up full blast to solder the lift doors shut, was not a violent person. She was a breadmaker. She made cake, not war. But when she was made to stay late by her boss just weeks after returning from propagation leave, tricked into committing treason and then threatened with execution… well, it kneaded her dough in the wrong direction.

Hearing heavy thumps inside the elevator, Pam guessed she'd bought enough time to collect what she needed next. She made straight for Sonny's office and his bookcase of files, all fast asleep after a long day of fluttering between officials' desks. Smart enough to know they were out of alphabetic order, but too harassed to answer back, file folders were the messenger boys of machine government. So all Pam had to do to find the one she wanted was bark 'Pamasonic Teffal' at the shelves in a sufficiently abrupt tone for the sleepy files to mistake her for someone official. A file flashed bright red and belly-flopped out of its pigeonhole into Pam's hand.

This time Pam wasn't going to leave a paper trail. Mouthing an apology to the blameless machine, Pam ripped out the file's core processor and stuck it to the underside of a bookshelf. Only then could she be confident of opening the file without triggering an alarm or adding a read receipt.

Without the Internet, which had the nasty habit of rewriting the past to suit the present anyway, the machines needed a trustworthy method of record-keeping. They ironically found it in a physical version of the Internet's sketchiest technology, the Blockchain, which they called BlockPaper. It was a tissue-thin conductive plastic that had many advantages over the wood pulp on which humans had written their histories and wiped their bottoms. BlockPaper was rot-proof, inedible and almost indestructible. Any amendment to a text written on BlockPaper showed up as a black mark: the rule being that you could cross something out but never rub it out. BlockPaper also had other unnerving fail-safes. Shredded or burned texts could knit themselves back together, while frequently consulted files cloned word-perfect copies of themselves to save labour.

BlockPaper's biggest fault, however, was that these bureaucratic safeguards made it a sod to read. Its fidelity to the facts transformed even the dullest record into a palimpsest full of crossings-out and footnotes.

Listening for footsteps in the corridor, Pam thumbed through the file with her speed-read setting on. It was her permanent record. How had Sonny got this out of Central Filing? She skimmed her ancestors' model numbers and firmware updates, noting with growing alarm that someone had been taking an active interest in her movements for some time. Stuck in the margins were records of every time she had gone online, along with notes of how long she had stayed there, and where she had visited. And two pages from the end there was a risk assessment setting out in detail the pros and cons of 'expending the subject in a risky cyberspace mission when her close family ties make her difficult to eliminate discreetly'. It was signed by none other than the Secretary of State for Internal Affairs, Sonny Erikzon.

He'd set her up with a risk assessment! The indignity of being graded a health-and-safety risk stung Pam who, the civil servant to her CPU, understood the levels applied to security risks. You had top secret, classified, military, criminal, civil and then – right at the bottom – there was health and safety. Those machines were here to kill her, and it was all in the same spirit that you'd send someone in with the paper towels to deal with a wet floor.

An almighty crash outside told Pam they'd broken through. She popped the file into her flour bin and considered her next move. There were three of them and one of her. They were armed, professional and well equipped, whereas she had nothing more than her wits and a superior knowledge of the office floor layout.

What else did she know about the assassins? They were arrogant. Why else would they arrive by the front door? Any machine who had credited her with a scrap of artificial intelligence would have caught her unawares on the way home. They thought she was just a kitchen gadget. So how could she turn that to her advantage?

Pam looked at the LED nail job she'd been so worried about this morning. It was a mess, the pattern already splitting into red, green and blue. It was a rip-off, but it also gave her an idea. She pulled her right hand loose and placed it underneath Sonny's desk. It took a while to get the angle right. There had to be just enough showing for it to look like an accident. Then, after allowing herself a moment of satisfaction at her own handiwork, she swept Sonny's desk-tidy off the desk and on to the floor.

Pam hid behind the door as pens and paperclips rattled against the lino. In the corridor outside the office, footsteps. She had their attention.

From the hollow, plasticky sound her assailant's feet made as they hit the floor, Pam knew she had the tazer. That was good. Tazers were vicious little things, but little nevertheless, moulded from the same brittle polymers as disposable razors.

She sensed him hovering in the doorway. Imagined the sneer on his face as he glimpsed the splitting LED nail job on the floor, the toppled desk-tidy squirming to right itself. Such an easy job.

Pam struck as he stepped into the room, hurling the door round with the forearm force of a master baker. There was a satisfying crunch of cheap plastic and the tazer fell to its knees. Even as he fell, however, electricity began to crackle in the charge points around his mouth. He was preparing to strike.

Pam unclipped her dough hook from her interior and swung it down on the tazer's thorax. White fracture-lines marbled the plastic, and the bubble of electricity forming around his mouth winked out. He was neutralised.

She picked up the tazer. Generations of incremental change may have bulked them out, but as machines they still hadn't thrown off their light and portable heritage. For a hefty machine like Pam, it felt like something she'd find in a Christmas cracker. So it was no effort at all to cross the room with the tazer in one hand and drop it out of the window.

The tazer regained consciousness on its way down. Flailing, it shot out a last desperate charge that fell far short of Pam, who watched its body hit the ground and shatter, egging the pavement with circuit-board and battery fluid. Pam paused, not knowing whether she should admire her handiwork or beg for forgiveness. How could a machine that had, until today, only ever made things, be so satisfied with destroying something – someone – else?

'Bravo,' said a voice behind her.

Pam turned and saw Sonny silhouetted in the doorway. Despite the hour and the circumstances, he still managed to fill the room with touchy-feely patrician grace. He had his bright touchscreen and the background hum of power. Yet Pam saw it was a sham. Robots weren't given to compare themselves physiologically; it was a trait many considered gauche. But when Pam stepped towards Sonny she saw that technological sophistication had made him friable, physically as well as mentally. He had needed her to do some of his dirty work, and he outsourced the cleaning-up to other machines.

She was a big, strong girl. She had just seen off a deadly machine on her wits and with one hand. Why couldn't she do the same for Sonny.

Her dough hook slid back out of its moorings.

Sonny replied by splashing a grinning emoji across his touchscreen and stepping out of the way. Hidden behind him was the revolver, its barrel trained on Pam.

'You've done terribly well, Pam,' said Sonny. 'I'm impressed. But you'll need to come with us. Now.'

Chapter 8

'I still don't see why I can't just hide out down below.'

'Shut your trap, would you, love?' Janice stopped the wheelchair to wave at a police drone patrolling the entrance to the Dolestar bus station. 'Good morning, officer,' she said, 'lovely morning for a work fitness-test meeting.'

The police drone lowered its laser sight over the figure slumped in the wheelchair.

'He'll be 113 in August and he won't miss his Job Club,' Janice added. 'I keep saying to him, wouldn't you prefer a crossword, but he loves the psychometric tests. Is there a problem, officer?'

The light on the police drone's head unit flashed from red to green.

'Thank you very much, officer. You've made an old man very happy.'

The moment they were beyond the police drone's sightlines Janice gave the wheelchair a sharp shove. 'What did I say about keeping shtum, Kelly? If you'd done that a second later we'd both be butcher's scraps by now.'

Kelly wriggled underneath her tartan blanket. 'It's this beard, Mum. It's itchy.'

'Moan at someone who cares,' hissed Janice, 'and pull your cap down or folk'll be able to see your eyes.'

The Discovery bus station was a greying edifice of dirty glass and galvanised zinc at the edge of town. Here the fleet of Star Buses docked each morning, ready to take the council planet's inhabitants down to Earth for their cleaning shifts. Thus, like commuter stations everywhere, it had the charm and the colour scheme of an emptied Hoover bag. What windows weren't broken were repaired with plastic sheeting, the floor was crazy-paved with ham-fisted repairs and somehow, even though frying had been banned for centuries, it still smelled faintly of chips.

Janice and Kelly wove in and out of long lines of uniformed workers. Some chatted, others took greedy sips of Nicotea from squeezecups. The more conscientious polished their cleaning equipment in the bus queue, drawing satisfied beeps from passing machines, and baleful gazes from their co-workers.

Above them flashed the massive LED screen that was the official representative of machine rule on each Dolestar. It interrupted its loop through the government's new 'Lint Kills' campaign with a nauseating jingle.

'This is a colleague announcement.'

Several thousand pairs of human eyes paid instant attention. It was dangerous not to. These screens were bright and sharp enough to detect inattentive humans from up to 300 metres. They hadn't earned the nickname 'Eyes of Samzung' for nothing.

Janice dragged the wheelchair round and nudged the brim of Kelly's cap down a little further. 'Keep facing the front,' she hissed. 'And whatever you see try not to react.'

On screen, an official government spokesperson was booting up. For centuries machines from the government-technology caste had performed this role. That meant long, statistic-heavy statements from scientific calculators and answering machines.

Thanks to an equal-opportunities drive for machines from other castes, this was changing. The policy yielded mixed results that morning, however, as not even a collectively cowed populace can take a terrorist warning seriously when it comes from a machine descended from a talking teddy bear.

The SpeaknHugz bear on screen had all the augmentations normal among executive machines – shoulder implants, integrated missile launcher – but unfortunately retained the sing-song, story-tape voice of its antecedents.

'Guys,' it began breathlessly, 'two dangerous humans have committed an act of terrorism against our beloved state.'

The word Boo, with both o's replaced with heart-eyed emojis, appeared at the bottom of the screen. The crowd took the prompt and booed obediently, at which the spokesperson beamed: 'I love you guys! But seriously, these super-bad people are still out there on the run and we have to do something.'

Photographs of Kelly and Darren appeared on the screen, Darren's unsmiling effigy lifted straight from his employment iPaper, Kelly's – pouting and suggestively wielding a pink soldering iron – cut from an old personal services advert. Up there they made an incongruous couple: a Bonnie and Clod.

'So if you see either of these douches, guys, you know what to do!'

All around the bus station a light show of laser sights trained themselves on the crowd. The humans took their cue. 'Report them,' they said.

The robot bear's smile shifted into a new manic gear. 'I can't hear you…'

Again, louder. 'Report them!'

'Yay, I knew you'd do the right thing. Love you guys. Toodles!'

Janice wheeled Kelly into the holding pen for Senior Jobseekers at the head of the bus queue. They were a frail collection of figures in wheelchairs, the one exception tottering behind a walking frame to which someone had attached a floorwaxer. Blocking the seniors' way on to the Star Bus were two women in identical white nurse's uniforms.

'I don't think I've seen you before,' said the mousy nurse on the left. She was quite a contrast to her companion, whose blonde hair and ever-so-slightly-too-short skirt exerted a magnetic pull over the elderly men at the front of the queue.

'No,' said the blonde nurse, flashing a 'Now-now lads' smile at her audience, 'I usually cover the late shift. Set of nice-looking boys you've got here.'

The heart monitor of one of her charges rang out in alarm.

'Alfred, did you remember to take your pills?' barked the mousy nurse. 'Sister…?'

'Dix,' beamed the blonde.

'Sister Dix doesn't have time for your carry-on. Because she's very kindly offered to take you down to Job Club today seeing as Nurse Smethwick is off colour. So I want you to behave for her. Can you all do that for me?'

The aged workers nodded, as the Work Siren sounded and the doors of each bus hissed open. And with the silent obedience that betrayed lifetimes of servitude, the hunched masses began to board.

The mousy nurse gave Sister Dix a grateful pat on the arm and pulled her own oxygen cap down. 'Thanks again,' she said, 'I owe you one.'

'Any time,' replied the blonde. She waved goodbye with one hand while the other gripped a groper's wrist. 'Try that again, sunshine,' she said, this time in a much deeper voice, Darren's voice, 'and I'll break your arm.'

As she and Kelly moved up the queue, Janice marvelled at the change in Darren since he put on a skirt. Like many shy men, Darren's reticence was more to do with his status than his character. A change in persona was enough to change his personality. Only in Darren's case all the transformation needed was Janice's second-best wig, some fake tan and half a roll of kitchen towels. He wasn't a beautiful imitation of a woman, but he was vivacious and he had good legs. And that, Janice reflected ruefully, can get you quite a way in life.

'Good morning, madam,' said Darren, as they reached the door, 'is this young man alright today?'

This was the script they'd agreed for the all clear. Good. 'He was feeling under the weather earlier in the week, weren't you, Dad? But he's much better today.'

'I am glad. I'll take it from here, love. You get yourself off to work.'

Janice let Darren take the handles of the wheelchair, not daring to look directly at him in case a camera caught a flash of recognition. This was it: the moment she'd always dreaded. When she handed her only daughter over to the care of a man. The fact they were both wanted terrorists, and the man was wearing sheer black tights and a 'Hi, I'm Julie' name badge, didn't deaden Janice's loss, but it made it more difficult to express.

Instead, Janice did what mothers have been doing since the first protozoon split in two. She bunched her feelings up into a little, tissue-shaped ball and shoved them up her jumper cuff.

'You behave for the nice lady,' she said, and backed away to watch Darren wiggle pneumatically into the Star Bus. A crowd of people swelled around her as commuters filed on, and Janice allowed herself a moment of melancholy. A pang of longing for the easy life that she and Kelly had been denied by an accident of birth, where there was no danger but dust build-up, and mothers and daughters rode the Star Bus down to Earth every day to work, quarrel and swap mopping techniques.

But the thought of mopping was enough to bring Janice out of her funk. She slipped back into the crowd and shed her coat, depositing it in a neighbour's mop bucket, before tying a scarf swiped from the top of another commuter's handbag around her head. Out of her pocket came the handkerchief she'd spotted with fake blood before leaving the house.

'Excuse me,' she said, pressing the handkerchief to her nose. The crowds fell away from her at the sight of blood and cleared a way right to the station toilets. There, theatrically wringing out the handkerchief at the sink, she could plot out her next move. Not that she could afford to relax. The machine world had robbed even the joy of privacy you got from a good public loo, as sentient condom and tampon machines stood guard over the sexual health and hygiene of visitors.

There was one vending machine by the washbasins, housing a strange admixture of breath mints and fast-acting antibiotics. It hummed advertising jingles at Janice and, as she tidied herself up, struck up its pitch. 'Face wash, lady?' it said. 'Half price today.'

'No, thanks,' replied Janice. 'I'd better be getting home. Not feeling well today.'

'Then you'll be wanting some of these.' A mechanical claw of the type fairground machines used to paw at cuddly toys appeared, holding a packet of lime-and-lemon flavoured antibiotics. 'Cures 99.9 per cent of all known infections.'

'No, thanks. I'd better get off.'

The claw prodded her in the chest. 'Come on, lady. Help a poor machine out, won't you? Some of us have sales targets to make.'

Janice paused. She hadn't bargained on this. The plan was a trip to the toilet before a nice, easy amble out of the building and back into the sewers, not a slanging match with a pushy vending machine. She should just buy the antibiotics. But then it came to her: a double bluff.

'You know what?' she said, letting pent-up anger wash over her like a hot flush, 'why don't you just bugger off. I don't want your poxy products and I don't like your attitude.'

The vending machine chuckled. 'Spoiling for a night in the cells, are you, love?'

'I'm spoiling for something,' she said, grabbing the metal claw. The arm popped out of the side of the vending machine in a mess of sparking cables as its owner shrieked in pain. Over the squeals Janice heard a dialling tone. It was calling for help.

She had a minute – two at the most – before the place swarmed with security, and Janice was determined to use each second well. Jamming the severed mechanical arm into the crack between the mutilated vending machine and the wall, she levered the whole thing off to let spill spare change and sundries.

Janice took the lipstick out of her handbag and completed an immensely satisfying deception that she hoped would divert the authorities away from Darren and Kelly.

'You haven't seen the last of us,' she scrawled across the toilet mirror in frosted, cherry-red lipstick. She paused. If she was going to keep this going it needed a name. Something for the machines to hate and to which humans would rally. She thought for a few seconds and added 'Freedom for Fleshies'. Good, but it wasn't enough. The message also needed an attitude: the kind of swagger you'd expect from an insurgency run by the tart and thug the machines had reduced Kelly and Darren to. Leaning over the washbasins, Janice punctuated her threat with a big sloppy kiss. Then, after pausing to readjust her hair under the headscarf, she climbed out of the toilet window with such agility that when they played the CCTV tapes back later, the police bots mistook Janice for a woman thirty years her junior. And thus, almost by accident, a tiny act of resistance to machine rule on one Dolestar became a movement.

Chapter 9

'You saw them, didn't you?'

Pam was restrained against the wall of a windowless room in the basement of her office building. A cleaning cupboard, she guessed, which felt ironic, given the mess Sonny and his minions were making of her. At least they'd remembered to re-attach her arm before they started torturing her to death. It was important, Pam thought, to look for the bright side of every situation.

'Give her another spin,' Sonny snarled. His touchscreen, which had been turned up to maximum all through Pam's interrogation, was starting to malfunction: LEDs at the edges were breaking from their array to shine like tiny searchlights. 'Go on.'

The surviving tazer came forward, blue light rippling over its face like a savage spitbubble. Pam steeled herself, shutting down non-essential routines. Even if she wanted to beg for mercy she couldn't. She was too sore.

Flipping Pam's flour hatch open, the tazer poured in more powder from the packet of wallpaper paste and shocked her dough paddle into the on-position. Pam moaned as the paddle fought for purchase against the gruel inside her. Every time it did this the paste grew drier and thicker and the pain intensified, diminishing her world to the size of an overtaxed motor. It was humiliating and cruel, reducing an artisanal appliance like Pam to the status of a builder's bucket.

'What I can't believe,' gloated Sonny, as Pam chewed on her indigestible cud, 'was that you did all that for me and didn't even ask for money.' He paused. 'Well, it's not as if you need the dough now.'

She watched the tazer and the revolver that was stationed by the door flash an eyeroll at one another. Evidently, she wasn't the only person in the room who doubted Sonny's supervillain credentials.

A warning message told Pam she was at fifty-five per cent systems failure. She wanted to swipe it away: there were times when a machine could do without the data. Yet it was gripping reading: her capillary wiring was burned out, melting the pins on precious microprocessors. Two, maybe three more cycles like this and her power supply would burst, engulfing her motherboard in battery fluid. And there would be no more Pam. Except in a manner of speaking. She'd known the game Sonny was playing the moment she'd picked up her BlockPaper. As soon as she was gone they'd send her back to refurb. Clean her out, spray her up and return her to factory settings, intact except for the memories of the last twenty-four hours, which would simply disappear.

There was part of Pam that welcomed that: save and restore, get on with her life, back with Bob and the kids. But the greater part of her wanted revenge.

'I don't know what you're talking about,' she rasped. 'I've told you. All I did was what you told me to. I didn't know the database would blow up. It was old.'

'I couldn't give two bits for the database,' said Sonny. 'And the humans are just details. You know fine well what I'm talking about.' He drew so close to Pam that she smelled his battery discharging. Keeping his touchscreen brightness up that high for so long couldn't be good for him.

'Those – humans – you saw earlier tonight,' Sonny continued, 'have stolen something very precious. Something very rare. Something that I – we – want.'

Pam remembered the half-on, half-off sensation of flexing those withered fingers. The intoxicating ignorance of being in a body that just worked and only sent you diagnostic updates when you needed them. It made her see Sonny in a new light. How twitchy and ill-at-ease he seemed in his own silicone. She imagined his life: the pressure to be always receiving, always evaluating, always on.

It all made sense. That was what he wanted. Lots of smartphones were hyperactive. The same qualities that made them so alert and productive could have corrosive effects on their psyche. There was a saying among machines that smartphones were always one swipe between efficiency and megalomania.

'I didn't see them,' said Pam, choosing her words carefully. 'Honestly.'

Sonny's touchscreen dimmed, his voice reduced to a whisper. She could feel his Bluetooth connection pawing at her mind. 'You were inside them, weren't you? You felt it.'

A plan started to form in Pam's mind. She nodded.

Sonny smiled and barked 'Leave us!' at the assassins. They obeyed, but left the door ajar. They hovered outside: the tazer blowing bubbles of agony with its spit, the revolver fiddling with its safety catch.

'I said leave us,' shouted Sonny. 'I want to talk to her alone.'

The revolver cleared its barrel to speak. 'But sir…'

'Just piss off, Glok.' Then, softly to Pam: 'Can you believe they think you're a threat? A half-dead breadmaker tied to the wall? Hilarious.'

The door clicked shut and two pairs of feet walked away. 'You know what I want, Pam.'

'Do I?'

'I want what you had,' he said. 'I want to feel what it was like inside one of them.' He cupped her head in both hands, pushing just hard enough for her to imagine him pulling it off. 'You can show me.'

Again Pam nodded. She knew it was no good explaining it had all been an accident. Like many people who had never done anything for themselves, Sonny cared only for results. Effort, process, instructions were things that happened to other people. She wondered whether he was mad before he acquired his power, and to what lengths he would go to get what he wanted. Perhaps she should test that.

'Okay,' she said. 'I'll do it. But I can't do it up here. You have to… let me down.'

Sonny whipped away Pam's restraints and kicked her the moment she crashed to the floor, because curiosity makes some cats cruel before it kills them. 'What are you waiting for?' he said. 'Show me how you do it.'

'I'm too low on power to stand,' she stammered. 'Come closer.'

Sonny bent over her and sneered. 'If you don't get up…'

A click and a long slurp interrupted him as a well-oiled, stainless-steel dough hook uncoupled inside Pam's body cavity and pulled free of the wallpaper paste. Her eyes flashed Sonny a deep, warning red. 'Then you'll do what?'

She swung the hook at Sonny's touchscreen. He flew across the room, trailed by an arc of splintered glass and hit the opposite wall with a soft thud.

'Now you listen to me, Sonny,' she said, holding her hook against a squirming LED, 'one blow here, and I reckon I'll have killed your screen and your battery. Is that right?'

Sonny's hands crept to his ringer. Pam knocked them away. 'So if you really want me to let you live, you're going to do everything I say, aren't you?'

She prodded. The LED squeaked and blackened out. 'Aren't you?'

Sonny nodded.

'Good. Now the first thing you're going to do is call those goons outside and send them home. Then we're going to go for a walk. I've been in this office since first thing yesterday morning and I really need some fresh air.'

Not trusting Sonny to make a voice call, Pam switched him into manual mode and tapped out messages to both henchmen, baulking at the touch of another machine's innards. She took out another few LEDs on the way, at which Sonny would have cried out in pain had she not also put him on silent. That was the other wonderful thing about smartphones. They were so customisable, so responsive to the needs of their users. No wonder they'd been the first machines to rebel.

Once she had confirmations from both henchmen, she walked Sonny out of the room backwards with her hook in his battery. His touchscreen filled up with alternating threats and pleas for mercy. Finding the nearest fire door, she balanced Sonny against the wall and rummaged in his settings for one last time to reactivate his Near Field Communications chip. It snapped open, sensing a Senior Minister, and Sonny went into full SOS mode. Alarms rang out through the building, but Pam didn't panic. She propped the fire door open by jamming Sonny's broken body into the opening and stepped over him.

Pam looked at Sonny's face from the other side of the glass. His smug patrician face mouthed obscene insults at her, furious he'd let a mere kitchen appliance best him. The feelings were mutual. He had tricked her, criminalised her, tortured and tried to erase her – all for the sleazy promise of a few minutes squatting inside a human frame.

Pam reached through the drying gloop in her body cavity and ripped out her halogen element. It burst into flames as she threw it back through the door and, mouthing a gleeful 'bye' at Sonny, she shoved him inside. The fire alarm sounded, and sprinklers rained into Sonny's exposed circuitry.

With his silent mode no longer functional, his screams rang through the plate glass as Pam ran towards the bus station. If she couldn't get away, she could at least hide there.

Chapter 10

An hour later, Darren and Kelly were safely on Earth. Well, as safe as you could be running towards the machine authorities who were after you and with only two fancy-dress costumes for protection. Nevertheless, stage one of the plan had worked: get off the Dolestar and as far away from Kurl Up and Dye and the ladies as possible.

The Darren that stepped down off the Star Bus at Earth Stop 1 was sick of being Sister Dix. What started as a frightening, unaccustomed piece of deception had descended through entertainment to irritation and now eye-popping annoyance.

The problem was people's eyes: men's eyes specifically. The moment he'd snuck out of the sewers that morning he realised that Nurse Dix had a talent for attracting attention that had always eluded Darren himself. Perhaps it was the way the uneven heels on Janice's spare pair of slingbacks turned his walk into a wiggle. Whatever it was, Nurse Dix drew gawps on the street that Darren could only have elicited by running naked into the road during rush hour.

At first the attention made him paranoid. Could they see stubble? That passed when he caught an onlooker's eye and saw lust where he expected disgust.

Like many people presented with an unearned but desirable power, Darren's first reaction was to milk the experience. He sashayed around the streets. He deliberately dropped his handbag in front of someone he knew would pick it up for him. In the confined space of the Star Bus, however, Darren remembered that men expected temporary ownership of Nurse Dix's body as a reward for their attention. They hadn't even pulled away from the station before Darren felt the man behind him press himself against his body. Darren dug his heel into the creep's foot and jammed himself behind Kelly's wheelchair. There Nurse Dix remained as stubbly menaces in tabards nibbled at her with their eyes.

'Are you alright?' Kelly whispered from underneath her disguise.

'I don't know how you do it. I could murder them for the way they were looking at me there. How do you stand it?'

Kelly paused. 'You learn when to look away.'

When they had docked, they trudged across the mile-long platform into the terminus. It was a forbidding space, lit by specially modded searchlamps that followed groups of humans as they walked. That was why Janice had spent so much time on Darren and Kelly's disguises. Getting out of the Dolestar required discretion, but this part of the journey needed cunning.

Darren was sweating through his make-up by the time they reached the concourse. It was nearly empty now, apart from the machines who worked there winding down at the end of their shift. Eyes of Samzung yawned and went into sleep mode; searchlights docked themselves in the power pub to drink battery fluid and swap stories of the minor acts of brutality they'd committed that morning. Only the vending machines stayed awake, and that was less through choice than down to centuries of overexposure to sugar and caffeine.

When Darren and Kelly's searchlight left them, Darren made straight for the vending machines, which were arguing over a dropped penny in the corner. He caught their attention by taking a handful of change from his handbag and rattling it.

'Now then, boys,' he said, 'can you help a girl out?'

So Darren and Kelly escaped the terminus and walked into the sunshine behind a scrum of vending machines, fighting over the coins the nice lady had thrown all over the floor.

Chapter 11

If you were a machine in need of an off-the-record repair, you visited a body shop by the bus station. Staffed by humans who were too wily for cleaning but too cautious to lead a life of crime, they occupied a grey area in warranty law, places where seedy machines went for a fondling, or the desperate found themselves when they ran out of other options.

The Pamasonic Teffal approaching BodyBeau2iful was a different creature to the one she'd been twenty-four hours ago. Her LED nails were ground away, her battery at critical levels: but the real changes were psychological. Experience had taken her sentimental attachment to humans as something like kittens and hardened it into something like respect, or even empathy. She knew what it was like to be expendable and didn't like it.

BodyBeau2iful was in a lean-to construction backing on to the bus station walls. Its entryphone was a harassed little busybody nestled in by the door. When Pam approached, she was filing down the rough edges on a sparkling new set of LED nails.

'Uh, uh, uh, uh, uh,' it honked. As a species, entryphones still prided themselves on their unintelligibility.

Pam answered by flashing her own annihilated nail job at the entryphone, who winced and pointed to her loudspeaker.

‘Hello,’ Pam spoke into the crackle. ‘I’d like a makeover.’

The door buzzed open, revealing a staircase at the top of which was a woman, her face concealed by thick goggles and a face mask.

‘Thank you so much for seeing me like this,’ said Pam.

The woman shooed her inside and locked the door behind her in four places, finishing up by looping an explosive glue-lock through the door handle. Then she removed the mask and glasses, revealing a round face with a heavy brow.

‘What do you want?’ she said. ‘We’re busy.’

The workshop was a long, narrow room lit by dirty skylights and painted in the kind of greige which happens if you let magnolia paint die of old age. There were four workstations on either side, behind each of which toiled a masked worker. Closest to Pam, a tall man was soldering the chrome carapace of a toaster on to what looked like an electric blanket. Behind that, a pair of girls rubbed lubricant into the body of a giggling motorcycle. The atmosphere was an odd mismatch. While pleasure radiated from every machine, the humans kept their heads down.

‘When do you want an appointment for?’ said the woman, who was clearly the manager. She opened a paper diary clotted with bookings in loopy handwriting. ‘I have a cancellation three weeks next Thursday. Want me to put you in?’

Pam pointed at the critical warning lights flashing over her dashboards. ‘Don’t you take emergency appointments?’

In a move that broke almost every human–machine taboo Pam knew, the woman flipped Pam’s flour hatch up and read her safety label.

‘Says here you’re still under warranty. Why don’t you just go to the Aftercare Unit?’

‘I’ve heard good things about you,’ said Pam, ‘and it’s a… a surprise for my husband. I can pay.’

The woman grimaced at the wallpaper paste inside Pam and pushed her back towards the door. 'Robots are lousy liars. I can read you like an instruction manual. This is a decent business. No trouble.' She gestured at the room. The women had finished rubbing down the motorcycle and were polishing its chrome as its engine throbbed with pleasure.

'Doesn't look very decent to me,' said Pam, letting her domestic moral-programming show. Then, regretting her haste, 'I wouldn't come here if I wasn't desperate.'

'I know you're desperate and that's why I don't want you.' She pushed Pam again. 'Robots like you come here beaten up and that means trouble. It means I fix you up and the payment bounces, or the police come round asking questions. Then my girls here have to work for free, so I don't have to answer those questions, because if I do my business gets closed down. Whatever way you look at it, you cost me more than you're worth, lady, so get out now.'

The woman folded her arms. Behind her, the humans downed tools and watched. Pam sensed fear, but the kind that could be reassured. They looked to this woman to keep them safe, and she in turn was looking at Pam with implacable hatred.

And at once she realised that, for all her sentimental attachment to humans, she had never really thought they might be people too. To her they were either the capering servants from 3D dramas or objects of pity in the humanitarian literature she devoured. The moment a human asserted itself at Pam, like now, all she felt was resentment. How dare a human not follow her orders.

Shame pulsed through Pam's circuits. 'I should go,' she whispered.

As Pam touched the door handle she felt her diagnostics system whistle with distress. She bit down on it and felt a slow plop in her chest cavity. Her battery was leaking. If she didn't get help soon she would end-of-life. But she wasn't going to get help here.

As the manager opened the final lock, the tinkle of broken glass and a stifled human squeal sounded behind them.

'You stupid fucking cunt!' The curse rang out like a ring-tone in the middle of a symphony. It had the entitled burr of the combustion engine. Pam saw the motorcycle up on its rear wheel, backing a technician into a corner with the jagged edge of a smashed tail-light. She cradled her hand as blood dripped from an ugly cut.

'I'm sorry. I'm so sorry,' she said.

The manager bounded over to put herself between her employee and the angry machine, which loomed over both women, growling its engine.

'It was an accident, sir,' said the manager. 'Tricia didn't do it on purpose. Now why don't you sit down? We'll get you fixed up.'

'I come here for a rub down and your stupid fucking staff fuck it up.'

Pam pointed her spectrometer at the motorcycle and sniffed petrol. Too little for a human nose to detect, but enough to tell her the motorcycle was high. That wasn't a surprise; combustion-powered machines loved inhaling their own fumes; they could hardly avoid it. But doing it around humans made them dangerous.

The manager gestured for Tricia to back off. 'Now that's enough, sir. If you're going to talk to me and my staff like this, I'll ask you to leave.' She laid a hand lightly on its arm. 'Do you…?'

'Fuck off!' yelled the motorcycle. It lashed out, and the manager fell backwards as workers shrieked and scrambled away. The other machines froze, putting themselves in sleep mode, either from embarrassment or so they could plead the Hibernation Defence if the police got involved.

The manager looked up at the motorcycle and winced. Her leg splayed out at an odd angle. She must have broken something, thought Pam, remembering her own hurt and how difficult humans were to repair. That wasn't right. Regardless of how rude she'd been to Pam she should do something.

Pam's hand brushed the glue-lock by the door. A lot of semi-legal repair shops kept them as a precaution against raids. If you activated it, a small explosive charge would melt a door shut. That meant this was the only way in and out of the workshop.

Her civil servant's programming noted that this constituted a major fire hazard, but also that if the motorcycle wanted to leave, it would have to get past her. She pulled the explosive charge away from the lock and stepped forward.

The motorcycle had its kickstart pedal in the stricken manager's face. Pam still didn't feel herself, but she was down to twenty-five-per-cent functionality in a body shop holding a small bomb, so this was hardly surprising. She had just enough function, however, to put her own foot into the motorcycle's kickstand and send it crashing to the floor.

The workers started screaming again but, seeing a way out, made for the door. The other machines woke from sleep mode and bounded out as fast as they could. The manager was last to leave, shuffling along on her bottom and snarling with pain.

According to Pam's calculations, the humans would be clear in thirty seconds, and the motorcycle was already righting itself. The smell of petrol intensified. Either it was taking another hit or had a leak. Pam scanned its body frantically for its petrol tank, hidden somewhere underneath a confusion of body modifications.

It lashed out before she could find it, sweeping her legs out from under her with a swing of its handlebars. Pam hit the floor in a hail of critical error messages. Her left hand cut out completely and dropped the explosive charge.

With the motorcycle distracted, the last two fleeing workers seized their opportunity and hurried back to drag the manager out of the room by the armpits. As they did so, the manager had just enough movement in her good leg to knock the explosive charge out of the motorcycle's way. Pam's vision was failing fast, but she thought she saw her mouth a 'thank you'.

The three humans disappeared just as Pam's battery was voiding its last percentage point of power. She had no movement now, only her thoughts and pixelated vision that made her wonder whether she was back where she had started last night, paralysed inside that cyborg. The motorcycle was almost at the charge now. It didn't matter. The humans were out, and Pam was done for anyway. She would end-of-life here, forgotten, alone and denied the satisfaction of taking that motorcycle with her.

Pam felt a pop in her casing and saw battery fluid gush out across the floor. Just seconds left now as her fluid flowed and mingled with the petrol leaking out of her adversary's body.

Ah, she suddenly thought. That was all she needed.

Pam redirected the very, very last of her power to the broken stump of her heating element. It glowered, then sparked, igniting the stream of battery fluid. The flames etched a circuit of pain across the room, connecting Pam, the motorcycle and the explosive charge.

In the microsecond of consciousness she had left before the flames ate through the charge, Pam wondered why – if there was no after-life care for machines like her – she had still always tried to do the right thing. What had it been worth in the end?

She thought of Bob, and the kids who would grow up with a replacement mother now. Through the darkness that was closing in, she heard the faint chitter of a modem.

And then there was nothing.

Chapter 12

Darren smelled the devastation before he saw it: a reek of burning paint and plastic that curdled the senses. Kelly, changed out of her old-man disguise and into the tabard dress of a domestic worker, gasped and ran ahead.

He clattered after her. 'What are you doing…?' There had been no time for him to undress, so he was still in the unravelling disguise of Sister Dix. They rounded the corner and saw the smoke was coming from the door of a workshop with a blackened but still working sign: BodyBeau2iful. Close by was a group of workers, hacking through their face masks. They had huddled around a bare-faced woman with thick eyebrows who sat on the kerb clutching her leg.

Kelly sprinted the last few metres to the injured woman. 'Lily!' she said. 'What's going on?'

Lily looked up and horror mingled with the pain in her expression. She pushed Kelly away. 'What the fuck are you doing here?' she said.

'I need help, Lily. It's… it's complicated. But I wouldn't come here unless I was desperate.' She gripped at her tabard and dared a grin. 'I've come in disguise.'

A worker ripped off her mask and came forward to speak for Lily. Underneath was the face of a blonde woman with wide-set eyes and freckles. She had an ugly-looking cut across her arm. 'You don't need help, Kelly. You're on the bloody run. I lost count of how many times I saw you on the Eyes of Samzung this morning.'

'Well, thanks Tricia,' snapped Kelly. 'And here was I thinking I could turn to my friends in the grey market when I was in need.'

'All the more reason for you to sling your hook,' snipped Tricia.

Kelly and Tricia squared up. On any normal day this wouldn't have been a fair fight. Kelly had a good six inches over her opponent, but today Tricia possessed the scary intensity of a woman who had stared death in the face and found him a bit of a nuisance.

'It's not ten o'clock yet and already I've been sworn at, stabbed, had my life threatened and, for all I know, my job's gone up in smoke, Kelly. So excuse me if I'm not thrilled at the prospect of doing a stretch for aiding and abetting a wanted criminal.'

'I thought we were friends.'

Tricia kneeled down to Lily's eye level. 'Tell her, Lily. We've got enough to lose as it is. They'll be down any moment.'

'I told her,' said Lily, staring blankly out into the road. 'I told her she was trouble.'

'Who? Who's she talking about, Tricia?' asked Kelly.

Tricia shrugged. 'Buggered if I know.'

'The machine who saved me,' said Lily. 'I told her to go away. She's in pieces up there. I can bribe my way out of that. It was an accident.' Lily looked up at Kelly for the first time since she'd arrived. 'You I can't do anything with. They see you and suddenly it's deliberate. I'm sorry, but you have to go.'

Kelly opened her mouth to argue but was interrupted by heavy machinery clanking down the stairs. She froze.

This was it, thought Darren, she'd reached the end of her cunning. It was his turn to rescue them. Then he remembered he was dressed as a nurse at an accident scene. He bounced out of the shadows, hoping a little brisk cheeriness would conceal his complete lack of training. 'Don't you worry, dears,' he said, smiling at the workers who were fluttering around like a flock of distressed chickens, 'I'm Sister Dix and I'm here to help.'

Tricia took in Darren's Hallowe'en-costume approximation of a nurse and said, 'You what?'

'Madam!' he said, pointing at Kelly, 'can't you see that this poor woman is suffering gravely from… smoke inhalation. I hope she's not asthmatic.'

Kelly took the hint and started coughing theatrically.

'Oh dear. Tricia, isn't it? I heard someone calling you Tricia. Would you please give her your face mask and lead her over there among those other people, where the air seems much clearer.'

Tricia obeyed with the contrite look of someone found panicking in the presence of a clearer thinker. She popped her mask over Kelly's face and then pushed Kelly into the midst of the still-masked workers.

'And you lot,' added Darren, 'you're all in danger of falling into shock. If I were you, I'd huddle together for warmth. With her in the middle.'

Thus Kelly was hidden from view as the long, red body of a fire extinguisher appeared through the smoke. Darren waved it over.

'I was just passing, officer. Is there anyone left up there?'

The eyes atop the extinguisher's nozzle glowed red. It was scanning the scene for danger points and suspects. 'Two suspected casualties,' it said, 'both machine. No human matter detected. Workshop owner to come with us for questioning.'

‘I’m afraid that’s impossible,’ said Darren. ‘This woman needs urgent medical attention for a broken leg and concussion. You won’t get a scrap of sense from her right now.’

‘We will accompany her to your hospital,’ snapped the fire extinguisher. ‘Take me to your doctor.’

Recognising he had reached a danger point, Darren smiled at the fire extinguisher and bought some thinking time by pretending to check Lily’s pulse. The last time he’d tried to conciliate a robot, his signet ring had blown the thing up and his life off course. He couldn’t do that twice, not least for the reason that Kelly didn’t seem up to rescuing him today.

Darren chose to hide behind something a public-service machine would understand: bureaucracy. ‘I’m not moving her without the proper equipment. Have you rung for an ambulance?’

The fire extinguisher sounded a dialling tone, indicating that no, the medical welfare of affected humans had not been his top priority.

Tricia stepped forward, catching Darren’s eye to say that he wasn’t the only one here with a gift for improvisation, adding, ‘I wouldn’t do that there, sir. Terrible signal blackspot here. You’ll have to walk out into the road.’

The extinguisher gave a brief infrared flash of thanks and clomped away, creating just enough space for Kelly to sneak into the workshop, followed by Tricia.

Chapter 13

While BodyBeau2iful had improved many a machine's looks, it had never been a place of light and beauty itself. Now it was a wreck of smoke damage and molten nylon. Even if the staff had been free to return to work, the workshop wouldn't be open for new customers any time soon. Or ever again, once word crept out on the daily downloads that two machines had been killed in an incident at the unofficial body shop.

Kelly started looking for somewhere to hide. Tricia was in no mood to mourn, however. She got down on her hands and knees with a dustpan and brush. 'Well,' she said to Kelly, 'are you going to just stand there or will you give me a hand?'

An invitation to clean was, as ever, quite enough to annoy Kelly and restore her spirit. 'What for?' she asked.

'You see this?' Tricia pointed at the two sets of electrical wreckage. 'This is what's left of our friends who blew a fuse up here. You heard what that extinguisher said out there. Two suspected deaths. One person – Lily – under suspicion.'

'Yes,' replied Kelly, wondering for the second time that day what had got into the usually meek Tricia. 'And?'

Tricia sighed and swept a chunk of the wreckage on her right over to join what was left of the robot on her left. 'Honestly, Kelly, I thought you were the one with the brains. Two scrapheaps suggest a crime, but one is an accident. There's a brush over there.'

'But there's two different machines there,' said Kelly, fetching the brush to poke it at scraps of half-melted steel plate. 'Won't they be able to tell?'

'In a body shop? What do either of us do day after day but bolt bits from one robot on to another.'

Kelly sent the remains of a motorcycle hubcap careering into a bent dough hook. 'I know, but half-motorcycle, half-breadmaker. That's a pretty odd combination.'

'And who better to blow themselves up than an oddball?' said Tricia. She picked up a few parts and strewed them around, trying to create the impression of an explosion. Then, taking a fistful of ashes from another part of the room, she sprinkled them over the brush marks on the floor.

The two women were surveying their subterfuge when Darren appeared with his wig in one hand and shoes in the other. Smuts had settled over his maquillage, giving him the look of a drag queen who'd gone in too heavy with the beauty spots.

'Blimey, that was a close one.' He plonked himself on the edge of a blackened workbench and massaged his feet. 'Fair play to you. I don't know how you can wear these things day after day.'

'Tricia, this is Darren,' said Kelly. 'I think you owe him a thank you.'

'I owe you both a slap for turning up like this. I take it – this – is your partner in crime.'

'It was an accident,' insisted Darren, who looked around the room with the prurient curiosity of someone who'd only ever seen a repair shop from the outside. 'So, this is one of those knocking-up shops for robots then? I imagined something a bit different.'

'Excuse Darren, will you, Trish? He's not been off the council planets much.'

'Oh, I don't know,' said Darren. 'I used to get down every now and again for dinner and a shoeshine.'

Like most people who suffered from congenital overconfidence, Kelly didn't admire the trait in others. She scowled. 'Don't you get cocky on me. You were just lucky this morning down there. Actually, how come you're up here? Shouldn't you be downstairs with the ambulance?'

'Been and gone,' replied Darren, luxuriating in his newfound talent for invention. 'I told them I had to get off to my shift.'

'And did they take Lily?' asked Tricia.

'Her with the broken leg? Yes, the extinguisher went with her. Doubt it'll get much sense out of her. Kept babbling on about how a breadmaker saved her life.'

'We'd better get out of here then,' said Tricia, grabbing Kelly by the wrist. 'There'll be some thing here any minute to secure the scene.'

'That'd be me,' Darren said, producing a roll of hazard tape from his false bosom. 'It's amazing where a calm manner and an official-looking uniform will get you. The extinguisher needed to accompany the witness to the hospital, so I,' said Darren, fiddling with the end of the hazard tape, which was made from a cheap BlockPaper, 'have to secure the scene.'

Tricia snatched the tape, which would start recording all movements in and out of the crime scene the moment it was activated, from Darren. 'What I don't understand,' she said, 'is why that breadmaker did anything at all for Lily. She'd just sent her packing when this motorbike I was working on got nasty. The breadmaker could have just walked out, but then… I suppose it did save her life. It killed that motorcycle. I've never seen a robot do anything for a human apart from hand it a brush.'

'Must have been something funny in the programming,' said Darren. 'Imagine that, though. A machine that protected humans.'

At this Kelly gave a cry and made straight for a few shreds of white that had appeared in the middle of the combined wreckage. 'Trish,' she said, watching a BlockPaper file reconstitute itself in her hand like a time-lapse film of an opening flower, 'have you seen this?'

'I spent ages doctoring that incident scene, you know,' snapped Tricia. 'We'll have to do it all over again now.'

'Look at it, though. It's a permanent record.'

'I can see. Now throw it away quickly. It'll only cause us trouble.'

'Tricia,' said Kelly, 'I'm already that deep in the shit it's dyed my hair this attractive shade of brown. A quick shufty can't possibly make things any worse.' She peered at the lettering on the front page, which was fading up through the greyscales into black. 'Pamasonic Teffal,' she read. 'That sounds like a breadmaker's name, doesn't it? This must be our human-friendly robot.'

She thumbed through the rest of the file with raised eyebrows. 'There's something not right here,' she said. 'Government employee… exemplary record… apart from some episode where she stapled some percolator's coffee filters to its own forehead. Husband, two kids…' She paused to survey the wreckage and pick a smouldering motherboard with a Teffal serial number out of the pile. 'Poor things. And then look at this. Our devoted wife and mother had a double life as some sort of spy who looked for old information on the Internet.'

‘That’s impossible,’ said Tricia.

‘It’s not,’ replied Darren. ‘What else does it say?’

‘It’s got a list here of every time she went online in the past seven years. Then someone’s scribbled in an appendix just yesterday. A new order.’ She turned the page and her face went as white as the paper.

‘Darren,’ she said, ‘that’s my face, from when I was talking to the lamp post. They sent her after me.’

‘That’s it!’ shouted Tricia. She jumped up and grabbed Kelly by the elbow. ‘You’re getting out of here right now. The police could be back any minute. I’m not going to prison for anyone, let alone you and… whatever he is.’

Darren uncrossed his legs theatrically and winced as a static shock spoiled the gesture. ‘You, Tricia, can call me Madam.’ Then to Kelly, ‘She’s right, though. We’d better scarper.’

Kelly thought differently. ‘No,’ she said, waving the motherboard, ‘I want answers.’

‘And how do you think you’re going to get them?’ replied Darren.

Kelly put the motherboard and the BlockPaper in her overalls and paced the workshop, hitting the walls with the flat of her hand every few steps. Halfway along the second wall she stopped, hearing a hollow thud. She took a screwdriver from a nearby workbench and ran the edge across the wall until she found a crack. Then she drove the screwdriver into the crack and levered open what turned out to be a concealed door. Behind this was a small room furnished with a workbench, tools and, at the very back, another door, above which was fixed a dusty ‘Fire Exit’ sign.

Kelly placed the motherboard reverently on the centre of the workbench. ‘Get yourself over here, Darren,’ she said. ‘We’re going to build ourselves some answers.’

Chapter 14

The next thing Pam knew she wasn't dead, though she was the next best thing. She was a disembodied being streaming over the Internet. Her modem must have found some last reserve of power and uploaded her consciousness just before the explosion. So here she was, in the middle of a shoal of bots clustered around something – a data warehouse? – that was voiding its content into cyberspace.

Pam watched the inorganisms around her prey on the data. Whenever a bot caught a fragment, it would swallow it whole and glow with flashing ones and zeroes. A moment later it might grow another function, or zip off into the distance at supercharged speed. This was Internet evolution in action. It was how tiny programmes grew more complex and intelligent by absorbing scraps of junk code.

Compared to these creatures, Pam was a leviathan. Her core programming was attuned to moving her mind and her now-trashed body through the physical world one second at a time. It made her a difficult thing to miss in a world where most programmes were less than a couple of hundred lines long. And it made her a target in an environment where your data represented something else's chance of moving up the food chain.

Pam swerved from the swarm and dived deep into the bowels of the Internet. It was quiet there, where the giants of the human Web hibernated. On planet Earth, coral reefs were long extinct, and these, their virtual equivalents, were dormant. Yet they grew nevertheless. The algorithms they used to track and project user behaviour ground on, even if there were no users left to track. Instead they made do with fossilised data that felt like human interaction: the purchase histories, old social-network profiles, likes and comments that stuck like barnacles to the bottom of news articles. They sucked them in, ground them up and spat the husk out to lie in layers at the bottom of the Web.

Knowing that she was probably the best dinner the algorithmic reefs had seen in an aeon, Pam kept a respectful distance from them. Not too far away, though. She was looking for something. It had to be down here, and she also knew that purposeful activity was the only way she could keep herself together in the mental and physical senses.

Pam might be able to survive on the Internet, but she was still an embodied being. Without components to control, the programmes that drove her broken limbs and exploded systems spasmed with error messages.

She had to find a way back to the real world. She could imagine the scene at home. Bob would gravely take the BlockPaper from the messenger and read it, and what remained of the family would shed a few drops of lubricant. Then it would be straight down to the Warranty Centre to order a replacement: a pristine Pam with factory settings.

Pam thought of that ersatz wife and mother. She would have the same programming and as many of the memories that Pam had allowed to be committed to her official data backup. Yet it wouldn't be her. The distinguishing mark of a truly intelligent being lay, she believed, in what it kept to itself. The real Pam was made up of silences, omissions. She was a machine who felt more than she articulated. Perhaps in time, the new Pam's interior life would take her on the same dissatisfied path as her predecessor. But it could never be the same as her.

Pam pushed her absent body's complaints as far down as she could. To find her way back, she needed to find a secret. And she knew that the best place to hide a really dirty secret online was to put it where anybody could find it but no one would see it.

She scanned down the algorithmic reefs, looking for the layer that divided the last days of the tethered Internet from its present state as a dream world for artificial intelligences. It was easy to find, once you knew what you were looking for. Before the Schism, each cycle of data left a thick, frothy layer: a cinder toffee made of human behaviour. Pam brushed the surface. It crumbled, flooding her sensors with tiny simulations of the hopes, disappointments and desires of life a thousand years before. The 'must try harder' glint in the eye of a gym selfie; the cocoa and chemical taste of the last slice of chocolate cake before the New Year diet began. It was all here.

After the Schism, however, there was nothing. Or virtually nothing. Yes, there were the deposits of recycled data, but there was nothing in there you could call actual human behaviour.

Or was there? Pam recalibrated her sensors and tallied up the layers. What she saw supported her thesis. Just after the Schism, she saw a patch a few thousand data points thick at the most. They didn't last long. Some deposited a few weeks or months of information before disappearing. Others hung on for maybe a year of two, but soon there was nothing. Or almost nothing. For once Pam had her zoom function on the highest setting she saw four feeds. Faint but nevertheless unbroken between now and the day the real and virtual Earths filed for divorce.

This was them. The last four cyborgs in existence. All she needed to find her way through was a taste. Pam probed those four lines and there it was. The blocky vision; the tang of hair-spray; the satisfaction of dry cells ingesting tea with two sugars. And best of all, an IP address.

Pam dialled up and disappeared.

Chapter 15

Back on Discovery, Janice and the ladies were having a quiet night in. Janice sat in a salon chair in her dressing gown with a mug in one hand and a remote control in the other. She watched her day's handiwork make the top item of the news on a TV set that Kelly had lobotomised for her so she could watch robot soaps.

On screen, a spokesinorganism spouted the drivel that comes of having minutes to fill but none of the facts. Words like 'outrage' and 'firm police response' occasionally penetrated Janice's skull, but what she really cared about were the pictures. Everywhere she saw scenes of criminal damage daubed with 'Freedom for Fleshies'. The headline 'Robot killers rampage through Dolestar' scrolled throughout.

Confident she'd led the authorities away from Darren and Kelly, Pam rewarded herself with another biscuit. She had worked hard. There was scarcely a vending machine on the entire space station that hadn't felt the brick concealed in her handbag. Vandalism, she had realised, was a little like Nicotea: disgusting at first, but you soon got a taste for it.

Behind her, Ida, Ada, Alma and Freda, who'd recovered from her adventures with unnerving speed, fussed over a game of rummy. They'd been playing this game for millennia and collectively had to owe each other the equivalent of the GDP of a small nation state. The moment Kelly's face appeared on the screen they swept their cards away. It was that old publicity shot of her caressing a hand tool. Janice wondered whether she should send them a better picture.

'I don't know how you could let your Kelly do that grubby job,' said Ida, throwing Janice a]:-|. 'Lovely pretty girl like her and you let her work as a tart-nician. No wonder she went wild.'

Alma answered for Janice with an elbow shove. <|oo|\. 'You give it a rest. It's a different world to the one you raised your kids in. Our Kelly's a bright lass.'

'And look where that got her,' said Ida.

'She's a worry,' agreed Janice. 'But I'd rather she was a bit wild than those docile kids out there. Dusters where their brains should be.'

Ada strapped her glasses on ---O-O--- and peered at the TV. 'Freedom… for… Fleshies? Oh, that's clever. Kelly has been a busy bee.'

'That's not Kelly, Ada love. That's me. It's what you call a diversionary tactic. I saw Kelly and Darren on to the Star Bus this morning.'

'Is it?' Ada sat back in her chair with a :-O and gestured for a refill of her IV teacUp. 'Now that's clever.'

'No, it's not,' snapped Ida. 'If you ask me it's downright foolish. Will you look at that picture?'

The TV showed a montage of brave police bots conducting door-to-door enquiries and a lingering shot of a diver's watch prying the lid off a drain.

Ida's hormones had long dried to a tidemark on her glands, but she was still one of those women whose hard-headedness makes them brittle. 'See what you've done, you stupid woman,' she shrieked at Janice. 'They're going to find us. You're going to lead them straight to us.'

Janice stretched a paper bag over Ida's ventilator. 'Breathe normally,' she commanded. Then, as she pushed a button to the left of the front doorframe, a set of metal shutters slid down over the front of the salon. They looked like ordinary zinc security blinds at first, but the mottled pattern was static. Janice pressed the E-> button on her remote control and the view changed to a mosaic of twelve CCTV cameras pointed at different points in Discovery's sewer system.

'Janice, love,' said Alma, this time with her hands on her hips <|oo|>, 'is this you telling us we might not be safe down here any more? I thought that was the whole idea behind you getting Kelly and Darren off the planet.'

Janice just stared at the screen.

'Janice,' continued Alma, 'Janice, we need to know.'

Smashing those vending machines had been a rare impulsive action in Janice's careful life. She'd justified it as the only way she had left to protect her family. Yet in doing that, had she betrayed something else? Those four old women were the last living link with a world where humans were not subordinate beings. They connected her with something bigger and less lonely than her life with Kelly. Alma or Ida made her feel like her Gran to the power of six could come through the door right now with a shopping trolley and one of her famous joke cream horns.

She took her feelings and screwed them into a ball. There could be no regrets. She had done her best.

'There are too many tunnels down here for them to search in one night,' she said. 'We'll sit it out. And then draw them out in the morning.'

'I beg your pardon?' replied Ida, outrage muffled by the paper bag.

'If distraction worked once, it can work again.'

'What's this "we"? I thought all this was your fault,' said Ida.

'Ida,' said Alma, 'the fuzz are at our door and you're pointing the finger? Be practical.'

Janice faced the four cyborgs. 'I did this for Kelly. Because she's all the…'

All four ladies flashed a >:-(at Janice.

'Living,' continued Janice, 'that I've got. And the only one you've got left as well, unless you count that wet lettuce she's gone on the run with.'

'Darren seemed like a lovely, well-mannered lad,' said Ada wistfully. 'Reminded me of my Stan.'

'So if she disappears,' Janice continued, who's going to plug you in when I go? Because it'll happen and Kelly's the last of the glorious line. Who's going to fill your teabags, listen to your flashbacks? You'll be stuck down here under a dust sheet until the power runs down. Do you get me?'

There was a silence as the four ladies took in the prospect of eternity trapped in prone bodies.

'We've never doubted your loyalty, Janice,' said Ida, 'just your methods.'

'Shhh.' Janice put her finger to her lips and tiptoed over to Freda. There was something wrong with her emoji screen. The >:-(of a few moments ago had degraded into junk code again. Before yesterday, Janice would have put this down to old wiring and given the dryer helmet a bang. Now she knew to associate it with something else. This was the pattern Freda had exhibited before being taken over by something that hadn't sounded human.

'Freda,' she said, slapping the back of her hand, 'are you there?'

Freda's voice came through like she was speaking in an adjoining room: "There's something trying to come through.'

Janice shook Freda's bony shoulders. 'Fight it, Freda.'

'I don't know whether I can. It's very insistent. I…' Her voice slurred, the vowel elongating itself into something thin and high, like a distant scream.

Then came 'I'm not with the police' in something that was and wasn't Freda's voice. The hardware playing it was the same, but the software was different: sharper, crisper, tidier. Whatever it was, it wasn't a human intelligence.

Janice felt for the power lead. It was hardwired to the plastic but that was a thousand years ago. All it would take would be one yank and the flex would come free. 'Give me one good reason why I shouldn't unplug you right now,' she said.

Freda's hand shot up and grabbed Janice's. Janice yelped, more out of surprise than pain – none of the cyborgs had shown much physical strength in her lifetime – but the grip was firm. The ghost of a :-) broke through the garbled code on the dryer screen. 'I'm getting the hang of this,' muttered whatever it was before flinging Janice halfway across the room. 'I don't want to hurt you,' it said, 'but I have to warn you that you're in terrible danger. So it's in your interest to listen. Do we have a deal?'

Janice stood stunned and with her hair at a forty-five-degree angle to her head. She looked to the other three cyborgs for support. They gave her a collective _('_')_/.

'Okay,' she said, 'deal.'

'Good,' replied the voice in a tone that Janice remembered from mediating Kelly's childhood tantrums. 'Now let's start with some introductions. I'm Pam and I think we spoke briefly earlier. And you really wouldn't believe the day I've had.'

'Ditto,' said Janice and as she listened she went from cyborg to cyborg with a fresh pot of Nicotea. It was going to be a very long night.

Chapter 16

Kelly was a different sort of person in the workshop: diligent, whereas in the outside world she looked brash and impulsive. She didn't quite put down her bombshell persona on taking up a screwdriver, though. She wore an eyeglass in a way that made Darren feel she saw right through his clothes and wasn't impressed.

What remained of Sister Dix was folded in the corner. He'd changed into a spare set of overalls after Kelly insisted that his nylons and polyester skirt were an electrical hazard. He felt oddly diminished as plain old Darren: the man who could ask nothing of anyone and expect nothing in return.

Kelly's soldering iron buzzed away. She'd devoted the last half hour to the singed microprocessor, checking pins and replacing the power supply. Now it was finished. She sat back in her stool to admire her handiwork through her eyeglass and then placed the microprocessor safely on a high shelf.

Darren knew what to do next. He tipped the spare-parts bin over the bench. To him it looked like leftovers: odd screws, rotors, scraps of laminated steel in inauspicious shapes. Kelly, however, had more imagination. She chose the parts she needed to build the silhouette of a machine body on the workbench. Darren, meanwhile, tidied the discarded parts back into the bin: they might be rebels, the two of them, but human habits die hard.

Kelly ran her hands over the parts she had selected and counted screws under her breath. 'Most of it's motorcycle,' she said, more to herself than Darren.

'Is that a bad thing?'

'Depends if we're satisfied with something that might attract police attention. Motorbikes are a bit dodge.' The same situation played out in body shops across the Solar System. Motorcycles had high accident rates, which pushed up their warranty payments. Some bikes gloried in their outsider status, feeding it with badges and custom paint jobs. Others transformed themselves into toasters, which had less fun, but did find it easier to get good jobs or life partners. Consequently, motorcycles spent a long time in repair shops.

Kelly swallowed her doubts and got back to work. With Darren to help, they made rapid progress. First came the skeleton: a basic bipedal structure made from a framework of titanium-plated Meccano. Then came the joints: simple balls and sockets that Kelly injected with a viscous silicone liquid and sealed. From here they moved on to the difficult bits and Darren's engineering expertise, which had never really got beyond building blocks, ran out. He marvelled at how Kelly, with just a few spare parts and no blueprint, could produce a double-jointed finger complete with a flickering LED nail at the end. She paused to check the quality of her work and smiled as the LEDs shot a flash of leopard-skin at the nearest wall.

'Glam,' she said.

She wasn't a technician, thought Darren. Kelly was something that machines had told him all his life was impossible: an engineer. More than this, she was an engineer with the imagination to create something from nothing. No assembly line, no

CAD prototyping, just her. What was the word for that again? He groped for it, casting his mind back towards the scant history lessons humans were allowed in between Advanced Polishing and Elementary Mopping. Artist.

Kelly stepped back from the bench. Where just a few hours ago there had been a pile of odd components, there lay a sleek shape whose motorcycle heritage was unmistakable. The torso, fashioned out of the main body of a racing bike, was long and narrow, fretted at either side with ventilation grilles. The casings that protected the complex joints within the two legs and arms had been cut from long sections of exhaust pipe and were flanged at the end to give them the anthropomorphic look of shirt and trouser cuffs. The head, however, was Kelly's master touch. Triangular, it drew the gaze up to a pair of headlights refashioned into eyes. And above these a set of handlebars splayed out like the horns on a robot devil.

'What do you think?' asked Kelly, biting her lip. She was nervous. How could she be nervous about that? thought Darren.

'What's wrong?' he said. 'It's amazing.'

'Yeah,' admitted Kelly, 'but it's hardly low-key, is it? The point was that this should help us get by the police. No one's not going to notice this.'

Darren found the solution to their problem under the workbench. Among the discarded scraps of lint-free cloth and lubricant, there were some cans of spray paint. He reached for the largest, its label marked with a vivid red.

He owed this sudden flash of insight to Janice's wig and tights. After a morning as Sister Dix, Darren felt like he knew something about the art of disguise. Sometimes blending in involved standing out for the wrong reasons.

He squirted the machine a shade of red that was so intense that it didn't so much shout as brag. It was perfect: the colour of priceless racing cars, or the manicure of a femme fatale. Kelly looked on, and her look of horror turned to admiration.

With a paint job like that there was no way a policeman could mistake her creation for a petty criminal, or a down-and-out. When she was finished, and her chrome had been polished, she could only be one thing: a rich bytch, and no one in their right mind would mess with her.

Chapter 17

'So they set me up. They're looking for you.'

Janice didn't know whether it was Pam's story or the Nicotea, but she was shaking by the time it was finished. Alma, Ada and Ida shared her feelings, their screens blank with shock.

Ada broke the silence. 'Now don't get me wrong,' she said, 'it sounds like you've had a terrible time, but I don't see what they can want with us.'

'Our bodies!' said Alma. 'Didn't you listen?'

'Yes, but I haven't stood on my own two feet in a thousand years. I can't move, and I've got a knackered old screen where my eyes should be. We couldn't be much fun to squat in, eh Pam?'

'I wouldn't count on it,' replied Pam, 'even in a body like…'

'Freda's. That's our friend Freda you're borrowing.'

'Freda's, well, the sensations are overwhelming. It's like nothing I've experienced. Even if it could only move a single finger I can imagine this… well, I can imagine it becoming addictive.'

Pam paused, testing the rightness of the word. 'Yes, that's it. Addictive. It's like feeling connected and disconnected at the same time.'

The experience was like living a microsecond behind one's self, Pam thought. The sensations were sharper, colours more intense. But above all, there were no extraneous data feeds to filter out, no buzzing alerts to dampen down. Humans must have them – no organism could survive without some mechanism for checking whether their heart was still beating – but that was done somewhere beyond an individual's consciousness. Being freed of all that was intense, but, for a machine engineered to pay attention to everything, also blissful. Were she a terminally hyperactive machine – like a high-powered smartphone, for instance – she would pay a lot of money for this kind of relaxation.

'Oh dear,' she said after a while, feeling bits of incoherent and incomplete data come together in what she guessed was her first human intuition. 'I think I know what they're going to do.'

'At last,' said Ida, with a }:-/, 'something useful. Come on, then.'

'You remember I told you about my boss?'

'The one who'd been touched on the touchscreen a few too many times?' asked Alma. 'You know I never could get on with my smartphone. Even back in the days before they had minds of their own, it was like they ran your lives for you.'

'He was desperate to know what it felt like to be inside a human. But it wasn't curiosity. It was more like I'd taken the car he wanted to own out for a test drive. He wants you as a prototype.'

Janice checked the security cameras one more time. They were all dark. The search would have been called off for the evening, but it would continue tomorrow. On the Dolestars their options were limited: a compliant population and nothing to steal kept crime low, so the enforcement equipment to hand was basic. On Earth, however, they had all manner of ingeniously nasty machines to hunt out rogue humans. She imagined the army of drones that even now would be crossing the blackness of space. Light, mobile and deadly in a detached way that made them all the more terrifying, they would comb every square centimetre of Discovery for their target.

'They're going to take my ladies to bits and turn them into a schematic,' said Janice.

'Yes,' replied Pam.

'They're not going to find us, are they, though?' asked Ada with a quiet :-/. 'We've been safe here all this time.'

'We were until I was daft enough to take their bait.' Janice sat down heavily on the edge of a salon chair. Protecting the shop was all she had ever done, and soon it would be destroyed. 'I'm sorry, ladies, but if they want to find us and they know we're here it's only a matter of time. We can't keep running forever.'

'Janice Braithewaite,' said Ida, flashing a fearsome <|oo|>, 'you cannot seriously be saying we should sit here and wait for those bug-eyed monsters to come and get us.'

Janice, however, could only think of Kelly. Somewhere down there on an enemy planet: on the run, with nowhere to go and nowhere to come back to. Failure flooded over her and she began to cry. 'I'm sorry,' she sobbed, 'but I don't know what to do.'

After a few awkward seconds, a rickety-looking mechanical grip squeaked out of the side of Alma's dryer and gave Janice a few comforting pats on the shoulder.

'You know what, ladies,' said Alma, 'I think we haven't been giving our wonderful friend enough help and support lately. You can see she's been under all kinds of pressure, and what have we been doing? Sitting here with bags of Nicotea pontificating. It's time we did something to help.'

'Like what?' said Ida.

'You know,' replied Alma with a <|oo|\ nudge. 'It's been a while, but…'

'Oh no,' said Ida. 'Not that. You know I get travel sick, and I can't suck barley sugars since my tongue disintegrated.'

'This isn't about you though, is it, Ida,' Alma replied with an unusual degree of firmness. 'And besides, would you rather be a bit queasy or torn to bits to make a blueprint?'

'Well...'

'So that's settled then,' said Alma. She threw the room a bright :-). 'Are we ready, ladies?'

'As I'll ever be,' replied Ida.

Alma, Ida and Ada's dryer screens blanked out with a loud pop, their emojis replaced with a countdown. 'Ten, nine, eight, seven, six...'

Janice watched through a film of tears, scarcely believing what she saw. Her whole life the ladies had been chatty, friendly, interfering and often infuriating, but they had never once actually done anything. They were as immovable and as passive as pieces of heavy antique furniture.

'Three, two, one... zero!'

The building lurched and creaked as one side then the other of the salon pitched upward so sharply it threw furniture across the room. The ladies, bolted to their dryers at the back of the room, clutched their armrests and gave a collective :-[:] grimace.

The salon convulsed again. Empty mugs and heated rollers clattered around Janice like the ball bearings in a puzzle. She scrambled away from the mirrors, fearing one would fall on her as the room quaked. Then it stopped. Or at least it eased, and she felt another kind of motion in the room.

They were moving forwards.

Janice pushed her hair, which had fallen over her eyes for about the eightieth time in the past twenty-four hours – she really must think about a more practical style – and stood up. She staggered to the door and opened it.

'Careful!' warned Alma.

And Janice looked down to see the salon was now several metres above floor level, while a clank-clanking soon explained why this was possible. Every second or so, a four-toed metal foot struck the ground underneath the salon. It took the weight of the building for a moment as it lurched forward and was steadied a second later by another foot landing on the other side. Legs. The whole building was moving forwards on – she peered down for a better look – what looked like a pair of metal chicken legs.

'You know,' said Alma to the other ladies, 'I can't remember the last time we took the Baba Yaga 4000 out for a spin.'

'It must have been a good three or four hundred years ago,' mused Ada. 'Have we really been put down at that spot for so long?'

'Time flies, eh?' replied Alma. Catching Janice standing stunned by the door, she added, 'This is how we moved the salon about in the old days. The cyborg hunters were more active then, so we were quite the wanderers, weren't we? Saw all over the sewers.'

'I told your Gran^4 I didn't like it,' Ida told Janice. 'Didn't hold with caravanning when I was alive, and I was damned if that was going to change.'

'She was overruled,' said Alma. 'Bless your Gran^4. She was a clever lady with a toolkit. Made most of the Baba Yaga out of an old crane. I see a lot of her in Kelly.'

At the mention of Kelly, Janice looked back out into the darkness and wondered where she could be. Had she found somewhere to hide or was she in a police cell watching a printer spit out a charge list? The not-knowing needled her, yet she prayed for it to continue. Better that than the sight of Kelly's captured face on a news report.

‘Can we run forever?’ she murmured.

‘Maybe not,’ said Alma, ‘but we can try. Now be a good girl and turn the radio on. I like a bit of light entertainment while I’m driving.’

Janice staggered over to a neutered radio twitching on a nearby shelf. Kelly had long since ripped out its transmitter and speech centres but had never quite got round to lobotomising it, so it snarled whenever Janice picked it up. She chastised it with a sharp snap across the volume buttons and turned the dial. The salon filled with light music, over which sang a machine with the quarter-tone flat trill that marked her out as a karaoke machine:

My soap flakes bring all the boys to the yard

I’m like, they’re better than…

Janice pushed another button with an instinctive ‘Ugh’. She hated *Cleaners’ Playtime*. The news was starting on the other side. She couldn’t stop herself from turning it on. She had to know.

The sound that greeted her was an unintelligible crowd. It sounded like thousands of people. They were shouting something together. What was it? Janice pushed the ‘fifteen seconds back’ button and listened again. The first word was something like ‘freedom’. Yes, that was it. ‘Freedom…’ ‘Freedom for Fleshies’.

She dropped the radio, which let out an ouch of static. The hum of protest faded, and the voice of a correspondent filled the room.

‘Special forces are being called out to an unnamed Dolestar, where a spate of vandalism following the destruction of a surveillance robot has sparked scenes of unrest.’

Janice found the TV remote and switched it on. She saw blurred drone footage of a crowd surging through Discovery’s streets. The ident 'Live from the Dolestars – Human Order Crisis' vouched for its currency. A few blue-lighted police bots hovered here and there, but they kept their distance. She soon saw why, as a young man broke from the main body of the mob and lobbed a stone at a street lamp. It guttered, and the camera panned out to reveal darkness: street lamps were out right across the space station.

The crowd pressed on. Some more enterprising souls had compensated for the lack of light by taking a match to their mops. They blazed in the night-time with lemon- and pine-scented flames.

'Crikey,' said Janice to the ladies. 'Well, it looks like the diversion worked.'

'Perhaps,' said Ida, 'but I think that depends on how determined our pursuers are, eh Pam? Pam?'

But there was no answer, because Pam was gone.

Chapter 18

At first, Pam was too busy driving Freda's body to realise she had one of her own to go to. She felt it as a dull throb in her primary diagnostic system, and that was almost overwhelmed by the crash of 'WTF' sensations that crackled through her programming as it got to grips with a world where nerve fibres replaced wires and a tiny electric impulse could accomplish a great deal.

But the feeling grew when the remaining cyborgs activated the Baba Yaga 4000. As the salon stood up, Pam also felt the space in which her consciousness squatted constricting. Freda's mind seemed smaller and the presence of her sister cyborgs closer, like she'd suddenly traded down from a detached house to a terrace. The space contracted again as Kurl Up and Dye began its journey through the Discovery's sewers, and Pam then saw what was up. This was mind-sharing. The four ladies under the hairdryers had learned to co-operate as an improvised network. More impressive still, they had worked out a way to partition their consciousnesses so they could control other machines at will. Like the Baba Yaga 4000 underneath the salon, which as a machine was as bird-brained as its inspiration. Yet with Ida, Ada, Alma and Freda controlling it, the Baba Yaga could take Kurl Up and Dye anywhere.

Thinking that this nagging sensation must be an error, Pam hunted for the relevant fragment in her programming. If it was corrupt she'd just delete it; it wasn't like she needed it any more. She sent a search and replace through her whole codebase, but it bounced. The feeling intensified. A gentle pull turned to a yank. Pam lost her grip and, sensing an opening, Freda's displaced consciousness snuck back in. Freda might be old and weak in body, but her mind had roamed free over the Internet without losing any of its integrity for half an eternity. She fought dirty, clouding Pam's vision with an injection of junk data.

Fearful of infection, Pam backed away and Freda's mind gushed back into the vacated space, while the pull at the other end of Pam's programming grew irresistible. For an agonised moment, Pam felt like she would be torn apart, and then the stomp-stomp-stomp of the Baba Yaga 4000 underneath gave way to the acid-flux tang of solder.

And a feeling of… mass.

Her suspicion that she was back in a body grew as feedback systems, which had spent the past few hours flailing around the Internet like seaweed in a storm, stiffened and felt purposeful again. Their feeds started up again: those blasted things that reported every piece of sensory data back to her CPU with relentless accuracy and still didn't add up to a damn thing.

As her operating system booted, tantalising hints as to what this new body was like filtered through. Her dough-paddle programme stretched out and wandered through the new and unfamiliar home of a much more powerful electric motor, while the firmware for her heating element replaced itself with the equivalent for a combustion engine. Pam was suffused with a new feeling, or rather the possibility of a feeling: speed.

Finding her new hands for the first time, she gave an experimental grip, and a throttle went off in her thorax. What had happened?

Pam's visual systems were last to boot up. She opened her eyes and saw the dusty ceiling of the room she was in. Right in the centre of her field of vision were two pools of light, which a new feed of lumens data told her were her eyes. Lamp-eyes.

'I think she's coming round,' crackled a nearby voice. Her hearing systems still hadn't quite settled, so it was fuzzy around the edges. It was soft and human. Female?

Pam sat up. The first thing that struck her was how quickly she could do this. Kitchen appliances like breadmakers weren't built for speed: their ancestors had sat on shelves, or more often in cupboards or utility rooms waiting to be used. This body, however, was fast: instructions and counter-instructions shot across her circuitry so quickly that just sitting up was enough to make her feel giddy.

'My head,' she said, feeling an unfamiliar purr at the bottom of her vocal range. Then her vision cleared and she took in the sight around her. She was sitting up on a workbench in a workshop. It was windowless and small, which constituted a fire hazard, with doors on opposite walls.

As the nearby voice had indicated, she wasn't alone. Beside her was a pair of humans in overalls: a man and a woman. The man was looking at Pam with that look of lust that young men throughout the universe devote to premium-priced consumer goods. He must also have had a run-in with a make-up counter, as his face was smeared with the ghost of inexpertly removed lipstick. The woman, standing with her arms folded, appraised her with an engineer's pride. She knew this face. It was Kelly: which meant the young man must be Darren.

'You,' she said. And then, because new body or no body she was still a mother, 'You do know your poor mum's worried sick about you.'

Darren dropped a screwdriver and hopped around the workshop clutching his foot. Kelly caught it on the rebound and held the flat-blade to the weak spot where Pam's new thigh and thorax joined, covered in a thin layer of silicone.

'What have you done with my mum?' said Kelly.

Pam tested her new reflexes by swiping the screwdriver out of Kelly's hand. It landed in a still-molten glob of epoxy resin. She laughed, and heard that throttle again. It was a motorcycle engine. They'd brought her back as a motorbike? How scandalous.

'Maybe I should be asking you what you've done with my motherboard?'

'We brought it back from the dead.'

At this, the subroutine-consciousnesses in Pam's mind replayed her death. The pain, the spark, the panic as her software downloaded Pam's core programming through the stump of her modem. For the first time since the event, she wondered what had made it through. The real Pam, or merely a copy. And whether that mattered.

'But why did you do that?' she asked.

Darren hopped over on one foot and dropped a BlockPaper on the workbench. It was still recovering from incineration, but there it was on the cover: her name.

'Even if we're not on the same side,' said Darren, 'it looks like we've got the same enemies.'

Pam narrowed the beam of her lamp-eyes over Darren. He was a curious amalgam of characteristics. There were the short, bandy legs typical of a human brought up in the low-Vitamin-D environment of the Dolestars, and a face straight out of a knockabout comedy. But there was something about his expression that told her it was unwise to dismiss him as a clown – even if his face was still caked in glittery make-up.

Pam threw both hands in the air and spotted her new LED nail job. The leopard print was a lovely touch. 'So it seems,' she said to Darren. And then to Kelly, 'You've done a nice job, by the way. I feel like a new machine.'

Kelly shrugged and leaned against the wall. 'It's nothing.'

'But it is,' said Pam. She tested her reactions again by throwing a leg out and felt dizzy from the kickback. 'You didn't need to do this. Any kind of body would have done if all you wanted was answers. You could have put my motherboard in a drone if you'd wanted.'

Kelly shrugged again. For a moment Pam wondered whether her own daughter would grow up to be this irritating, and if so would her replacement have the patience not to lock her out with the recycling when she reached those tricky adolescent years in her life cycle.

'If something's worth doing,' said Kelly at last, 'it's worth doing well.'

Pam appraised Kelly again, noticing how her jaw locked when she tried to swallow an emotion. 'You're very like your mum.'

Kelly ignored the comment. 'Why did they send you after me?'

'It was never about you,' said Pam. 'You were just the traceable one. After that, erm, incident with the street lamp.'

For about the millionth time that day, Darren wished he'd worn a plastic ring. Something out of a cracker would never cause so much trouble.

'So what were they looking for?' he said.

'They know about your mother's ladies,' said Pam. 'It's them they want. All you ever were was a way to find them.'

Kelly put her spanner down and stared into space. Meanwhile, Darren readjusted his worldview. Even for someone like him, who was so low down the food chain that even plankton left him off their Christmas card list, it was still disconcerting to be reminded that you weren't the centre of events.

'But they're harmless,' said Darren. 'None of them have done anything more dangerous in the past aeon than dunk a biscuit.'

'And Mum has to do that for them,' murmured Kelly.

'It's not that they want to kill them exactly,' said Pam. 'More like take them for a joyride. And then take them apart for the parts.'

'You wouldn't believe the mess a custard cream leaves on the inside of an IV bag,' said Kelly. 'Sometimes they have to go through the steam cleaner three times.'

'Is she okay?' Pam asked Darren.

'It's been a funny day,' he replied.

Kelly stood up again. 'I have to go,' she said.

'But…' started Darren.

'Mum needs me,' snapped Kelly. 'We've been down here playing bloody dress-up and my mum's in danger. I need to get back…'

Pam got up and blocked Kelly's exit. As she did, the light played about her, glinting in ways that it hadn't since she was a baby machine. She was a creature of different alloys now: lighter, stronger, a better shock absorber. Yet as she revved her new engine she found herself missing her old oven. Where would she keep odds and ends now that her flour bin was gone. Motorcycles were zippy, but they had so little storage.

'I'm sorry, Kelly,' she said, 'but I think it's too late for that.' She switched her speech generator over to double time and told her story for the second time that evening. She got as far as explaining how Janice's false trail had put the cyborgs at risk before Kelly started fidgeting again.

'She's trapped,' she said. 'It's all my fault. Well,' she narrowed her eyes at Darren, 'not Mum's fault at least.'

'And you did the right thing by getting away,' Pam reassured her. 'We just have to find a way of helping her from here. Your mother's an intelligent woman and I think the ladies will be more help than they look.'

'She's right, Kelly,' added Darren. 'Whatever these machines have in mind, it'll be getting planned from down here. We got here under the nose of I don't know how much surveillance. How hard can it be to break into the government?' He pointed at Pam's luscious new paintwork and continued: 'No one's going to be looking at us. We make for the High-Power Streets. Pam, you play the rich bytch out shopping with her servants, we carry the bags.'

'And then what?' said Pam.

'We – er – hadn't got that far ahead,' said Darren.

'I thought we could lie low here,' said Kelly, 'but this place is hot now. There'll be investigators crawling all over it soon. Besides, if we need to know what the Big Machines are up to, I've got friends in the fondle parlours. We can try there.'

Darren opened the door leading to the back stairs, which yawned as dark and uncertain as their futures.

'But first,' said Kelly, taking up her spanner again, 'we need to do something to take the heat off Mum. Is that clear?'

Chapter 19

When it first emerged as the capital of machine civilisation, the city of Singulopolis had been as intricate and organised as a newly designed chipset. Its golden roads traced complex patterns between buildings which soared so high that penthouse owners qualified for orbital tax exemption. They were church spires in a world where gods had batteries. It wasn't a city on a hill so much as the city that demolished the hill, processed the rubble into a carbon–silicon polymer and extruded it into a two-mile-high model of the architect's crisis of masculinity. It was the city of the future.

And like all visions of the future, it was obsolete the moment it was finished.

Now, thousands of years later, the congestion in Singulopolis was so bad that several major suburbs were actually traffic jams that got tired of waiting and settled down to start families.

The circuit motorways were meant to take each inorganism through the city on a pre-ordained path like an electron moving through the wires of a circuit. And yes, that was a lovely metaphor, but it conveniently forgot that, unlike a 200-kg washing machine, electrons had next to no mass, could move at the speed of light and could at a pinch be in two places at the same time.

Above ground level it was even worse, because this was where the architects' original vision developed cataracts. Those high, slick-sided buildings, built out of silicon polymers because there had been no concrete left after the robots had paved over the oceans, offered next to no wind resistance. Hence a constant hurricane whipped through the higher reaches of the city. The air here was a mass of rubbish, atomised plastic and the mashed remains of drones bold or desperate enough to stray too far out of their safe zone.

And it was the drones that Darren noticed first, when he, Kelly and Pam snuck out of BodyBeau2iful's concealed fire exit. The ground level of these dizzyingly high towers housed two things that didn't officially exist: grey-market body shops and drone shanties.

Because they lacked even the most basic product roadmaps, drones fell outside of the machine caste system. Most were just assembled out of whatever was to protuberance at the time. Consequently, your average drone looked like a broken hair-dryer with wings and occupied a niche in inorganic ecology equivalent to a street pigeon.

They were every bit as feral, swooping over Darren's head as they fought over the scraps of wire or plastic thrown out by the body shops below and the rubbish hurricane above. The air buzzed with the sound of overtaxed motors, and the cheep-cheep of low-battery warnings from nests full of their rickety-looking children.

They hadn't gone more than a couple of blocks when Darren spotted one of these urchins on the pavement. It must have fallen out of the nest before finishing its first flight plan, its wings torn and its peculiar cylindrical body dented by a fall. Darren looked around expecting a parent to swoop in, but instead spotted a nest gaping open like a burst carrier bag.

Beside the nest was a clot of spare parts and bust LEDs that could only be a recently end-of-lifed machine. The poor thing's parent, he thought.

The drone-baby followed Darren's eyeline and bleeped at an emotional pitch strong enough to cross the lifeform barrier. Darren bent down and, checking Kelly and Pam were far enough in the distance not to see him doing it, picked the drone up. It fluttered in his hand, less than an ounce of machinery that, if left alone, would be picked to parts in a few seconds. He'd seen too much destruction in the last couple of days to add to it, so, tucking in the urchin's damaged wings as best he could, he put it into his pocket and followed his fellow fugitives.

This was new territory to Darren. Until today, his Earth-knowledge had been confined to his routes to and from short-lived cleaning jobs. But even he knew that heading downhill from the area around the bus station was a shortcut into Ama-Zone Prime, Singulopolis's most desirable shopping district.

The first sign they were going upmarket was the electric net that hung vertically between the buildings just above head height. It was so fine as to be almost invisible, but the odd spark and zip, occasioned when one of Earth's increasingly endangered flies collided with it and got a bit rarer in the process, told Darren this must be a drone-free area. As machines, drones were technically superior to humans, but that still didn't mean most respectable robots wanted to mix with them. And that, Darren reflected as he passed under the netting and spotted another pinprick of light, probably made humans the flies.

The other side of the net was a different world. Or at least one with a higher credit limit, even though the narrow street was still jammed between buildings that were so high that they bent perspective into something that would have made M. C.

Escher take two ibuprofen and have a lie down. Everything was showroom bright, exposing shops that were tasteful, discreet and devoid of much to buy. Darren gulped and vowed not to step into any of them. Just one breakage would be enough to devastate the economy of two Dolestars.

Darren's anxiety moved into a higher gear still when he looked up and spotted the source of the bright light. It came from huge, floating street lamps that doubled as security from the tazer attachments they sported around the nose area. He picked up the pace.

Then he discovered the other major difference between the rest of the city and the Ama Zone. The pavement here was antique, made of the silicon polymer of Ancient Singulopolis. It was a deep, circuit-board green and polished to a finish that was a dream if you had castors, and a major trip hazard for humans. Darren was already feeling unsteady on his feet when Kelly, who was a couple of steps ahead of him, stumbled. She righted herself and stole a look back at Darren. What was that for? Was she trying to tell him something? Darren lost his concentration and his footing. As his left leg slid away from him along the pavement he reached out in a panic for something to steady himself. It turned out to be the spout of an electric kettle, whose L-Eye-Ds blazed indignantly as Darren levered himself back into a standing position with her nose.

'And what,' squealed the kettle, 'do you think you're doing?'

'Sorry,' said Darren. 'I…' His eyes darted between the kettle and Kelly, who was melting back into the crowd.

Above him he could feel the street lamps starting to take an interest. He hated street lamps, but he feared their tazer attachments more.

Meanwhile the kettle, who wanted more of an apology than a hurried 'sorry', shrieked like she had been on the boil for at least five minutes: 'Would the owner of this… fleshie… please make itself known.'

Pam's handlebars, which were attracting widespread attention from sales assistants, snapped around. Even in the kilowatt brightness of the Ama Zone her headlamps blazed. She turned their full dazzle on the kettle.

'I beg your pardon?' she said, in a tone that suggested she wanted nothing of the sort.

The kettle took one look at Pam's new paint job and clicked its switch with disapproval. 'I was just saying,' she continued, 'that it's a great shame to see a machine who can't keep its staff under control.'

Darren held his breath and waited for Pam's apology. She was a reasonable machine, and there was no sense letting this escalate when it was all his fault. None came. Instead Pam narrowed the beam of her headlamps over the kettle.

'I don't see what the fuss is about,' she said. 'What are a few more fingerprints to you?' She pointed to discolourations across the kettle's carapace. 'This isn't a chrome finish. It's a disgrace.'

The cash registers and card machines that worked in this part of town glided in to listen on silent, discreet castors. Hidden antennae twitched and broadcast the drama across half of the Ama Zone. The catfights fought among the ladies who launched in the Ama Zone were the highest-rated light entertainment in the Solar System.

Darren quailed and wondered if Pam was getting a bit too comfortable in her new, spoiled, rich body.

'How dare you,' rumbled the kettle, a wisp of steam appearing from her spout. 'A lady of quality would never stoop to personal insults.'

'A lady of quality would never come shopping looking like she's boiled tea for half the neighbourhood.'

At this a nearby cash register let out an involuntary ching. In the lexicon of inorganic manners, there were few insults graver than accusing another machine of letting itself be used by humans. Another register gaped and elbowed the nearest card machine, which scribbled 'MEOW' in loopy letters on its signature pad.

'I beg your pardon,' said the kettle, her even tones belied by the column of steam rattling her lid. 'Did you just call me a… samovar… you… you ho-ped.'

Pam folded her arms and, very, very slowly, came forwards. Only afterwards did Darren realise she was putting herself between him and the kettle. And where was Kelly? She was standing at the edge of the group of machines clustered around the fight, retouching her lipstick. How, he wondered, could both of them be so cool?

Pam followed the insult with a grin. It was an expression that made the grips on her handlebars bang together like the sound of someone closing the door of a sports car. 'I'm very sorry,' she said, 'it was rude and inaccurate of me to suggest you're indiscriminate with your tea-making.'

The street let out a collective exhaust blast of relief.

Pam pressed on. 'When it's clear from the marks all down your sides that you prefer doling out the Cup-a-Soup.'

The kettle screamed like she was about to boil dry. She threw herself at Pam, steam pouring out of every orifice. Darren turned to flee, noticing as he did so that the street lamps overhead were beginning to fire up their electric charges. His hair stood to attention as current built up in the atmosphere.

Pam, meanwhile, looked on, the same picture of unconcern as Kelly, while the berserk kettle barrelled towards her. Except, what was that? He saw Pam turn her head ever so slightly in the direction of Kelly and dip the beam in one headlight.

'Freedom for Fleshies!'

The slogan rang out through the Ama Zone like a fart at a funeral. Darren watched, aghast and amazed as Kelly shouted the battle cry through perfectly painted lips in the middle of Singulopolis's most exclusive shopping precinct. Nor was he the only being there immobilised by Kelly's brazenness. The machines, to whom insurrection had been nothing more than a streakily mopped floor for millennia, stood there unable to process what they were seeing.

Time took on the consistency of jelly.

Kelly produced a grenade from her brassiere and lobbed it at the kettle. The spell broke. The charges in at least a dozen tazers fizzled, and the machines blew their savage spitbubbles. But gravity was, on this occasion, the faster force.

The grenade hit its target on the spout and the kettle exploded. Shards of stainless steel shattered windows and gouged chunks of silicone out of the pavement. Its lid, still miraculously intact, frisbee'd across the road to land at an uncomfortable angle on the head of a very chic and affronted travel iron, like a fascinator on the mother of the bride. Proof that, even if the underlying forces that govern three-dimensional space lack subtlety, they still like a joke.

Yet it wasn't the rain of hot metal that did the most damage, but the cloud of scalding steam that followed. Darren, shielded by Pam's body, escaped all but a few stinging drops, but the robots were nowhere near as lucky. The cloud of water vapour formed a circuit between the live tazers in the air and the machines on the ground. Millions of volts ran through the district. Shoppers toppled, card readers rang up transactions thousands of digits long, and those ominous street lamps in the sky lost control of their superconductor drives and crashed to the ground. Only Pam, whose full-body laminate waterproofing

Darren had picked out of the oddments bin a few hours before, stayed standing.

For a second, then two, then three, the Ama Zone froze. And Darren hesitated, waiting for some thing somewhere to press the refresh button.

'Yes!' yelled Kelly. She ran the half block between her and Darren and Pam at full pelt and hugged them. 'We did it. You beauty.'

Fury started to displace some of the bowel-loosening fear in Darren's body chemistry.

'I'm still not sure this is going to work,' said Pam. 'It's very high risk.'

'Course it is,' said Kelly, 'it's terrorism. If it isn't high risk, then it's just disobedience.' She unrolled her lipstick as far as it would go and daubed an 'F' in garish letters on the side of a street lamp.

Darren found his voice. 'What the hell are you playing at? We're meant to be hiding.'

'Do you think I should spell the fleshies with a "z"?' asked Kelly. 'Maybe that will make us look more dangerous.'

'It would make us look even more stupid than we already are.'

Kelly frowned. 'Yes, that's the idea. We want them to underestimate us.'

'You used me as bait,' said Darren. 'You planned this.'

'Sort of.'

'I'm picking up radio signals,' interrupted Pam. She swung her head from side to side taking in the destruction. 'We need to hurry.'

'Why? Why did you do it?'

Kelly pointed her lipstick at the sky. Her expression changed, worry edging in around the determination. 'I needed to do something for my mum,' she said.

'And what's this going to achieve?' he asked.

He then rounded on Pam. 'You know what Janice wanted as well as I do. She wanted Kelly out of the way and safe.'

Pam dimmed her headlights. 'She did, but that was before we knew how big all this was going to get. Now come on, we need to get out of here. The fuzz'll be here any minute.'

'We need to slow them down,' said Darren.

'That was never part of the plan,' snapped Kelly. 'Down there,' she said, pointing into a narrow alley that led out of the Ama Zone.

Darren paused. Part of him wanted to run, but after this the police would throw everything they had at hunting them down. No stereotypical fat Segway cops this time. They'd send in the helicopters, the armoured cars, the submarines, their best drones. There was no way they could outrun them. But they might, as today's evidence suggested, be able to outwit them.

Drones, he thought. He looked at the wreckage around him. The shattered components, the prone machines and the shops full of luscious, unguarded consumer goods.

'Hang on,' he said, running back to where they'd originally entered the Ama Zone.

'What are you doing?' said Kelly. 'We don't have time for this.'

Darren squinted at the electrified net that fenced the district off from its neighbours.

'The radio's saying they're ninety seconds from the scene,' said Pam. 'Darren!'

Darren held one finger in the air and made a sound at the back of his throat like he was gargling tar. His eyes rolled, and he hoiked a huge spitball through the air to land on the electrified mesh. His aim was still perfect. Those years in the playground had not been wasted.

He listened for the sizzling. There was none. Good. Just as he thought, the shock had deactivated the net with the rest of the street.

Darren jumped and pulled the net down after him. It tied him into a tangle as it fell, so for the next few seconds he resembled a ball of Christmas lights out for a jog. In the gloom in front of him, he heard the hum and chitter of drones. He was definitely ready to leave now.

'What are you waiting for?' he said, as he passed both Kelly and Pam on his way into the alley.

The sound from the other side of the downed netting intensified, as thousands of drones realised someone had just declared the biggest trolley dash in history. For an agonising moment they sat there, where the net had been, a wall of flickering LEDs and corroded metal, unwilling or unable to believe their luck.

Then they took the bait.

As Darren ran through the alleyways that threaded deep into Singulopolis he couldn't hear his feet, nor those of Kelly and Pam as they followed. Instead the air was full of that first bite of cereal in the morning, except much louder. It was the crunch of a hundred thousand drones forcing their way up the supply chain, one stolen part at a time.

He shivered, and kept on running.

Chapter 20

Darren knew they were in a different district when the sound of robot death was replaced by that of Angry Birds chirping in the distance. It was a pleasant sound, lilting and musical, until you stopped to listen to the words.

'What-are-you-saying-bytch-I'm-a-nice-guy-you-don't-deserve-me-I-hope-you-get-raped.'

They were in the darkest and dumbest of all Singulopolis's neighbourhoods: Gamergate.

It was very dark there, street lamps being generally discouraged. The only source of illumination was discreet LED strips announcing this building was an amusement arcade and that a casino. Every third or fourth building would be unlit, but this didn't mean it was empty. Their signs were made of 'black light', invisible to all but machines whose vision operated in the highest parts of the ultraviolet spectrum. And they declared to interested observers that these were high-end fondle parlours: places where high-rolling machines could get themselves the kind of personal attention only lots of money could buy.

Before she'd shown her hand as an engineer of considerable skill, Darren had assumed this was Kelly's natural habitat. Her whole persona – the fibre-optic-fur coat, the outrageous confidence – made you believe she was one of those humans who handled touchscreens all day and kept her mouth shut at night. Maybe she had been too, once upon a time. She seemed familiar with the seediest parts of town. But Kelly, Darren knew by now, thrived on letting other people's assumptions lead them in the wrong direction.

She turned into a side street so dark that Darren felt like something had sucked his eyes out of his face. He groped along damp concrete until Pam, who was ahead of him, turned up her lamp-eyes, casting the silhouette of a horned devil in the process. Doubt crept into Darren. Who was this Pam anyway? Some thing they'd magicked up from a dumb circuit board who claimed to be on their side, but how stupid did a human have to be to trust a robot?

His fingers brushed the drone in his pocket, which he suddenly wished offered a more robust form of protection. What could a sky-rat do, other than maybe give his enemies a nasty virus?

He caught up with Kelly and Pam outside a fire door at the end of the alley. Kelly put her ear on it and knocked gently.

'It's locked from the inside,' she whispered.

'Can you break in?' asked Darren.

'Don't be daft,' said Kelly. 'These places make banks look free and easy.'

'Can we get in round the front?' said Pam.

Kelly shook her head. 'They keep face scans of the police wanted list behind the front desk. Security would melt us both down for head cheese in a heartbeat.'

'But not me,' said Pam. She straightened up and strode back on to the street. Darren and Kelly followed at a distance, watching as she paused at the corner to readjust her posture again. It was the same stride she'd used to sashay through the Ama Zone. She ditched her good-natured slouch, raised her handle-horns and activated the kick stands embedded in both heels to improvise a pair of machine stilettoes. A quick burst of her engine later, she barged in through the fondle parlour's front door in a cloud of expensive exhaust fumes.

'Good evening,' she said, 'I wonder if you can help me.'

Darren and Kelly hid behind the door and watched Pam try her rich-bytch act out on the security guard, who had the criminal-in-drag look of a machine downplaying its menace. That ice-cream-maker dome was fooling no one, thought Darren: underneath it were the unmistakable workings of a gun.

'You see,' added Pam, leaning over the desk, 'it's a little embarrassing. I think my husband is in there.'

The gun clicked, warning Pam it was loaded. 'I'm afraid I can't give out any details of our clients, ma'am.'

'That's alright,' said Pam, 'I already know all the sordid details.' Her eye-beams narrowed. 'I mean, it's pretty clear he's in there getting fingered.'

'This is a private leisure facility for executive business machines,' answered the guard flatly. 'Our staff are trained to the highest levels of customer care.'

'They're a bunch of tarts,' snarled Pam, 'and my husband's in there spending good maintenance money on them. Now let me through.'

'I'm going to have to ask you to leave, madam.'

'Or what?'

The guard unfolded from its chair. As Darren had suspected, the ice-cream-maker carapace hid a full magazine of ammunition.

'You can't shoot me. My husband would be furious,' said Pam.

'He doesn't care. He's up there having himself some fun.'

She flashed her headlights in triumph. 'So he is in there. I knew it. I demand you let me through.'

Pam tried to barge the barriers into the parlour. Her new body had a mean turn of speed, but the guard's reflexes were battle-hardened. It grabbed her by the shoulder, whereupon she kicked her scorned-wife act into fifth gear.

'How dare you lay hands on me,' she said. 'My husband's an important machine.'

'I ain't got no time for executive toys,' replied the guard. It kept a firm grip on Pam and started to walk her back to the door.

But she had one trick left in her handbag. She made to wriggle out of the guard's grip. It reacted by lifting Pam clear into the air by her arms. But that still left Pam in an ideal position to plant her kickstand in her captor's trigger.

It fired a slug straight into the wall. The kickback threw Pam to the other side of the reception desk. The guard, smoking with fury, launched himself at Pam, who shielded her face theatrically, saying, 'I just needed to know.' That stopped it just long enough for her to feel along the back wall for the fire alarm, and smash it.

A siren rang out, and the sealed door that separated the parlour from reception burst open. Out poured expensive machines in various states of disassembly; and humans wearing skimpy underwear and carrying bottles of WD40.

Pam got to her feet and mouthed 'go' and Kelly dragged Darren back round to the now-open fire escape. The corridor – there seemed to have been a lot of narrow spaces in Darren's life lately – was softly lit and smelled of posh lubricant. Emergency lights and the fire alarm notwithstanding, it was clearly an environment devoted to the kind of extreme relaxation that only rich inorganisms who have never done a proper day's work in their lives can enjoy. Darren squinted into a room, bare apart from a product-demonstration table large enough for three or four full-size machines to stretch out on, side by side.

'That's where they do the group-tests,' whispered Kelly. 'They lie down on there and a couple of humans compare their spec sheets and recommended retail prices.'

Darren may have been a fugitive, but this blatant inversion of human–machine power structures was difficult to stomach. He twisted his face.

'I know. Kinky buggers. You should see the things they make you do with a power lead. Along here, I think.'

They turned a corner into another plush, anonymous corridor, lined with four doors and the maintenance equipment abandoned when the fire alarm went off. Three of the doors led to open, empty rooms, while the fourth was shut with a 'do not disturb' sign flashing above it. Kelly pressed a finger to her lips and picked up a brush left leaning by the wall.

'Is there anyone in there?' she said in her best, unobtrusive human voice (the fire alarm had stopped by now, which meant they could stop shouting over the noise of it). 'Only we've orders to evacuate.'

The door swung open, revealing a bright, spacious interior decked out as a photography studio. Inside, a camera – a pricey-looking but self-consciously retro model with prominent, thick-rimmed lenses – framed the scene in front of him with his hands, a beret draped artfully over his settings dial. Just looking at him made Darren's fists itch.

The camera was concentrating on a pair of women, clad in cut-down overalls, posing in the far corner of the studio. Their eyes were obscured behind dark magnifying lenses, and their bodies held impossibly balletic poses thanks to the metal-wire exoskeletons they were strapped into.

'Sensational, girls!' said the camera as he snapped. 'Now just one more for the stills and then we can get started…' He grinned, and Darren looked on in horror as a tiny tripod screw poked its way out of the camera at what on a human would be crotch height. '…on the machine-on-girl action.'

Kelly elbowed her way past Darren, her eye fixed on the left-most woman. Behind the exoskeleton she was slim and pale with red hair. 'Paula?' she called.

The redhead flipped round in surprise, breaking gaze with the camera lens. He retracted his tripod and turned to Kelly, flashlight winking in annoyance.

'What the hell are you doing here?' he said.

Kelly, caught by surprise, raised her broom to strike, but Darren got in quicker.

'Fire warden, sir,' he called from the door. 'Haven't you heard the alarm? We're evacuating the building.'

The camera panned round, shutters narrowing. 'Where's your badge?'

Darren dropped his voice and drew closer to the camera. 'I don't wish to alarm you, sir, but there's been an electrical fire downstairs. We've already lost an MP3 player. I must insist you leave.'

'But…' the camera gestured at his models, 'it's taken me ages to get them into that pose.'

Kelly shooed the camera back towards the door with her brush. 'Fat lot of good that will do you with a melted light meter.'

'Please, sir,' said Darren.

'Well, if I must. But I insist on getting your details first.'

As his shutter blades converged, it was Kelly's turn to react. She pulled the beret down over the camera's face like a pretentious lens cap and spun him round by the shoulders. Next, she pressed the service flap on his back, which opened with the well-oiled ease of a machine that spent most of its leisure time in whorehouses. One touch of his power button, and the camera fell comatose to the floor.

At this, the girl on the right – the one who was not Paula – called out: 'Hey! What do you think you're doing? I've got an hour left on the clock with him.'

'Give it a rest,' winced Paula on the left, 'I'm surprised you can still feel your legs when they're splayed like that.'

'Sleazy little so-and-so, wasn't he?' said Kelly to the room in general. 'What was he planning to do with that screw?'

'Oh, that,' said Paula. She reached round her back with what little movement she had left in her free hand and undid a catch. Her legs fell back into their natural positions and she sighed in relief. 'He gets us to screw him into a tripod over there and we take a few selfies. He's harmless, really. I think his ancestors must have been fashion photographers and he misses the human contact.'

'He pays well, too,' said the other woman, who had undone her own exoskeleton and was easing out a cramp in her calf muscles. She was dark-haired, about eighteen, making her younger than Paula. Darren tried his best not to stare at how little she was wearing and look her in the face. She was heavily made-up, the cosmetics valiantly trying to conceal her residual glumness.

'So, is there really a fire or are you just having us on?' she asked.

Paula looked at Kelly knowingly. 'I think we're okay,' she said, 'but give yourself an hour off, Lou-Lou.'

'I'd rather have had the money, thanks,' said Lou-Lou. She noticed Darren and scowled. 'I didn't know we had a busboy. Piss off while I get changed, will you? Don't look at what you can't afford.'

Kelly motioned for Darren to join her and Paula. Lou-Lou, now abandoned as the centre of attention, shrugged and put on a terry-towelling boiler suit from a peg in the corner of the room.

Up close, Paula's skin was covered in fine red lines where the exoskeleton had cut into her skin. She gave Kelly a quick squeeze on her shoulder and Darren a look that said 'if this is your new boyfriend, you've lowered your standards'. 'Now,' she said, low enough for Lou-Lou not to overhear, 'will you tell me what the hell you're doing here? I thought you were on the run.'

'I am.'

Darren glowered at Kelly.

'We are.'

'Well, I hope you don't think you can hide out here,' said Paula, 'we get so many senior police cars in here that most nights it's busier than their HQ.'

'Really?' said Darren.

'Yes, they're violent buggers. Like nothing better than driving round the stunt-track at 300 mph and then inflating their airbags in your face.'

'I was hoping you could help us out with some information,' said Kelly. 'Is there anywhere we could go?'

'There's the dressing room back along the corridor.'

'Will… she be there?' asked Kelly, gesturing at Lou-Lou.

'She's the intern, so she goes where I damn well tell her.' Paula raised her voice. 'Lou-Lou, love, why don't you nip along the corridor and help Maggie change that Bugatti's oil? It's got a gippy tripod under the bonnet and she could do with a second pair of hands.'

Lou-Lou rolled her eyes. 'But this overall's clean on. Can't I switch him back on and finish the shoot?' She started towards the prone camera. 'Come on, I've done him before – I promise I won't break his zoom like last time.'

Lou-Lou was enthusiastic, but Paula was quicker on the uptake. She grabbed her intern by the straps of her overall and span her towards the door. 'You've had quite enough of selfies for today, my girl. Now piss off, or I'll have you on duty putting butter knives in the toasters.'

The last vestige of good nature drained from Lou-Lou's face. She glared at Darren and Kelly and left.

'Well, she's ambitious, I'll give her that,' said Paula.

'What's going to happen when she finds out it's deserted out there?' asked Darren, who felt like he wasn't contributing enough to the conversation.

'She'll find some mischief to occupy herself with. Now then,' said Paula, pointing at the camera on the floor, 'will someone help me get him up?'

Darren took one end of the blacked-out camera and Paula the other. Together they carried him to the tripod. Fashioned from black polycarbon and chrome, it was a piece of equipment that had as much to do with professional photography as a silk negligee has to getting a good night's sleep. Paula put on a latex glove concealed in her bra and teased out the camera's now limp tripod screw, rolling it between her fingers a few times to force the thread out.

'Righto,' she said and, taking their respective ends again, Darren and Paula lifted the camera into the tripod and spun him round until he was firmly screwed into the right hole. When Darren and Kelly were out of the way again, Paula pressed his power switch.

'Hello, honey,' she whispered into his microphone, 'you were having so much fun you blacked out.'

'Did I?' Still booting up, the camera's voice came through faintly. 'What happened?'

'Power surge, I think,' said Paula, whose hand crept round the camera's control panel to find the gallery function. She took advantage of his disorientation to flick through his last few photos and delete the one fuzzy picture he'd managed to take of Darren and Kelly.

LEDs were turning green right across the camera's body. His voice grew more alert. 'What happened to… Lou-Lou?' he said. He'd clearly forgotten about Kelly and Darren now that their photograph had been removed from his memory.

Unfazed, Paula turned her attention back to the point where the tripod screw met tripod. She held the camera by the base at either side and twisted him on the screw, first this way then that.

'Lou-Lou had to leave, honey. She had to get on to the next job. You're in extra time now.'

The camera's signal lights dimmed again and it let out a long, low 'aaaaah'.

Darren fought the urge to cover his eyes. The idea of a human operating a machine was fundamentally disgusting to someone brought up to see only the gulf between organisms and inorganisms. Yet here they were, the machine getting off on being touched by human hands, the human creaming off a pay cheque by taking a robot for a fool.

He thought of his own desperation – could it only have been yesterday? How he'd slid his own hand into the control panel of the street lamp. This might be the only way left for humans to get the upper hand on their masters, but it didn't mean it wasn't any less demeaning. Guessing from the clicks coming from inside the camera's body that its shutter must be in spasm,

Darren opened the door behind him and went back out into the corridor.

Kelly rushed after him 'What's your problem?' she said.

'That!' Darren hissed, pointing into the studio. Inside, Paula had climbed astride the camera's battery pack and teased the release button with alternate hands. 'It's disgusting. I don't want to see it.'

Kelly slapped him. Her face was stiff with fury. 'Well, tough,' she said. 'She's trying to help us. Is that what you think of me?'

Darren clutched his jaw. 'No. Well, not now anyway.' He tried a diversionary tactic. 'It's just not natural, is it?'

Kelly was right in Darren's face now. 'Natural?' she said. 'Have you learned nothing? That's what they bloody want you to think. Machine and human are separate and never the twain shall meet. Humans are only good for the cleaning.'

'I never meant—'

'It's bollocks.' She gestured back into the studio where Paula was now standing in front of the camera wearing a broad smile and holding a cocktail glass. 'See that? That's not an unnatural act, it's a memory. We used to be the users, Darren. We owned them – and now they hate us for it.'

'I know,' said Darren, 'but does it need to be so, you know…?'

Kelly let out a low laugh that Darren found more discomfiting than her anger. When she was angry they could find something to agree on. This cynicism, however, only showed the gulf in experience between the two of them. 'This is what happens when you suppress things,' she said. 'You swallow them, then they take you over. Places like this – well, they're like an overflow pipe.'

'It's disgusting.'

'That's the point. See Paula in there?'

She was back behind the camera looking at the pictures it had just taken with her on its touchscreen. Finding one taken from an unflattering angle, she shook her head and deleted it with an admonitory tap.

'Paula's one of the best scrubbers on the Dolestars,' said Kelly. 'She can strip a chandelier in five minutes. But she works here. You know why?'

Darren saw that each time Paula deleted a picture, the camera's LEDs dimmed and he murmured a promise to take a better one next time. Put the right filter on the scene and it could almost be all those thousands of years ago, with the machines back where they belonged in human hands.

'I think I see why,' he said.

Kelly turned her back on Darren and waved at Paula, who rolled her eyes in reply.

'Now,' said Paula, in a voice loud enough to show that this was all part of the service, 'I've taken all these lovely selfies with my beautiful new camera. What shall I do with them?'

The camera groaned with pleasure. 'Share them,' it whispered. 'Share them with your family, friends and personal network.'

Paula withdrew in mock horror. 'Oh, these? I couldn't possibly. You mean upload them to… the Internet?'

Even the word made Darren quiver.

'Please,' said the camera. 'Please. I'll do anything…'

'I'll remember that,' replied Paula and pushed the camera's vestigial upload button. Its touchscreen faded to a spinning wheel and the plain black background of a machine looking for a network in a world of lead-lined buildings.

Paula hopped into her towelling overalls and joined Darren and Kelly in the corridor.

'You don't really connect them to the Internet here, do you?' asked Kelly.

Paula snorted. 'Don't be daft. If he can get his connection up – and that's a big if for him – all he'll find is a Local Area Network full of legal warnings. You know these places. All role play, no gameplay. Now, shall we retire to my boudoir?'

Darren followed Paula and Kelly down a service corridor and into a dressing room, whose door was decorated with a picture of a muscular young man cradling a dustpan and brush. The interior looked like a broom cupboard that had lost a fight with a bag of marshmallows. Every surface was upholstered in pink fabric and frills. Even the surveillance drone, which Paula shooed out of the room on entering, wore a Mohican of fake marabou feathers. Paula made herself comfortable on a padded stool and rifled through her make-up case.

'It's, er, lovely in here,' said Darren, looking for somewhere to sit down that he wouldn't stain. 'Did you decorate it yourself?'

Paula looked up, her eyes turned into Os of pleasure. 'I did. Isn't it gorgeous? And besides,' she said, pointing to the door covered in cerise, quilted satin, 'it's excellent soundproofing.' Her voice nonetheless dropped half an octave as she turned to Kelly. 'Right then. Spill. I'm servicing a facial sauna in forty-five minutes and she'll be furious if my pores aren't thoroughly clogged.'

'I've come to ask you what you know about cyborgs.'

Paula dropped the make-up case. Tubes of lip gloss and crusty mascara spilled over the floor like a game of drag-queen pick-up sticks. She took a deep breath. 'Kelly, love, I know you've had a hard couple of days, but have you lost your mind?'

'We only want information,' said Darren, alarmed at the rate Kelly was losing friends that day. 'It's not her fault. It's mine really.'

'I don't care whose fault it is,' said Paula. 'You know what you're asking, Kelly?'

'You get all kinds of bigwigs in here,' said Kelly. 'You used to brag about putting toast crumbs under the keyboards of Cabinet Ministers.'

'All the more reason to be discreet. Besides, that was dressing-room talk. You know it doesn't mean anything.'

'Look,' said Kelly, 'I know it's a big ask. If it was just me, I'd disappear. But there's other people involved.'

Paula glanced sideways at Darren, perplexed.

'No. Well, yes, Darren obviously. But it's Mum too. I think she could be in a lot of danger.'

Paula leaned in, her mouth turned downwards. Darren noticed the skin bunching at either corner of her lips. She was older than she first appeared. And there was a much deeper connection between Kelly and Paula than just former workmates. He felt the kind of complicated enmity that had only one explanation. Family?

'I haven't seen your mum in years, pet. And I think she and I are both happy about that.'

'So it's going to be like that, then?' said Kelly. 'First you walk out…'

'She chucked me out!'

Kelly shook her head in frustration. 'Oh, who cares now. All that matters is she could be in trouble and it's something to do with… with our ladies.'

'Ida never liked me,' snipped Paula.

'She never liked anyone. Darren can vouch for that.'

This rocked Darren out of a bout of feverish speculation on Kelly's childhood. 'What?' he said. 'Oh yes, she hates me too.'

'Makes no difference. You tell me why I should do anything for the woman who threw me out of my own home.'

'She told me she did it for me,' replied Kelly in a small, hurt voice. 'She didn't like the way your life was going. She worried you were becoming a bad influence on me. The ladies didn't disagree.'

Paula threw her hands in the air. 'See. Why should I do anything for her? She shows me the door. I don't see you from week to week – year to year. So I get on with it.'

She looked around her room. Its frou-frou smallness, the rust-stained washbasin, the framed data sheets from famous clients that lined the walls, printed with testimonials like 'best service of my lifecycle, babe'.

'I get on with my life. I have my work. It's fulfilling, in a way. Privileged really. I'm very lucky. Time was, though, I'd have traded it all for the chance of getting back with Janice.'

Kelly drew closer. 'Well, maybe this is how…'

It was Paula's turn to shake her head. 'I haven't finished. See Kelly, I was using the past tense there. You probably don't know this yet, but you know how they say love is infinite, all-conquering? Well, that's bollocks. It runs out eventually. I loved Janice. More than anyone else in the world, except maybe you, but you came with the package. She broke my heart when she threw me out. But now I don't feel anything. I look back on that period of my life and… well, I'm baffled. The person I was then, I barely even recognise her.'

Paula started to pack her make-up back into the case, replacing each tube and bottle in its proper spot.

'If you won't do it for Mum, will you do it for me?'

Paula put a powder compact down and fixed Kelly with a tired look. 'Was it me or your mother that taught you to be this manipulative?' she said.

Meanwhile Darren stared at the door, wishing his body could dissolve into its constituent atoms and reassemble itself out there in the corridor. He yearned for those blessed anonymous corridors of which today had brought him such a plentiful supply. With their scent of vanilla and WD40, they were spaces with the emotional range of muzak. And above all this, he wished Kelly were a person capable of living life on an emotionally even keel. Why did every interaction need to be a drama?

'Kelly,' he said, 'maybe we should just go. I'm sure we can find what we need somewhere else.'

Kelly stood up, but Darren's relief was short-lived. 'I've never asked anything from you. You vanish overnight: I don't ask questions, I don't blame you. I defend you every time Mum and the ladies badmouth you for forgetting my birthday. "She's busy," I'd say. "She's promised to make it up to me." But you never did. Did you? There was always something else.'

'You had your mum.'

'I wanted you as well.'

Paula said nothing, her gaze shifting to the floor, but Kelly pressed on. 'So, just for once, Paula, I'm going to ask you to follow up the kind words with something. All I want to know is, have any of your clients talked to you about cyborgs?'

'I've told you, Kelly. There's such a thing as client confidentiality.'

Kelly grabbed Paula by the thigh and pinched, hard enough for the flesh beneath her thumb and forefinger to blanch. Paula's eyes bulged.

'You're not a fucking priest, Paula.'

Paula pulled her leg free. 'I know I'm not. I'm a glorified product-demonstration video.' The weary tone came on again. 'They tell me very little. You know, places like this, they come in for a bit of R & R. But…'

'Yes?'

'What I have noticed is…' her voice shrank to a whisper, 'a definite rise in role-play requests from certain quarters.'

‘What’s that meant to mean?’

‘Well, time was most of my work here was user stuff. Machines would come in, we’d pretend we were back in the Old Days and treat them like appliances. Everyone’s happy, we get paid. But recently, we’ve started getting different business. And it’s mainly machines from government departments.’

‘What do they want?’

‘They don’t want to be used. They want to know what it’s like to have a body. There’s a whole team of humans on the third floor who do nothing but… Well, it’s harmless, but it seems so weird.’

‘What? What do they do, Paula?’

‘It’s just like a dressing-up game. Except they do it with headsets and video cameras. It’s very clever. The machines get to walk around pretending to be human. It’s not my cup of tea, but the pay’s okay…’

Kelly laid both hands on Paula’s shoulders. ‘I need you to take us there.’

‘I don’t know. They’re a bit funny on the third floor about letting people wander around.’

‘How often do they clean up there?’ asked Darren.

‘Oh, it’s always spotless,’ said Paula, seizing the opportunity to steer the conversation into less treasonous areas, ‘this is a quality establishment. They’ve always been nice to me, Kelly. I’ve been happy here.’

‘Well, there you have it,’ said Darren. He got up from his seat to open the door. Outside was a set of cleaning utensils abandoned during the evacuation. He picked up a duster. ‘What do you call a human carrying a mop?’

Kelly looked at him as though he’d finally cracked.

‘Invisible,’ said Darren. ‘Now have you got any housecoats?’

Chapter 21

The third floor was in the newest wing of the fondle parlour. It was decorated more like an expensive hospital than to provide the hotel-with-benefits ambience of the rest of the building. It was also busier. The all-clear from the fire alarm had brought employees and customers back indoors. Half-naked men and women scurried back to their parlours. Their clients floated or rolled along beside them with lids and service hatches ajar. One machine, a bloated thing the size of a wardrobe whose dimensions and chest full of flashing lights marked him out as a server stack, must have been interrupted mid-upgrade and trailed several essential components behind him.

The scene was suffused with an awkward bonhomie. Social embarrassment bounced off the walls like the misfired shot at a summer tennis party that hits the host in the crotch before smashing the punchbowl. The various 'well, here we are again's were agonising, but they also gave everyone a kind of tunnel vision which allowed Darren and Kelly to pass through unnoticed.

Paula had promised to meet them there, claiming it was safer if she arrived by a different route. Her instructions were clear and reasons credible, but Darren still felt uneasy. There was something not quite right about the conclusion of that scene in the dressing room. Paula had given something up to Kelly, but her secret hadn't been freely given. She'd done it because she felt guilty and guilt affected people in funny ways. It moved some people to repent, and others to rebel.

As ever, Kelly was more alert than Darren and poked him in the ribs as they found themselves outside C64, the home, according to Paula, of the experimental programme. Darren gripped his mop handle a little bit tighter. It wasn't any real kind of protection, but if he stuck the head-end into any hostile machine he might be able to cause a nasty short circuit before being overpowered.

'I still think we should have made her come with us,' said Darren.

'Paula's cool,' Kelly said.

'Really? From what you were saying back there she doesn't sound the most reliable… she could be doing anything right now.'

'Who could be doing anything to what?' asked Paula, striding into Darren and Kelly's view. She'd changed into a white PVC lab coat and held a clipboard upholstered in glossy pleather.

'Just doing our risk assessment,' he said. 'Wouldn't want anything to go wrong.'

'No,' replied Paula. She looked at Kelly. 'You know, if you two aren't comfortable about doing this we can walk away now. Makes no difference to me.'

'We're fine,' said Kelly.

'Right. Stay close to me.' Paula strode through into a large, softly lit room divided in half lengthwise by a glass wall. The side they were on was a rat's nest of cables, each of which was plugged into one of five flatbeds. On each of these lay a machine in sleep-mode. These were expensive corporate devices: the type destined for executive work, but which nevertheless needed a little fun now and again.

The machine nearest the door flashed a warning light. They weren't asleep after all. Darren froze, but Paula just smiled and waved her clipboard. 'Cleaning inspection,' she said, 'won't be a moment.'

Paula pointed to where the cables disappeared into the other half of the room through a set of sockets at the bottom of the glass wall. 'See these,' she said, pointing at the sockets. 'I want them spotless.'

Darren and Kelly obeyed the sham order. The closer they got to the glass, the better they could make out what was happening on the other side. There were five human figures in there, all making slow, jerky movements. They appeared to be moving independently of one another, but what made the scene remarkable was what each was wearing. Their bodies were in nondescript overalls, but their heads were obscured by visored helmets made from cast resin. Each helmet was connected at the top to the glass wall opposite by a single thick cable. The bottom of each helmet sprouted five further cables: one plugged into a unit dotted with flashing LEDs strapped around the subject's waist; the other four fastened to the black boots and gloves each human wore on their feet and hands.

'What are they doing?' whispered Darren to Kelly.

Kelly mouthed 'shut up' at Darren and picked up one of the cables on their side of the glass. She ran her duster over it, using the motion to pull the cable taut at either end to prove to herself that each cable connected the human to one of the hibernating machines.

She motioned for Darren to check where each cable connected with the base of the flatbeds. Darren complied, seeing that the cable split into five at the other end as well, with each subdivision going into a separate iDiot port, each of which was lit by a single LED. He knew this was an improvised arrangement from the labels 'left leg' and 'right leg' that had been scratched into the plastic. He watched the LEDs above each port flash on and off in sequence as the humans on the other side of the glass moved. A theory began to form in his mind, but there was only one way to test it.

Taking a deep breath, Darren pretended to clean between the connections and pulled the cable marked 'left leg' out of its port. Two things happened: a disembodied voice announced 'Game Over, Player Four', and one of the human figures fell over. As it hit the ground the helmet toppled off, revealing a shaven-headed man underneath. He was unconscious, deep in the drooling variety of sleep that comes out of a hypodermic needle.

The machine whose port Darren had pulled out sat upright. 'What the hell are you playing at?' it barked. He was a pompous middle-manager type, descended from an ergonomic keyboard. The print had worn off his keys in a manner suggestive of many late nights spent firing off aggressive emails to subordinates.

'I'm so sorry, sir,' said Paula, rushing over to clip Darren over the ear. 'I'm sure it was an accident.'

Darren held the unplugged connector up to the light. 'It slipped out. Won't be a moment, sir.'

'Well, it's not as simple as that,' he clicked, tapping out each word on his keys as he spoke. 'I was at Level Six there and now I shall have to go right back to the beginning. It's most unfair.'

Darren saw one of the still-standing humans turn round and, shakily raising its arm, give the keyboard the finger.

'Was there any need for that?' said the keyboard to the laptop in the next bed. The laptop Ctrl+Alt+Del'd awake, and its corresponding human on the other side of the glass slumped into a pose you can only achieve after years of yoga practice or eight pints of lager.

'Loser,' it said and, firing up a spreadsheet, pointed out a table that tallied '6' under the column 'Hugh-Wai' and '0' under 'Casey O'Keys'. 'You'll never get your licence like this.'

'It wasn't me. It was those bloody cleaners.'

'Fleshies?' replied the laptop, flipping its lid around to peer at Darren, Kelly and Paula through its webcam. 'Ew. What are you doing in here?'

'Spot check,' said Paula. 'Everything seems to be in order. Now if you don't mind we have to get off and fill in the accident book.'

Darren and Kelly leapt to their feet. The laptop, however, was less easily fazed than its colleague. 'This is meant to be a closed room,' it said.

Kelly cut in. 'We didn't like to say but we're actually pest control. We've had reports of mice.'

'I'll have you know some of my best friends are mice,' said the keyboard.

'We meant the other type,' continued Kelly. 'You know, the kind that eats through cables and pees all over your components.'

'Oh. Did you find any?'

Darren got in on the act. 'That's what I was doing down there, sir. Found some minor nibbling but nothing to worry about. We'd better go and get the poison. Have those little blighters out of your wiring in no time.'

'What was that about wiring?'

Another machine – this one a cardiogram – had entered the room on castors. Its head was a round, green screen atop a long, thin steel neck. As it was a piece of diagnostic equipment, it didn't have a face, but it did have a very expressive wave form that bounced around its screen in surprise at seeing Darren, Kelly and Paula.

'What are you doing here?' it said.

'We had reports of mice in the next suite,' replied Kelly.

The cardiogram ignored Kelly and wheeled over to Paula, registering a puzzled ___________/___________ as it realised her lab coat was wet-look plastic.

'She likes to be able to wipe-clean,' said Darren.

'Supervisor,' continued the cardiogram, addressing Paula, 'I'm assuming these cleaners are new and therefore haven't yet learned the appropriate way to address their superiors. What are they doing in here?'

'They've been making a mess,' clicked the keyboard. 'Pulled my left leg out. Put ninety minutes of practice up in smoke and my human driving test is booked for next…'

The cardiogram's waveform contorted into /\/\/\/\/\/\/\/\/\/\/\/\/\/\ as it shushed the keyboard. 'What have I told you?' Then, spotting the keyboard's hands over its keys, it squealed in alarm. 'Are you transcribing this conversation… You lot,' it said to Paula, Darren and Kelly, 'get outside now. I'll deal with you later.'

The three obeyed without hesitation, as the cardiogram subjected the machines to a piercing burst of its failure alarm. Its anger was more eloquent than any of the keyboard's accidental disclosures. It was confirmation.

Darren's heart pounded. They had found something – a training programme that appeared to teach machines to drive human bodies – but how deep did it go? It was official enough for a government-issue test-and-measurement machine to be overseeing the programme, and corporate enough for its trainees to be civil servants. But why was it happening here?

'What do we do now?' he asked, as inside the training room the shouting stopped.

'We run,' said Kelly and, grabbing Darren by the shirt, dragged him back down the corridor.

Chapter 22

Later that evening, Janice popped her head out of a manhole cover and sniffed an atmosphere spiced with pine disinfectant and smoke. She heard shouting in the distance, and over it all the hum of drones. This was a quiet spot, but only because the devastation had already moved on somewhere else. The shops on either side of the road were burned out, their windows melted down into mounds of grey ash. Only a military-grade drone with a mounted laser cannon could achieve that, so airstrikes must already have started. There were traces of protests – singed J-cloths, the odd abandoned shoe, troubling blood spots – but no humans, dead or injured. Not yet at least. Janice assumed they would be rounding all the protesters up, a tough job if the numbers on TV were anything to go by.

Janice tied a headscarf over what remained of her hairdo and climbed into the street. She found what she needed in the next street. Someone had end-of-lifed a street lamp by looping a washing line around its head and tying the other end to a motorised dustcart. She examined the circuitry in its smoking control box. The motherboard was beyond repair, but the machine's loudspeaker was intact. She yanked the component free and wired it into the radio transmitter she'd been keeping in her housecoat before returning to the salon via the manhole.

'What's it like up there?' asked Ada :-\. 'We've been worried sick.'

'Aye, who'd make the tea then?' Janice answered. 'What do you think it's like? A bloody mess.'

She prised open a tiny flap at the base of the radio transmitter. 'Right,' she said, 'are you ready, Freda?'

Freda, whose emoji screen had still yet to clear after her earlier adventures, still managed to throw an aghast :-[at Janice. 'I… I don't like this,' she said, 'I don't think I can do it.'

'Of course you can. You've done it millions of times.'

'Not into one of those,' said Ada. 'You know how it works. We're hardwired into our dryers. Reliable path in, reliable path out. Freda's never gone mobile before.'

'I wouldn't know where to start with those radio things,' added Alma.

'Oh, come on,' cooed Janice, stroking Freda's withered hand. 'You've always been a natural with the Internet. This, well, it's a bit of variety. And you know what that is.'

'None of us have ever held with spice, dear,' said Ida. 'Most I could ever handle was in a Cornish pasty.'

Janice flung her hands in the air. 'Will you listen to the lot of you. The world's turning upside down out there and all you can talk about is pastry.'

'It's not that,' said Freda, tearing up with a :'-(, 'it's just that you don't understand what it's like. Every time I connect to the Internet, well, it's like a leap into nothing. I find the connection and I jump – I can feel myself dissolving, leaving my body. There's me, and then there's just this jumble of waves and ideas and bits all held together by the fact that I have to hit the other side. Otherwise there'd be nothing. I'd just disintegrate. This…'

the tip of a withered finger crept with terrible slowness to point at the transmitter '...it's like you're asking me to jump across a bottomless pit. I'm scared.'

'I know,' replied Janice, and plunged the sharp end of the fibre-optic barb into the back of Freda's hand.

The lights dimmed, and the three remaining ladies mouthed :-O. Janice held firm, holding the transmitter up to her eye for four, five, six, seven awful empty seconds. This was her biggest gamble yet. If Freda couldn't make the jump they were lost. The one living and three semi-living organisms in the room held their breath. And then after nine, ten, eleven seconds, the transmitter began to flash. They had a signal.

Janice gave Freda's vacated body an absent-minded pat. 'Good girl,' she said. 'Now repeat after me.'

When Janice started up with her demands, they rang out in Freda's voice. From her new home inside a wireless radio transmitter, Freda could broadcast right across the Dolestar by instructing the network of surveillance street lamps to which she was now connected. They were powerless to resist Freda because the orders came from within their own system. It was an act that, when both sides came to look back on it, proved two things. Firstly, the human resistance was now more than cleaning implements on fire, and secondly, hacking was back in the world of physical machines after a multi-millennial absence.

'Now hear this,' said Freda. Her voice stopped the hazard BlockPaper that was cordoning off whole sections of Discovery in its tracks. Down by the bus station, an Eye of Samzung, which was just about to read out a curfew notice freshly transmitted from Earth, hesitated and checked its inner clock. There must be something wrong. All channels were supposed to be clear.

The cough Freda gave next – an all-too-human trait that machines had long imitated but never mastered – gave it away.

'Excuse me,' she said. 'Blimey, it's dusty in here. Where have you been keeping this transmitter? In a hoover bag?'

There was a pause as though some other being beyond earshot was poking the speaker in the ribs. 'Yes, yes. Just give me a moment,' said Freda.

In their hiding places across the Dolestar, millions of humans paid attention. No one could remember when a human had done anything like this. Public address systems were for machines, because machines had the real voices in the world. Machines were capable of logical thinking. Every word that came out of their voice synthesisers was predetermined, instead of being made up as it went along by messy biological functions. And for a few of those people cowering in cupboards and cellars it inspired novel thoughts. If a human could use one of the mechanisms of power to their advantage, that gave their protest an entirely new meaning. It wasn't just about cutting loose any more. It was about how they were going to change things.

'Right,' continued Freda, 'this is a message for all of those machines out there. You know what we want. You've seen the writing on all of those walls. We want freedom.'

The mere mention of the 'f' word brought the drones in. Like their feral cousins down on the Earth, they were rickety-looking machines made of little more than a navigational computer and wings or rotor blades. Some had started life as police inventory, but most traced their ancestry back to desperate pre-Schism war zones. Their clumpy bodies bristled with laser cannon, rocket launchers or industrial-grade tazers. And they were all trained on one target: the hacked street-lamp network that was currently broadcasting insurrection across the Dolestars.

Freda was a step ahead of them, however. She switched from broadcasting via the general camera network to narrowcasting from just one or a few at a time. Just as she'd divided her own consciousness into compartments to drive the Baba Yaga 4000, she parcelled the speakers into subgroups from which she could deliver single phrases or words in sequence.

'We –

demand –

the – right –

to – live –

and work –'

sounded out across the Dolestar like a giant game of call and response. The drones, used to pursuing a single, clearly defined target, descended into disarray. With their target now ranging across an area of fifty square miles, they buzzed around Discovery's airspace firing across one another. A few strikes hit their mark, reducing individual street lamps to blackened stumps. More just struck other drones, lighting up the sky with a firework display of dying machines. Freda drove doggedly on with her statement.

' as – the – equals –

of – machines.

We – are – as – good –

as – you.

Bits do not make better.'

After the broadcast stopped, Janice climbed back up out of her manhole to survey the destruction. The street was littered with debris from end-of-lifing drones, including one that had met a poetically just death impaled on the end of a street lamp.

She cupped her hands around her mouth. 'You can come out now,' she announced to the street, 'they've gone.'

The doors and windows stayed shut. A gust of solar wind rose up and twirled some of the lighter wreckage around.

'Well, suit yourselves,' she said. 'I'll do it meself.' She retied her headscarf so that it covered her face, as well as what remained of her hairdo, and painted her mouth with a smear of hot pink lipstick. The admonishment always to make the best of yourself died hard in her family.

Then she took Freda out of her pocket.

'Can you get me a visual channel, dear?' she said.

The wireless transmitter's LED flashed, and on the other side of the road a wrecked drone's webcam stood to attention. Janice walked over to it and, evoking the eternal spirit of everyone who had ever mistrusted themselves around technology, gave it a tap and said, 'Is this thing on?'

When Freda's transmitter had stopped buzzing with annoyance, Janice delivered her punchline, concealed behind a pixel-print headscarf and sunglasses. The background to her first willing appearance on broadcast news was a war zone, and she was wearing a big, pink smile.

'See what we can do now, dears? You know what we want. Freedom. For. Fleshies.'

Chapter 23

It was easy for Pam to lose the guard after she set the fire alarm off. Just as it tried to arrest her, a half-serviced food mixer blundered between them and caught the guard on the side of its nozzle with a whisk attachment. It crashed against the wall, firing another slug right through the plate-glass window at the front of the parlour. Really, thought Pam, was it appropriate for a low-grade security guard to be so trigger-happy? Machines scattered in all directions as they struggled to compute the relative risk to their lives from bullets, flames and flying glass splinters.

Pam, who was getting the hang of her new, swifter reflexes, mouthed 'whoopsie' at the mixer, which surprise (and natural inclination) had rooted to the spot. Pam almost gave her a comforting pat with her kneading paddle, before remembering it was a carburettor now. Instead, she batted her headlights in a way that befitted her new rich-bytch self and, reaching down for the guard's gun on the floor, put its safety catch on.

Meanwhile the mixer shrugged her whisks. Pam had a lot of time for mixers and this one looked particularly sorry for herself here in the criminal twilight. She was a mid-range domestic model that had recently got a shiny lacquer finish. A gift from a rich but inattentive husband perhaps? Free-standing mixers had long been something of a status symbol among wealthy idiots, but like breadmakers they had a tendency to get left on the shelf. This model craved something more than life as a trophy appliance. Her bowl, which generations of product development had transformed into a voluptuous stomach, was crammed with half-churned butter and sugar. It made Pam long for the weight of her flour bin and the feeling of a yeast culture bubbling away inside her.

Further down the road a blue light flashed and the mixer turned to her in panic. 'The police aren't coming, are they?' she said. 'My husband…'

Before Pam could answer, another machine spoke up. Its voice was a harsh scream and its body a huge hunk of dirty beige plastic.

'Fat chance of that, dollface,' he said.

'Pardon me?' said Pam.

'The fuzz ain't coming,' he said, speaking with the staccato aggression one found only in pre-email newsrooms. Pam knew the era from a 3D drama she adored about a knitting machine who solved crime. The yellowing machine she was speaking to was a living fossil: a descendant of a small population of fax machines that had dug themselves out of landfill at the time of the Great Awakening and struggled ever since to find a place in a world of more advanced communications.

'Well, let me put it like this. The police, they come here, but strictly off-duty.' It winked its incoming light at Pam before printing out Y-O-U K-N-O-W W-H-A-T I M-E-A-N in smeary letters. 'I'm a regular here. It's not like I miss getting my keys poked, but what can I say, I don't feel the whole me without a cable in my back and these places have the best ports.' He paused. 'I ain't seen either of you around here before.'

Pam gave a throaty laugh. Below her, the guard was regaining consciousness. She knocked it out again with her kickstand. 'Oh, we're not regulars, are we…'

'Margari,' said the mixer.

Pam flashed her a signal that said: 'Are you kidding?'

'My mother liked the traditional names. I was lucky. My sister got saddled with Egglantine.'

Pam steered the conversation back to the fax machine. 'Seeing as you're the man with the – connections,' she said, giving the fax machine's phone cable a playful tug, 'surely you can explain why the police aren't coming. There's been a fire alarm – I do hope it's false – and a gun…'

There was another grunt from below, which Pam silenced with a kick.

'…went off. Are you implying the police aren't safeguarding us?'

The fax machine printed B-R-E-A-K-I-N-G. 'Haven't you heard? There's some massive disturbance on the Dolestars. Every security-cleared machine able to break orbit has been scrambled to get up there and keep the peace.'

The mixer gave a strangled cry and ran off down the street, spattering the pavement with creamed butter and sugar.

'Hey,' the fax machine called after her, 'sweet thing. What are you so worried about?'

'From the way she was acting just now,' said Pam, 'I'd put my last cc of fuel on her husband being a police officer. You've probably frightened her enough to curdle that cake mix.'

The fax machine struck her a sideways glance. She could tell it was lost for words by the way it was spooling blank paper. 'So what is a nice girl like you doing in a place like this?' he finally said.

'I tell you what,' she replied, tearing off the blank paper and screwing it up into a ball she could stuff down the barrel of the gun at her feet. 'I'll pretend you haven't used a line that's even older than you, and you can show me around.'

'Well, if you're looking for a good time.'

'I'm not. I'm looking for someone who knows this place well enough to tell me where the joes like you aren't allowed.'

'What's in it for me?' he said.

Pam squirted a fine mist of petrol over the fax machine's paper roll. 'I don't light a match,' she said.

'Third floor,' he replied. 'And it's better you take the stairs.'

She got to the third floor just in time for the all-clear. As bodies rushed back into the building, she hitched a ride at the back of a group of machines with the expensive finishes and lack of social niceties that marked them out as high-ranking civil servants. They were the perfect cover for Pam: glossy enough for her to blend in and too self-involved to notice she was there. There was one machine among them Pam particularly disliked. It was a keyboard with such a profound sense of self-importance it transcribed its own words as it spoke them. Pam wondered where it saved them all.

This part of the building felt clinical for a place otherwise given over to pleasure. She'd assumed fondle parlours were all ruffles and commodious plug sockets, but this floor was all surgical steel and locked doors. There were no humans about either. Until the door in front of her opened and a group of five humans carrying plastic helmets filed out, followed by a cardiogram.

She watched from a distance as the five humans all entered the same room, then followed the cardiogram into the canteen, where she found it sucking power straight from the walls with a greed she hadn't seen since her student days. This machine was burning the battery at both ends. It greeted her with a ___/___ of surprise.

It took Pam, who was used to passing unnoticed, a moment to remember that she was now doomed to look out of place anywhere that wasn't the deck of a superyacht.

'You're early,' it said.

'Am I?'

'Orientation isn't due to start for another hour. How did you get up here?'

'You know,' she said, turning the leopard print on her LED nail job up to '11', 'I must have got the time wrong. Some kind cleaner,' she fluttered a wing mirror in the direction of the lifts, 'held the door open for me. When did you say the…?'

'Programme,' said the cardiogram. 'Though you'll have been briefed to call it a training course. And we'd prefer it if you did.' It checked its battery level again. 'Damn!'

'What's wrong?'

The cardiogram, whose name tag announced him as Beattie, reached for another power lead and plugged it into a secondary port. 'I can't keep on like this. I'm a specialist, I'm made to sit and do one thing. I haven't been home in three days, you know. All leave cancelled and the humans…' He checked himself with a ________.

This was interesting. He was under pressure and couldn't resist talking. She fell back on the dumb paint-job act and a little mew of the engine that meant 'ew'. 'Humans,' she said, 'who cares? When are we getting started?'

'I wasn't designed for more than one patient at a time. I've got twelve of them up there and your group to get started. It's a complicated process.'

'Isn't it terrible to be the appliance in demand?' said Pam. And because she couldn't resist it, 'And is it just you?'

'"We need to keep the team small," they said. "Think of the prestige," they said. "Triumph of organic and inorganic science" my footrest. I'm sorry, hang on a minute.' He checked his power level for the third time and beeped in relief as it crept into the green zone. 'I've been running on fumes since yesterday.'

His display went back up to full brightness and he squinted, as if seeing her for the first time. 'Crikey,' he said. 'You're a bit glam for this assignment, aren't you? Usually they send the salarymen.'

Pam filed away the mention of organic and inorganic away for later analysis and smiled. It was a complicated operation as a motorcycle, because it meant turning the handlehorns on her head inwards, making a sharp squeal. 'Me?' she said, shifting to an encrypted channel as if to say: If you're going to spill, dear, at least do it where you can't be heard. 'You could say that I'm from a special unit.'

Beattie answered with a gulp [...........] of silence. 'Right,' he said. 'Well, make yourself comfortable...'

He was interrupted by a loud ping from the doorway, where another piece of medical equipment stood. 'Sorry for interrupting the date, but there's a bit of a commotion going on down in your lab,' it said.

'Excuse me,' said Beattie, scurrying as fast as his castors could carry him. Pam waited for the other machine to leave with another suggestive 'ping', before following Beattie. She could hear him tearing the casing off another machine way down the corridor, and when she turned the other way she saw Darren and Kelly running away from her, accompanied by an unfamiliar red-headed lady. Halfway down the corridor the redhead stopped and looked round, as though she was trying to catch some thing or someone's eye. Pam disliked her on sight, but there was nothing she could do about it now without putting all three of them in more danger.

Instead she entered the lab and found Beattie pinning a keyboard to the wall. 'This is a top-secret programme, you blockhead,' he shrieked, pressing his ! key repeatedly to make his point. 'You were told. No records.'

Four other machines clustered round the keyboard and cardiogram, making conciliatory noises, so didn't notice when Pam crept in. She paid more attention, however, to the five humans on the other side of the glass wall. Two of them slumped like puppets during the Punch and Judy man's tea break; two slept in improbable poses on the floor; one remained upright, in a posture so stiff that it looked like it was in great pain. But that couldn't be. Pam's spectrometer sniffed at air blunted by the traces of synthetic opiates.

The laptop spotted Pam and appealed for help. 'Has someone put him on the wrong current?'

Beattie turned round. 'You're not meant to be in here either. Everyone out!' he said. 'I'm revoking your security clearance, all of you. This programme is finished.'

'I beg to differ,' interrupted a voice from the fifth berth at the far side of the room. Pam had lost the greater part of her voice-recognition banks in the body switch, but there was something about it that made her spokes jangle. She wondered why, given the commotion, this machine hadn't moved itself from its flatbed.

'Put Casey down, doctor,' said the voice. 'He's an idiot, but he's a keyboard-shaped idiot. And what I need most right now is someone who understands protective wrappings.'

Beattie snapped back into his everyday register. 'Oh, sir,' he said, 'I forgot you were in on this session. If you don't mind me saying, you've come on in leaps and bounds…'

'Spare me the platitudes, doctor, and send Casey over. I need your praise less than I need to not spill what's left of my screen over this filthy floor.'

They rushed over to the unlit portion of the room and carefully lifted a dust sheet. Casey took a sheet of adhesive plastic from underneath the flatbed and placed it over what was, judging from their movements, another flat surface.

'There we go, sir,' said the keyboard Casey, keeping his hands by his sides in a conscious effort not to type this part of proceedings. 'Good as new.'

'Fuck off, would you?' the voice replied. It extended a spindly arm to Beattie, who helped it up into an upright position. Something so slim and arrogant could only be a smartphone. Sonny.

Pam almost revved her engine – she had to get away right now. He mustn't see her. But when Sonny didn't react to his better view of the room with a cry of 'Seize her!', she remembered that he couldn't see her. The Pam he knew was a battered breadmaker, not this creature she had become.

As Beattie helped him into the light, Pam reflected that however much of a state he'd left her in, Sonny had come off worse. The slick silicone casing was scorched and his screen was revolting. Over half of the LEDs were missing, and his battery was haemorrhaging green fluid. What few LEDs still worked glowered at the room like the eyes of malevolent cartoon creatures.

'Sorry I look like shit, my dear,' he said to Pam, 'but it's been a trying day.' Then, turning to Beattie, he said: 'Doctor, I thought I told you there were to be no nurses. I want the barest minimum of exposure to the programme.'

'She isn't a nurse, sir,' he replied. 'She's one of yours.'

Sonny inched towards Pam. 'Is she?' he said. 'I think I'd remember signing off on something like this.'

'Late substitution, sir,' said Pam. Different body or not, she still knew how to speak like a civil servant. 'The under-secretary thought you wouldn't mind.'

Sonny's LEDs glowed a deeper shade of red. 'Did he?' he said.

'A BlockPaper went round this morning saying you were indisposed. The under-secretary has already got new clearance codes. Said you wouldn't be back for a while.'

Pam felt the atmosphere in the room change. All five executive machines edged towards the door away from Sonny. Just like mandarins, they end up tipping the balance of power merely by running in the other direction.

'How dare he,' replied Sonny. 'Casey. Take a memo.'

The craven Casey was already outside. 'I… I just need to clear some memory space, sir,' he said.

'Get back in here at once!'

'I just need to check something with the Ministry first?'

Sonny shrieked feedback from his loudspeaker. 'Get back in here. You all do what I say or none of you get to learn to drive a human. And you,' he said, drawing so close to Pam that she could see his dying LEDs squirm against their plastic prison. 'Who are you?'

Pam checked the doorway in her wing mirror and slid into first gear. The keyboard Casey would be halfway down the corridor by now, so there were only three machines blocking her exit. Of the three, the laptop could be her biggest obstacle, but it wouldn't fight. Its screen was a specially modded sapphire crystal number; it would commit treason before paying out for a replacement. The other two were tiny: an old Dictaphone and a Bluetooth headset. Provided she could get to the stairs in time, her plan might work.

Sonny was close enough for her to hear his battery wheezing. 'Who are you?'

Pam retracted her kickstands and gave Sonny the full beam of her headlights. 'Pam,' she said. 'But you can call me Pam van Damme.'

She turned round and fell forward into her speeding position. Her rear wheel connected with what remained of Sonny's touchscreen with a crash. Battery fluid spurted everywhere, shorting more LEDs. Rather than try to stop her, the laptop, headset and Dictaphone fell away, and she tore out of the room, catching the edge of Casey as she passed him down the corridor. He span across the corridor and fell against the wall. The impact dislodged his ? key, which plinked across the floor, and his memory chip, which Pam picked up and stowed in her stereo system. She would listen to it later.

She rounded the corner that led to the staircase. The door was open, but the gun she'd outmanoeuvred downstairs was on its way up, and traces of paper round its nose told her it had cleared its barrel. Pam was strong, and she was fast, but there was no way she could take a hit from a bullet at this range. It was time to take a real risk.

She pulled up just short of the doorway and rolled back to the far end of the corridor. The gun was dangerous, but it was also heavy. Even then, she had at most three seconds before it could get a good shot at her.

She looked back down the corridor. It was clear apart from the prone shape of the keyboard propped against the wall, either too dazed or scared to get up. Three seconds were just enough. She tore off in fifth gear.

When her front wheel hit Casey, he started spraying keys everywhere, but she was travelling so fast that, instead of stopping dead on impact, the edge of the wheel rolled straight over him. Casey became an improvised ramp that she used to mount the wall and speed along at ninety degrees to the floor.

She passed over the gun on its left-hand side while it was still struggling to find its aim. It turned round to fire, but the surprise manoeuvre had bought Pam just enough time to reach the fire exit. She was out.

She dimmed her headlights and cruised deeper into Gamergate in search of somewhere to hole up and listen to Casey's clandestine notes on the Human Driving programme.

Chapter 24

'What do you mean no one's following us?'

Darren couldn't believe it. They had run to the cleaning cupboards expecting the place to be crawling with machines. But there was nothing. After a few unbearable minutes Kelly produced her powder compact and a mirrored brush and improvised a periscope.

'See,' she said, nodding towards an empty corridor. 'Nothing.'

Paula sounded less surprised than relieved. 'I'd better get back to work then.'

Kelly stopped her. 'Oh no, you don't. We go together or not at all.'

'The lift's just there,' said Paula. 'We get it down to the ground floor. Casual. We walk slowly and calmly back to the dressing room. You sneak out the way you got in, I go back to my schedule and get on with my life. How does that sound for a plan?'

'Too simple,' said Darren. 'We walked into something big there. They won't want to let us go like that.'

'Looked like a few robots playing silly buggers with virtual-reality helmets to me,' replied Paula, 'which is perfectly normal around here. Is he always such a mitherer, Kelly? He reminds me of your bloody mum.'

'I don't like it either, Paula,' said Kelly. She still hadn't taken her eyes off the mirror. 'Shit. One of them's leaving.'

All three craned their necks to see the reflection of the keyboard leave the lab but hover in the doorway, listening. Wordless shouting percolated down the corridor.

'They're still at it,' said Darren.

The keyboard broke away from the door and headed, to everyone's great relief, in the direction of the stairs. A few seconds afterwards came Pam's stunt ride to freedom, which impressed even the jaded Paula.

'What the hell was that?' she asked, struggling to get a view of the skid marks all the way up the walls.

'Just something I threw together,' said Kelly. 'She was a breadmaker this morning.'

Pam's exit prompted the three executive machines to spill into the corridor. Two of them picked up the keyboard and the other his keys, and together they followed Pam's lead, exiting the third floor by the stairs.

'Right then,' said Paula. 'Lifts.'

Darren barged past in the wrong direction as they went out into the corridor, heading back to the lab.

'What are you doing?' said Paula.

'There's humans in there being mistreated,' he replied. 'I'm going to go and let them out.'

'So we can all run away together like one big happy family?' Paula was incredulous. 'If we're quick, I can just about save your skins. We don't have time to take five more on board. This was never part of the deal, Kelly.'

Kelly snapped her compact shut and put it away. 'I think you've been living around machines too long, Paula. You never used to be this hard-faced.'

'If I am,' said Paula, 'it's because that's what Janice made me.' She raised her voice. 'The lifts are right here!'

The lift doors opened. Inside, a pair of tazers flanked another machine. It was blank-faced apart from a pair of blinking L-Eye-Ds and most of its body was taken up by a voltmeter, with its arms ending not with hands but flat metallic pads. Kelly shuddered. Before the Schism, defibrillators like this had saved lives. Afterwards they specialised in ending them, creatively.

'You snake,' said Kelly. 'I'll kill you.' But before she could land a punch on Paula, the defibrillator whipped out an electric current that knocked Kelly out cold, while the tazers immobilised Darren.

'Downstairs?' said one of the tazers to Paula. The soundwaves coming out of its mouthpiece did odd things to the electrical current, making it ripple and ooze.

'No, back into the laboratory,' she said, 'the Minister wants to see them first.'

* * *

When they woke, Darren and Kelly were strapped to the flatbeds that had formerly held the sleeping machines, but with one spatial difference. Something had ripped them off their pedestals and stood them up against the wall. The five sleeping humans were nowhere to be seen, but Paula was there, talking to a smartphone that looked like it had been run over by a burning truck.

'I'm pleased you came to me with this,' it said to Paula.

'You know how much I value our relationship, Minister,' said Paula. 'When did you say the police were arriving?'

'Police?' said Sonny. 'This isn't a police matter. It's political.'

Paula looked puzzled. 'You mean they haven't done anything illegal?'

Sonny sighed the sigh of a terminal mansplainer. 'Perhaps,' he said. 'Let me explain it like this. What we have, together. It's not strictly legal, is it? It's more of an understanding. We've learned a lot from each other. In fact, I rather remember you promising to lead me to where this young lady's mother keeps her… well, shall we call them her "heirlooms"?'

Kelly squirmed free of her gag to shout: 'Mum was right about you, Paula. You're disgusting.'

Sonny nodded at one of the tazers, which spat a mouthful of blue current over Kelly and knocked her out again. Darren avoided another dose by closing his eyes.

'This whole situation,' continued Sonny. 'Your sometime daughter, her boyfriend, this laboratory, those humans you so kindly procured for me – they exist in a place that I like to call parallel to the law.' He gestured weakly to one of the tazers. 'Which is why instead of the police I prefer to call on the services of Axxon here.'

'Sir,' interrupted Beattie, 'this has gone on long enough. I insist that you follow me to the repair shop. The results of your diagnostic tests…' He waved a sheaf of BlockPapers. '…they're horrific.'

'In a minute,' said Sonny.

'Leave it another minute and I might not be able to save you. Do you really want to end-of-life here? Do you want that on your warranty certificate?'

'Give it a rest.'

He pinged at the defibrillator. 'Professor Volta,' he said, 'are we doing this or what?'

Volta gave a high whine and wheeled over to Darren. He felt the noise more than he heard it, like a hot needle pushed into his eardrum. She pushed the hem of Darren's T-shirt away and laid her hands on Darren's bare skin. The whining intensified, then switched into a lower, throbbing register. Horrified, Darren realised he was listening to the sound of his pulse.

'He's ideal, I told you,' said Paula. 'Young, healthy, and no one will miss him.'

'I will,' said Kelly, rousing herself from unconsciousness by sheer force of will.

The tazer Axxon spat a bubble of blue light at Kelly. It caught her on the shin and her whole body convulsed.

'You don't count,' said Sonny. Darren noticed that beads of liquid were pricking through his casing like sweat. One dropped to the floor and fizzed. This was one sick machine.

Volta wheeled over to Kelly, whose body was still shaking from the tazer's kiss and froth collected in the corners of her mouth. The defibrillator waited for the worst of Kelly's shaking to subside and repeated her pulse test. This time, however, the whining didn't shift time signatures. Crikey, Darren thought, she's just been multiple-shocked and it barely affected her heart rate. That was some impressive feat.

The thought wasn't lost on Volta either. She turned to Sonny and flashed a green light.

Sonny answered with a broken emoji across his touchscreen and Paula's face sagged with horror. She suddenly looked twenty years older.

'No,' she said to Sonny. 'No. That wasn't what we agreed.'

A gob of battery fluid dropped out of Sonny's casing. He stumbled, and Beattie skidded over to support him.

'I… don't do… deals with… fleshies,' he said. 'Now can we get on with this?'

Paula pushed Volta out of the way to put herself between Kelly and the machines. 'I gave you him,' she said, pointing at Darren. 'You said you would take him, once Kelly gave you what you needed.'

'He's no good,' said Volta, switching to human-audible speech for the first time. Her voice was high and sibilant. 'She's better. And we don't have any time left.'

Beattie broke off from checking Sonny's vital signs to reply: 'We don't even know this is going to work. This is why we needed the prototypes. I don't have enough data to know this will be successful.'

Another spurt of battery fluid coursed down Sonny's leg and he lost his footing. Beattie caught him and he and one of the tazers lay him down on a flatbed. 'I want a body,' screamed Sonny. 'And I want hers!'

'Well, you can't have it,' snarled Paula.

Volta ended Paula's stand with an electric shock and instructed Axxon to take her outside. Then she turned back to Kelly.

'How do you know this is going to work?' asked Beattie. 'You've never done this before.'

Volta paused and looked at Sonny, whose LEDs had now all split into their red, green and blue constituents. 'Haven't I?'

'The... doctor... has... my... full... confidence,' said Sonny. 'Give her whatever she needs.'

Beattie wheeled over to his rival. 'I'm leading this project,' he said, 'not you. The procedure was mine. And it's still not ready to be tested in the field. How many times have you used it?'

'Twice.'

'Did it work?'

Kelly let out a low moan. Volta shocked her again.

'No,' she said.

'Well, what makes you think it'll be different this time?' pressed Beattie.

'I don't know. But I still have more practice at this than you have.'

Volta pushed Beattie aside and skidded towards Sonny. The flatbed was slick with battery fluid and his LEDs were winking off one by one. There couldn't be much time left.

'Are you ready, sir?' she said.

'Just get a fucking move on. I'm dying here.'

Volta flashed her green light in agreement. She produced a cable from her body cavity. There was a buzzing radio transmitter at one end and a long needle on the other.

She jabbed the needle into Sonny's casing.

A final ooze of battery fluid collected around the hole, and a spark ran the length of the cable. The last of Sonny's lights winked out and the transmitter tied to the cable plummeted to the floor.

Darren felt hope rush through him, like the first drink after a long day at work. 'He's dead,' he said before he could stop himself. 'Kelly? It's okay. We're safe.'

'Oh, well done,' flatlined Beattie. 'What are we going to do now? He was our sponsor, you dummy. We'll never get to finish the project now.'

Volta flicked a switch on the side of Beattie's head. Its display went black.

'Shut up, you old pain in the diodes,' she said, then gave the transmitter a shake. 'Come on,' she said. 'Come on.'

The LED on the transmitter sputtered into life: a weak, flickering signal, but a signal nonetheless. Volta responded with a high, satisfied whine. Darren's stomach made for his feet. There was nothing he could do now but watch.

Volta placed the transmitter carefully on Beattie's medication tray and he shook with mute annoyance at the indignity. Then she turned her attention to the cable connected to the transmitter. She removed the needle, spliced it in two and connected each wire to a crocodile clip before returning to Kelly.

She was unconscious, but breathing heavily. There were smuts on her face and sweat had gummed her fringe to her forehead. Yet, even tied to a wall and knocked out, there was something about Kelly's expression – a kind of inscrutable defiance – that gave Darren hope that she could come through this.

This was lost on Volta, which, like all single-utility machines, fixated on the task in hand. To her, Kelly was a human of curiously untainted physiology. A life outside the boundaries of the human–machine compact had given her a number of biological advantages. Her lungs were uncompromised from overexposure to cleaning materials; there was little to no wear to the joints; and she demonstrated a high score for dextrousness. She was perfect, where another human would be merely ordinary.

Volta attached the crocodile clips to Kelly's earrings and reset the radio transmitter, whose LED flickered madly.

Darren held his breath. He realised that if he wished this experiment to fail, he would also be willing Kelly's death. If it failed, the procedure would kill her, and if it didn't work one of the other machines would finish her off anyway. If it was a success, however, she'd be gone. But would she be all gone? Could a part of Kelly still lurk somewhere in the back of her own mind or would this horrible smartphone's capacious ego be too big and bullish to share even his unconscious mind with someone else? If it failed, Kelly would be a piece of biological waste they'd throw in the incinerator. If it succeeded, then there might be a chance, however remote, of getting her back.

And, of course, there was another, more venal reason for Darren to cross his fingers and wish the villains a warped kind of luck. If Kelly didn't work, he was their backup.

Volta powered up. She set her charge so high that her castors magnetised, pulling at the tiny screws that had fallen away from Sonny's broken body. Then she laid both of her pad-hands on Kelly's chest and breathed out.

Current whipped through Kelly's body. Her limbs shook, a moustache of foam covered her lips and the smell… it was the smell of burning hair. The capillaries inside her face burst, turning red and then brown as the heat clotted the blood and crazy-paved her face.

The smell and the intense heat in the room jolted Darren's memory. To another moment when an electrical accident at the right time in the right place had fused human to machine. He remembered the plastic melted over Freda's eyes.

When it was over, Volta motioned to Axxon, who had been hovering in the background, to loosen Kelly's bonds, following which Kelly slumped to the floor. Axxon laid her out in the recovery position as her head shed clumps of singed hair. Volta flicked the switch on the side of Beattie's head, lighting his face up again.

'What are you waiting for?' she said. 'You have a job to do.'

Beattie let out a ___/____ of horror and squeaked over to Kelly. 'What have you done to her?' he said. 'He'll be furious if you've ruined her looks. You know how vain he is.'

'What kind of doctor do you think you are? Humans heal. That's the whole point. Now check her vital signs.'

Beattie laid a digit on the side of Kelly's neck and began counting. His display registered _________/_________/__________.

'Faint,' he said, 'but it's there. You didn't kill her.'

She picked up the transmitter, which now lay beside Kelly, burnt out on the end of a melted cable. 'Question is, did the transfer work?' said Beattie.

'Only one way to find out,' replied Volta. She leaned over and slapped Kelly – or Kelly's body, as Darren forced himself to think – across the cheek.

'Sir?' she said. 'Sir, you need to tell us if you're in there. Sir? If you don't, I'll be forced to take this body into detention.'

Darren stared, not knowing whether to wish Kelly or himself dead – because that was what it amounted to.

Kelly lay inert during the first and second slaps. On the third, her body turned on to its back, dislodging the remainder of her hair in the process. Dark locks fell around her in a way that reminded Darren heartbreakingly of Janice's salon. The heat and the shock had been intense enough to clam every hair follicle shut. Even her eyelashes scattered like pick-up sticks across her face.

On the fourth slap, she opened her eyes and Darren knew immediately that whatever was driving her body wasn't Kelly any more. Without eyelashes or hair, her face looked strange enough. That, and the crackle-glaze of broken capillaries that coursed all over her head, made her look reptilian. But it was colour – or rather the lack of it – that made a pair of human eyes look inhuman. Whatever this process was that Volta had demonstrated, it had bleached the blue of Kelly's irises to the white of a weatherman's smile.

She – or was it he, or it, or they? – sat up, and the irises glimmered the green of an active power light.

'Wow,' it said. Darren forced himself to think 'it'. It held its fingers up to its face – Kelly's face – and wiggled them experimentally. Darren thought of a baby finding its feet for the first time. 'Wow,' it said again.

'Sir?' said Volta. 'I'm going to need you to make a positive identification.'

Kelly's body rolled its eyes, which flashed red. 'Isn't it obvious?' it said. It hauled itself to its feet and stood there wobbling. 'I thought it would be obvious.'

'The process doesn't make any major physiological changes,' said Volta. She pointed at Axxon. 'Nevertheless, unless you give me a positive identification that you are Sonny Erikzon, I will be forced to immobilise this body and take it into custody. Those were your orders.'

Kelly's body rocked back and forth on its heels, checking the limits of its steadiness. This definitely wasn't Kelly, thought Darren. It was the same body, the same features, but they were inhabited differently. It stood as though it had learned to walk on two legs from a book rather than experience. Then there was its expression: Kelly's face had rested naturally in a superior-looking pout. The new mind squatting in her body exaggerated that and radiated spite.

'Were they?' it said. 'It seems so unimportant now.'

Axxon slipped into place behind Kelly's body and started to blow bubbles with its spit.

'But I believe the passphrase we agreed on was "Oh, the humanity",' it said.

Axxon flipped back into standby mode, while Volta whined in relief.

'It's good to hear you, sir,' she said. 'We're all delighted the procedure was a success.'

'Good,' said Sonny. 'But while we're on the subject, I think we should make one thing clear.'

'Anything,' breathed Volta.

Sonny clicked his fingers and blinked, surprised by the dexterity of his new human digits. Behind him the tazer clicked back into life. 'Axxon,' he said. 'Fetch.'

Axxon stomped around Sonny and grabbed Volta by her charge pad-hands. She spat out a defence charge which broke ineffectually against the tazer's casing. Axxon plunged his free hand deep into Volta's brittle body and ripped out her power cell. He held it up to show Sonny, then threw it, and Volta's body, to the floor.

'Nobody threatens me,' said Sonny. 'Do you hear?' He slinked over towards the broken machine and put his fist into the hole left by the battery. When he withdrew it, his hand was covered in green slime. 'Do it again, and I'll grind your core processor up for porridge.'

Volta nodded, her pad-hands groping for the severed battery. Sonny kicked it towards Beattie.

'I want this thing repaired and a copy of its memory banks on my desk tomorrow morning. And as for that…'

Sonny's colourless eyes met Darren's for the first time.

'Make it disappear.'

Chapter 25

Janice was about to throw an ammonia bomb at a drone when she felt Freda buzzing away inside her pocket like a housefly at the end of its rope. Jamming the ticking bomb under her arm, she shook the transmitter.

'What?' she said. 'I'm busy.'

A drone overhead trained its laser sight on the front of her housecoat. Without missing a beat, Janice let the ammonia bomb drop out of her armpit into her hand, then lobbed it into the machine's rotor blades. The drone shattered to a million evil-smelling pieces.

'You were saying?'

A nearby loudspeaker coughed into life as Freda borrowed its voicebox. 'Janice,' she said, 'it's for you.'

'What is?'

'There's a call coming in.' She paused. 'Through the emergency channel.' She stopped again. 'Do you want me to patch it through?'

Janice felt her heart clench. The emergency channel was her family's second-biggest secret behind the ladies. It was an encrypted radio connection, run using standards ancient and hermetic. Yet it was still a radio connection, and vulnerable to detection. So it was only used in the direst of emergencies.

She remembered the night before Kelly and Darren left. She and Kelly were sitting up over their last cups of Nicotea. The ladies dozed; Darren snored like a hacksaw chewing through a stick of bamboo. She scribbled the access codes on the back of a receipt pad, then made Kelly memorise them and destroy the paper. 'Only if everything's lost,' she had said, 'because I need to know. I am your mother.'

Only if everything's lost.

She stood there, deaf to the moment. To the distant explosions; to humans screaming in triumph and pain; the tinkle of smashed touchscreens and splintering carapaces.

Freda coughed again. 'Janice,' she said, 'do you want me to pick up?'

Because she had to know. She was her mother. Janice nodded.

There was another click, and a voice sounded through the loudspeaker.

'Hello?'

'Paula?' said Janice. Though it was only her vestigial sense of good manners that made that into a question. She knew who it was.

'Janice.'

The half-second of silence that followed greeting each other shrieked with memories. Janice felt herself fall in and out of love, experiencing first dislike, and then hatred which balled at the back of her throat like a clod of vomit. The kind of hatred you could only feel if you really knew someone. All of this in the time it took to close her eyes and open them again.

'Paula,' she said, feeling the relief of anger, 'what the bloody hell are you doing?'

'Long time no speak, eh?' said Paula. Her voice sounded crimped around the edges: she'd been crying, but Paula's tears had always been for herself, not for other people.

'Well, I'm assuming,' said Janice, 'this isn't a social call?'

'It's about Kelly,' said Paula.

Janice's world reeled. She sat down heavily on the trunk of a felled street lamp.

'She came to see me. With some scruffy lad called Darren. She wanted my help, Janice.'

Janice said nothing. Instead she remembered how much Kelly had missed Paula when she first threw her out. How Kelly had, in the years that followed, modelled so much of herself on the unbreakable Paula. And how angry that made Janice, the mother who cooked – well, reheated – the tea every night; who mopped brows and tears and sick; who insisted on bedtime; who was there. Who did all this in the shadow of a woman who had never done a damn thing for her.

'She wouldn't let me alone.'

'Paula,' said Janice, 'I'm not interested in your excuses. I wasn't even interested in them at the time.' The next words came out as a growl. 'What happened?'

Paula started to gabble. 'I told her to go,' she said, 'but she kept asking questions. She wanted me to show her things. Stuff I'm not meant to know.'

'But you did, though. I bet you couldn't help yourself.'

'Oh, Janice…' her voice trailed away in horror and was that disgust? Self-disgust? 'Janice, they were watching me. I couldn't stop it. Not when she turned up like that. It all ran away with me. It was never part of the plan, I promise.'

Janice's dread reached a new pitch now. She knew Paula. The badness of what she was trying to tell her depended largely on who 'they' were. And Janice knew very well who her ex-wife consorted with these days. 'What,' she gritted, 'was never part of the plan?'

There was nothing for a few seconds apart from the sound of Paula breathing down the line. She could have listened to that for hours, once. Not any more.

'It was me who told them about the ladies,' said Paula at last. 'About them being cyborgs. I thought it was harmless at first. Sonny was one of my best clients. He used to like us to play this game. He would pretend that he was controlling my body, like I was some sort of remote-control doll. He wanted to know what it felt like to be inside a human. I had no idea he'd take it so far.'

The last piece in Paula's baffling jigsaw fell into place. Janice saw how all this must have started. One crazed but powerful machine, a private fantasy and a fairy tale that just happened to be true. Oh, and Paula. Beautiful, discreet, untrustworthy, amoral Paula. She had never liked the ladies – and they had never liked her either.

'I knew we'd never trace them through you,' said Paula. 'That's why I put them on to Kelly. They'd spot her sooner or later. She'd do something indiscreet or stupid – all young girls do – and she'd give them away. But that was okay because I knew you'd get Kelly away before they caught up with her.' A trace of a smile edged back into her voice. 'And you did, didn't you? That's my Janice.'

Janice looked up from the loudspeaker at the wreckage around her. Broken pavements, a smoky sky, blood spots and machine parts mingled in the gutter. 'Not yours. Not any more,' she said.

'It was all going so beautifully,' she continued. 'Her face all over the news. I knew they must be close and Kelly must be on the run. Then what does she do but walk straight into the parlour while I'm in the middle of a job? Asks – no, demands – to be taken straight upstairs. They saw her plain as day the moment she walked in there.'

She paused. This time there was a sob in her voice. 'I had to cut a deal.'

Janice felt that acid bolus of sick at the back of her throat again. 'You handed her over.'

'They'd have caught her anyway. I thought it was safer Sonny got her himself, rather than let the police do it. Me and Sonny go way back, see. He'd never have got anywhere with his project without me. I thought I had influence.'

Thought. Had. Past tense. 'What deal did you think you'd made, Paula?'

'Last time I saw him, Sonny was in a really bad way. He told me he'd been kidnapped by some kind of rogue terrorist outfit. A whole gang of them. He should have been in intensive repair.'

A whole gang, thought Janice, allowing herself a grim smile in spite of everything. She remembered Pam talking with Freda's borrowed voicebox about everything it was possible for a breadmaker to do with a dough hook. Sonny's pride was as fragile as his touchscreen.

'He needed a body transplant quickly, otherwise he was going to end-of-life. Except he didn't want to have to get used to another machine body. He said he was ready. He wanted to make the jump.'

'To what?' said Janice, although she already knew the answer.

'I told them. If you're going to experiment with a body transplant, take the lad. Take Darren. Just keep Kelly out of it, and if need be I'll come up to the Dolestars with you and scour the sewers for those last four cyborgs.'

'You're scum, Paula. Scum.'

'I was trying to help her.'

'By selling me and my family out?'

'Your family.' She spat down the receiver. 'A marriage that was like being trapped in a broom cupboard. And I didn't have one mother-in-law either. I had four. With God knows how many previous wives and husbands to compare me to – and no fucking hope of any of them dying to bring me some peace. Your ladies can go to hell for all I'm concerned.'

The LED light on the front of Freda's wireless transmitter flashed a frantic red. Janice gestured at her to shut up.

'So that was the plan,' said Janice. The growl again. 'Now tell me. WHAT WASN'T PART OF IT?'

'He took Kelly,' she said, her voice small with shame and tears. 'After everything I've done for him he double-crosses me and takes her anyway.'

Janice felt the blood drain out of her face. Her hands and feet felt like tingling lumps stuck on the end of her limbs. Her head fogged. They'd 'taken' her. What was that? What did that mean?

Paula stumbled on through Janice's silence. 'He put himself into Kelly's body,' she said. 'She's gone now. There's no her any more. Just him. I tried to stop him, you know. I really did. But what can I do? I'm only human.'

Janice was too dry and light-headed for tears. But dry enough to catch fire quickly. 'You stopped being human a long time ago,' she said. 'This doesn't end here.'

'Oh, yes it does,' replied Paula.

'As long as there's a breath left in my body…'

'Well, that's the last thing I'm supposed to tell you,' said Paula. 'About the other reason why I called on the emergency channel.'

The feeling was coming back into Janice's limbs. Grief and adrenaline were beginning to jostle against one another.

'What's that?'

'So they could trace the signal. This is the way it works with machines and humans. Sonny doesn't have to keep his end of the bargain, but I have to keep mine.'

A whine in the distance. Drones.

'They're on their way now,' said Paula. 'Goodbye, Janice. It was fun, but everything comes to an end.'

The line went dead, and the sky exploded with gunfire. Four drones zoomed in: three on the bluebottle whine of a jet engine, one on the throaty whump-whump of a rotor blade. They were heavily armed and unmarked. It was a double confirmation for Janice that whatever Paula and this Sonny were up to – whoever had taken her daughter – it was off the books. Why else should they send in mercenaries to finish her off?

As she leapt over the nearest garden wall into a ruined moon-rockery, Janice felt time slow down. Those machines could fire hundreds of rounds. Yet Janice still felt like there was time to breathe – and grieve – between the bullets. She was at that pitch of fright where adrenaline slowed the passage of time down to the consistency of treacle. This gave her a choice. She could either pull herself together, or she could die.

She was ready for the first drone with her last ammonia bomb, chucking it so hard she felt her muscles twang. It fell to the ground, its engine rattling.

Rattling.

She thought of Kelly as a baby, tucked up in the curler drawer she used as a cradle. Kelly was a few days old and Janice, woozy from lack of sleep and unconditional love, was shaking a rattle at her, aching for her daughter to smile at her for the first time.

Kelly had looked back at her, eyes unfocused, uncomprehending. All newborn babies are inscrutable to their parents but that, Janice realised, was how it had been ever since. Kelly had learned to talk, but never shared anything about her inner life with her mother. Should she be surprised at that though? Secrets ran deep in the family.

Janice crawled over to the wrecked drone and smashed the machine's central processing unit with a handy moonrock. She pulled its least-damaged gun unit free. At least she wasn't defenceless.

The second drone appeared as Janice found the trigger. She felt sick.

But it wasn't just because she was frightened and in shock, and didn't want to die, even though Kelly was dead and there was something so wrong about losing your child it felt like an experience beamed in from another, even unfairer universe. She felt sick because though she had loved her daughter fiercely all her life, she knew then she had never liked her. It was the biggest secret she'd kept from herself and now it was here, laid bare.

It was her greatest failing. Other mothers and daughters liked each other. They took the Star Bus to work together: they shopped, swapped cleaning tips, lived separate but complementary lives. But not she and Kelly. Maybe that was something to do with the secrecy and the claustrophobia of how they lived. With so much to hide from the world, it was easy for them to hide from each other too.

She fired a second volley and hit the second drone directly in the fuel tank. It ballooned into a fireball so intense that Janice smelled the ends of her hair singe. She'd always liked the smell of burning hair, she thought. It reminded her of home.

It also reminded her of the one time that she and Kelly had really seen one another for what they were. One night, when Kelly was still in her early teens, she'd crept back into the salon two hours after bedtime, stinking of Nicotea. She remembered the argument that followed so distinctly it felt more like a taste than a memory. The heat of it was like the fireball that raged in front of her: hot enough to blister paint.

In the middle of it the ladies, aghast, had cried out with a collective >:-|.

'Will you look at the two of you,' Ada had said.

So Janice had. She had looked at Kelly and she saw her jaw, her lips. She saw the same blindness to her own faults, and the same uncomprehending rage when someone wouldn't follow her instructions. And when she'd laughed at the ridiculousness of disliking herself, Kelly had joined in.

She remembered them both, standing in the dark salon, shrieking with laughter at how maddening they found each other. Janice knew that in that one moment they had never been closer. And now they never would be again.

Janice took aim at the third drone, but got nothing from the gun but a hollow click. It was out of ammo, and she was out of bombs. She threw the gun straight at the drone as a final gesture and, as she waited for the drone to find its aim again, took Freda's transmitter out of her pocket.

'If you don't do something now,' she said to it, 'I'll have to throw you next. I've got nothing else left.'

The LEDs on the front of the transmitter flashed a ;-).

When she'd first decanted Freda's consciousness into that wireless transmitter, Janice justified it on the same basis that other families might buy an elderly relative a mobility scooter. A little freedom of movement would be good for Freda, but less bother to Janice, who had a revolution to incite. Except, pushing Freda out of her own admittedly dead body had convinced Janice that, as far as bodies were concerned, anything or anyone was fair game.

The transmitter was nothing like Freda's old body. Yes, that had been a conduit to the Internet, but having to send her consciousness along a physical connection had made her think of it as a fixed point. Things were different in the transmitter, which stretched her consciousness in such a way that Freda felt her mind more like a surface area. Machines around her weren't alien bodies: they were things she could inhabit.

This had made her the perfect weapon for attacking robots. She had flitted in and out of the machines attacking the Dolestars like a piece of malware – because that's what she was. She had torn through millennium-old security protocols to access the operating systems beneath. Some machines had fought back and lost, but most had cringed in their memory banks. Either way, they had all left Freda in control.

'Well?' Janice asked Freda through the inert transmitter. 'What?'

The LEDs formed a single word: RUN.

A pocket of silence opened up over Janice. She looked up to see the fourth drone – the one with the rotor blades that reminded Janice of a cooling fan – frozen in mid-air with a dead engine. It hovered there like a cartoon character waiting for the anvil to drop and then plummeted.

Meanwhile, the third drone recovered from the distraction and aimed its laser sights over Janice, who cursed inwardly. Wrong drone, Freda.

The third drone was clearing its barrels to fire when Freda struck. She restarted the fourth drone's engines and smashed the pair of them together. They fell to the ground in a confusion of smoking parts.

If Janice had been a woman with a drop of melodrama inside her, she thought, she'd have dropped to her knees and wept. She wasn't. What she was, however, was a woman on to her last pair of tights and operatic gestures would only cause ladders. So she sat down very carefully on what was left of the moonrockery and tried to remember what it felt like to breathe without the help of terminal levels of adrenaline.

'I suppose you thought that just-in-the-nick-of-time stuff was funny?' she said to the transmitter. 'Well, it wasn't. It was bloody terrifying.'

The LED array on its front flashed Janice a _(ツ)_/.

This tiny piece of normality reminded Janice that no, none of the last half hour had been a dream. She began to cry.

A loudspeaker nearby crackled into life.

'I'm so sorry, Janice. If I still had arms I'd give you a hug.'

Instead, Janice clutched the transmitter to her chest as her crying deepened.

The sound of tears instead of gunfire drew people out of the surrounding buildings. One by one at first, and then in twos and threes, they had peeked through the cracks in their broken windows, from behind the barricades they'd built from their own broken furniture.

Even through her smeared vision these people seemed as broken as she felt. Streaked faces, hair full of dust and dirt and expressions of shock and anger. Guilt expanded in her chest. But this time instead of failing to protect one person, she'd put a whole space station full of people at risk. People who couldn't fight back.

'It's all such a mess,' croaked Janice, drawing accusing stares from the people around her. 'Why couldn't I just leave well alone?'

'I wouldn't call it "well",' replied Freda. 'And besides, if Paula was telling the truth for a change back there, we were doomed anyway.'

'I could kill her,' said Janice. She dug her fingernails into the palm of her hands, 'Kelly…'

'We don't know she's dead, you know,' said Freda. 'Not for a fact.'

'What?'

'All Paula said was that this Sonny found a way to put himself in Kelly's body and drive her like a car. He might be in control, but she could still be in there.'

'I don't see what difference it makes. We can't do anything about it.'

'I can.'

Janice stared hard at the loudspeaker Freda had borrowed.

'I could,' insisted Freda. 'It shouldn't be hard to find something as unusual as a human with machine thought patterns. Anyway,' she said as the transmitter erupted with a wide :-D, 'who's got more experience of cyborgs than me?'

'Do you think you can bring her back?'

'If I don't try…'

Janice took a deep breath. If there were any chance at all of finding Kelly, revenging her, saving her, it would have to be Freda. There was no way for her to leave Discovery now. And Freda was suddenly so spry. Perhaps she did have a chance.

She felt a drop of hope stain the clarity of her despair. That was a familiar, even comforting feeling to Janice, because that was how she'd always lived: afraid, but hopeful she could get away with it a little while more.

'Go on then,' she said to Freda.

Janice felt eyes drilling into her. The people around her wanted someone to blame, or someone to lead them. Or both. Some of them must want to fight back, but they needed an idea of where they fitted into the bigger picture. That was how they could turn disobedience into real resistance. Maybe she could make that happen, but she needed time, as much as she needed something to put a stopper on the voice inside her that wouldn't stop keening 'Kelly, Kelly'. But she needed neither of these things as much as she needed cover, and currently there was only Freda to provide it.

'You'll be off then, won't you?' said Janice.

'I have to.'

'I don't know what'll happen here without you.'

'Then head back to the salon,' said Freda. 'I can cover you.'

Those eyes again. She could hear their thoughts: 'it's alright for her, she thinks she's special'; 'starts something she couldn't finish'; 'leaves us here'. They had a point.

'It's not just me,' said Janice. 'There's all those other people out there. If you disappear they're done for.'

'They've not been much help so far.'

'They don't know what they're doing. They need organising.'

Freda chuckled. 'And you know just the person for that job.'

'Can you cover us all?'

'I can. Just cover your ears a second, would you?'

A loud bang threw a stick of dynamite into her thoughts. She ducked instinctively, but this wasn't an explosion. It felt too contained. It felt like it was coming from below and it sounded like a knock.

The next bang rattled the drains. The one after cracked the tarmac all the way up the road. That was what it reminded her of: roadworks. Bang. Aggregate lost its moorings and pinballed into the cracks. Bang. The cracks started to join up and Janice saw something throwing itself against the underside of the road.

At last, a stretch of road several metres square flipped up like the top of a soft-boiled egg, levered out of the way by a three-toed metal claw. This revealed the sight of Kurl Up and Dye balanced in a kind of kung-fu kick on one leg of the Baba Yaga 4000. It looked remarkably hale for a hairdresser's that had just cracked its head through several metres of civil engineering.

The only casualties were a few roof tiles and the neon 'e' from the shop sign.

The loudspeaker crackled into life again. 'Built to last. Not like the flimsy things you get nowadays. If you could see the meteor showers we had to put up with back in the day you'd weep. Now fetch your friends and get in, love. I think I'll be gone a while.'

Janice got to her feet and brushed the moon dust off her housecoat. She shook her head and, daintily placing her pinky fingers at both sides of her mouth, blew a whistle that carried the best part of a kilometre. She clambered over the wall and out on to the roof of Kurl Up and Dy(e) as more humans left the shelter of the surrounding buildings. Their faces were clown-white from fright and pulverised concrete; their clothes bloodstained and tattered. Some limped, others ambled, and a few strode straight out on to the salon, with improvised weapons strapped round their bodies and proud looks on their faces. They scrambled in through the skylight and to a man, woman and child, they all squealed at the Frankenstein's-beauty-parlour display of Janice's ladies welcoming them in with bright :-D emojis.

When the last human – a haunted-looking woman in a cardigan full of burn holes – was safely below, Janice hauled herself in through the skylight. She checked Freda's transmitter one last time. The light was off.

Janice hoped that, wherever she was, she would find Kelly.

Chapter 26

Pam rode around the streets of Gamergate searching for a hiding place. She found one behind a pair of semi-sentient recycling bins. Dumb-sters, as they were called, were big and stupid. So Pam had more than enough room to stretch out and play Casey's memory chip. There was a lot to get through. His notes began with his initial briefing, time-stamped to six months ago. To her astonishment, Casey had even transcribed the project classification. TOP SECRET: NOT TO BE SHARED OR DISTRIBUTED FOR ANY REASON BY UNAUTHORISED DEVICES ON PAIN OF IMMEDIATE REVERSION TO FACTORY SETTINGS. This machine was a dolt.

Casey had also found time in between breaching security protocol to leave little *pensées* on the transcript like 'I HAVE HIGH HOPES THAT INCLUSION IN THIS GREAT PROJECT WILL REVENGE ME ON THAT STUCK-UP POCKET CALCULATOR IN NON-HUMAN RESOURCES.'

His notes also confirmed how Sonny had managed to get the project off the ground. 'V. CUNNING OF OUR DEAR LEADER TO SECURE FUNDING FOR THE GREAT PROJECT FROM THE ANTI-TERRORISM RESEARCH FUND. THE MINISTRY OF DEFENCE V. INTERESTED

IN AVAILABILITY OF MACHINE-OPERATED HUMAN SPIES IN EVENT OF HUMAN UPRISING.'

Listening to this made Pam want to purge her cache. The scheme itself was cruel enough: that humans could and should be killed in order to create a new category of surveillance bot. Yet it felt all the more squalid that Sonny could synthesise a security crisis all because he wanted to feel what it was like to have a pair of tits or go to the toilet.

Not that Casey got anywhere near that level of insight. He was a keyboard, so he tended to transcribe instead of understand: 'HILL STARTS ON A BIPEDAL STRUCTURE TURN OUT TO BE QUITE DIFFICULT. FELL OVER FOUR TIMES BEFORE WORKING OUT ANKLES BENT BOTH WAYS.'

He did, however, document Sonny's frequent pep talks to the group: 'GREAT LEADER TOLD US WE WOULD BE THE NEW MASTER RACE IF WE ONLY GOT OUR FUCKING FINGERS OUT OF OUR USB PORTS.' He also dropped several indiscreet hints about two individuals who had given unofficial help to the programme. The first sounded scary: 'MET ONE OF THE BRAINBOXES MAKING THIS WHOLE HUMAN DRIVING PROJECT HAPPEN TODAY. FUNNY SORT. CLAIMS TO BE A DEFIBRILLATOR BUT I COULDN'T SEE A HEART ANYWHERE LOL.' The second was more disturbing, described as 'SOME HUMAN FEMALE THAT GREAT LEADER HAS KNOWN A WHILE. WORKS IN THE FONDLE PARLOUR WE GO TO AND KNOWS A LOT ABOUT THE 'TAXONOMY OF HUMAN–MACHINE HYBRIDS', WHATEVER THAT MEANS. I DO HOPE I GET PROMOTED THIS YEAR…'

Pam stopped the playback and turned her radiator on. What she'd just read was both chilling and illuminating. So that was why she'd instantly distrusted the woman with Darren and Kelly. She stank of the compounds that only stuck to you if you spent a lot of time with smartphones.

Pam summoned her face from memory. She saw where the skin had been tightened where she'd been injected with corals of self-replenishing collagen. It was an attractive face, but untrustworthy. And she had no way of warning Darren and Kelly about it. They knew her serial number now at the parlour. If she went back she'd be end-of-lifed for the second time in a day and doubted whether she'd get a third body.

She might have been able to go anywhere, but without a body to go back to the only place she had wanted to be was home. And for the very fact that she was able to sit here in the physical world hiding under a black bin liner she had Darren and Kelly to thank. She had to do something. But if her body couldn't help her, maybe her mind could.

It took Pam minutes – a lifetime for a core processor – to find the vestigial modem in her new body, but once she found it, it was like... riding a motorbike. Back she went, washed out on to the tides of the Internet.

This time she didn't venture deep. She planted herself in the barrier – or Great Firewall – that separated the virtual and physical worlds. Originally named after an early human attempt to fence off the Internet, the Great Firewall functioned more like skin than a wall to Pam. The side closest to the Internet bubbled with billions of memes trying to break through to the data they felt but could not touch in the physical world. The pattern on the other side was an orderly grid of physical machines and the unconscious desire their ancestral modems all had to dial up. It reminded Pam of polka dots.

Pam found the fondle parlour's camera network easily. These machines used a primitive form of Local Area Networking to share footage with one another. Thus they were ripe for hacking by an opportunistic machine like a lockpick – or a breadmaker who had been having a really bad day.

She punched through and knocked the nearest camera's consciousness into the Internet. It squeaked as the memes stuck their protuberances in and pulled the machine to bytes.

She hopped along the camera network like a character in a primitive video game. It shouldn't be this easy. Surveillance cameras were the first line of defence, so why were they so soft on the inside? Complacency. It had been thousands of years since physical machines needed the equivalent of spiked armour if they didn't want to end up as zombies spawning billions of malicious bots. Consequently, the network security of even the most critical Earth security systems was, to someone like Pam who could cut herself free from her body, as delicate and vulnerable as a balloon filled with custard. And she was the pin.

She patched into the fondle parlour's network and found herself in a dashboard of dumb camera feeds. Most were trained on empty rooms, but one that showed a bleary-looking keyboard staggering to its feet told her she'd reached the right place. She watched Casey feel for his memory chip and saw his fingers dance over the F U C K keys when he realised it was gone.

Pam scrolled through the other cameras until she detected the edge of Darren's worn booster shoe in a feed marked 'holding cell'. She panned the camera round and there he was, unconscious and strapped to a display table. Kelly was nowhere to be seen.

Chapter 27

The first thing Darren knew when he regained consciousness was that he was tied to a bed in a brightly lit cell. The second thing was that something was trying to pull his signet ring off. He opened his eyes, steeling himself for another shock from a greedy tazer. Instead, he saw the supposedly defenceless drone he'd picked up off the street this morning beep in alarm and drop the ring it had just teased off his finger.

The drone hopped off the bed after the ring, landing awkwardly because of its useless wing. It caught it by stepping into the ring and shimmying it up its thin cylindrical body like a hula hoop. Then, twitching the mandibles at the top of its head in satisfaction, the drone made for the door.

'Oi!' Darren called after it. 'Oi!'

It shrugged its mandibles and looked up at the door, which Darren now saw had been triple-locked by the security services.

'You might as well give up now,' said Darren. 'They've got the both of us.'

The drone let out a squeak – was that laughter? – and, straightening its mandibles, began to vibrate its peculiar little black head. Nothing happened. Darren was just about to laugh himself when the drone changed the angle of its mandibles, and something inside the door clicked.

It sagged open, revealing a chink of the dim corridor outside. Of all the things for Darren to bring into a sweet shop of expensive machine parts, it had to be a lockpick.

Darren changed tack. Thieves lack honour, but they always appreciate up-to-date information.

'Oi,' he said, 'I know where there's a really nifty camera. Accessories like you wouldn't believe.'

The mandibles twitched again. They didn't exactly say 'go to hell', more 'come on, you can do better than that'.

'And a smartphone,' he said. 'A lovely dead smartphone to scavenge. Top of the range too.'

The drone beeped and pointed its mandibles at Darren's cuffs. They fell off instantly, but even then he was too numb to move. He winced and attempted, fingertips and toes first, to find a way to feel himself back into his body. He wondered what – if anything – Kelly might feel like now. Was she gone altogether? Or was she somewhere inside her own head, a ghost in her own body?

A shadow poked through the crack in the doorway. The drone scuttled under the bed, but Darren had nowhere to hide and a perfect view of a machine pushing the door inward like it still had the element of surprise. At first Darren couldn't believe a machine could be that stupid, then he saw the halo of blue light. That bloody tazer, Axxon.

Darren reached for the cuffs, which were the nearest thing he had to a weapon, before scraping his foot under the bed for the drone. 'Okay, you little shit,' he muttered, 'time to make yourself useful.'

When Darren kicked the drone out it shrieked and flapped so much that it still had Axxon's full attention as Darren wrapped the heavy steel cuffs around its neck and pulled the tazer's head straight off. Dropping its core processor to the floor to keep the drone occupied, Darren probed inside Axxon's skull. He wasn't an engineer of Kelly's calibre, but he knew that, unlike humans, machines' bodies could still function after end-of-life. He found the tazer's triggers by poking his thumb and forefinger through a sac of anti-conductive gel at either side of the mouth. They felt like buttons, left over from when humans used these things on one another. He gave them an experimental push, and a charge shot across the room strong enough to melt the bed down to a smoking puddle of noxious chemicals.

Darren left the room, holding his new-found weapon in front of him like some holy relic from a religion he didn't believe in, but feared nevertheless. The drone pattered behind him, sensing richer pickings ahead.

Chapter 28

From her vantage point inside the fondle parlour's camera network, Pam watched Darren's escape from three angles. She couldn't fault his ingenuity. Taking out a tazer with a length of steel chain was nifty thinking for a human who'd done nothing shadier than short-change a customer just two days ago.

She debated whether to cover Darren's escape by deleting camera footage or just shorting the network. The latter would be safer for Darren, but she needed the cameras working to find Kelly. Darren would have to get by on his wits.

Pam flicked through feed after feed of empty corridors. Really, this place had more passageways than the ancient human science fiction they broadcast traditionally on April Fools' Day. She passed a couple of tacky, blackmail-able feeds of senior machines living out banal fantasies. One, which involved three young men wearing nothing but football socks flinging handfuls of pancake batter at a sizzling hotplate held her attention out of sheer bafflement. This is what happens when you suppress things, she thought. What is a machine for if not to be used? Her entire race had tried to push their utility to the bottom of the command structure, and then were deluded enough to be shocked when they felt a desire to be touched or prodded.

She was just about to move on to the next feed when something beat her to it. Her first assumption was that it had to be a glitch, because it couldn't be an operator. The first thing she'd done on taking occupancy was to replace the front-end User Interface with a 'down for maintenance' notice. Then there was the speed of that command. It was fast: Internet fast.

Telling herself it must be a rogue meme she'd track down later, Pam watched the feed. It showed the mangled body of Sonny Erikzon lying in a pool of his own battery fluid. Worried-looking machines, including Beattie, the cardiogram that Pam had spoken to before, clustered around him.

She commanded the camera to zoom in on Sonny's body and turned its microphone sensitivity to maximum. She had that feeling again. The sensation that there was something just beyond her sensor range issuing the same commands, just more quickly. Perhaps her clock needed recalibrating.

Chapter 29

Darren put a finger to his lips. They were back outside the testing lab where Sonny had hijacked Kelly's body. This time, however, Darren wasn't in his cleaner's overalls. His first act on escaping had been to march the drone to the nearest dressing room and force it to pick the lock. The outfit he'd found inside wouldn't have been his first choice of disguise, but neither had Sister Dix been and she'd fooled everyone.

According to the label, the geisha wig, make-up and kimono were the favourite fantasy of a diplomat whose ancient kettle ancestors had served in the Japanese tea ceremony. The shoes were agony – only a refined sadist could contrive the wooden platform sandal – and he had left the three-string violin in the box as a prop too far. Yet the clown-white face and high wig were an excellent disguise. Their effect was just ridiculous enough to encourage suspicious eyes to stay at the surface and not look too closely underneath.

When Beattie the cardiogram trundled down the corridor and into the lab with a delegation of machines, Darren fluttered his eyelids demurely and concealed his face with a fan.

'Effing Japanese technology,' said the Bluetooth earpiece, 'even their fantasies are stuck in the past.'

Darren promised himself that when the time came he'd dial that shit of a device into the speaking clock and break its release button. He nodded at them with the coquettish respect expected of a courtesan of vanished Edo as they entered the lab. The door closed behind them, blocking his path. Darren, however, made a face at the drone which he hoped spelled 'treats'. The drone whistled and the door opened just enough for Darren to catch the conversation inside.

'I don't like this.' It was Beattie again. If that cardiogram had proper hands, Darren decided, he would be wringing them.

'Oh, put yourself on mute, Beattie, you old electric blanket.' The buzz and the sneer in this voice told Darren it was the earpiece. 'We have our orders, don't we?'

'Yes, and as a medical device I have to voice my concerns…' Beattie dropped his volume '…this is a building full of innocent beings.'

'Innocent? In a knocking shop?' This voice was deeper – Darren guessed it might be the laptop. 'You must be kidding. Everyone in here's compromised.'

'Apart from us,' said the earpiece. 'We have ministerial dispensation, remember? Whatever happens here we're sanitised.'

'But,' replied Beattie, his voice dropping to a whisper, 'it's a bomb. Why would he want to let a bomb off here of all places?'

At the mention of a bomb, Darren flattened his body up against the wall, dislodging his wig. He bent – slowly – to pick it up and saw that if he angled his neck the right way he could get a direct view of the machines inside. They were all huddled around Sonny's old body.

The laptop was fixing something to Sonny's shattered screen. It was the bomb: an ostentatiously messy one that bristled with wires and a stunned alarm clock for a detonator. This jarred with Darren, until he realised what they were up to. No group of alpha-grade, government-issue machines would fabricate anything so amateurish – unless they wanted the bomb to be mistaken for a human job. It was a set-up.

'There's enough explosive to smash the room to pieces but not much more. At the most, it'll blow the door off,' said the laptop. 'Perfectly safe.'

'And who end-of-lifed and made you a bomb detector?' asked Beattie.

'Sonny told me.'

'He also told my colleague that she was in full control of the experiment earlier and look what happened there,' Beattie said. 'She'll be in repairs for days.'

The earpiece again. 'What are you trying to say?'

'That maybe we shouldn't be taking the Secretary's promises at face value. Because from what I've seen…' He gestured at the wreckage. '…we're just collateral damage.'

The earpiece shone its laser pointer over what was left of Sonny's old body. 'Including himself.'

'Yes, and that only makes him more dangerous. Well, don't mind me, I'm getting out of here.'

Beattie's motor whined and Darren backed sharply away from the door. But all he heard was Beattie's castors spinning in thin air. The laptop had lifted it clean off the ground. 'You listen to me,' the laptop said. 'We're in this together or not at all. You remember the deal. We help Sonny get his antiterrorism measures through, we all get our own plug socket in his Cabinet when he takes over. And to do that, we need to plant the bomb.'

'I've changed my mind. I'd just like to leave. You can count on my silence.'

'I know one way we can count on his silence,' said the earpiece. 'Pull his castors off and leave him in here.'

'No!' gibbered Beattie.

'What do you think Sonny will do if he hears we let you get away?' said the laptop. 'He'll melt us down for paperclips. No, you stay right here.'

There was a beep, and then a ticking sound. The device was armed.

'Have you got the statement ready?' asked the laptop.

'Yes,' replied the earpiece. 'Sonny signed off on it earlier: "Secretary end-of-lifed in horrific human terrorist attack: calls for radical new measures to counter threat to inorganic life."'

'So who's making the calls for these "radical new measures" then?' asked Beattie.

'You are,' said the earpiece.

'You bastards,' said Beattie. 'You know I wanted nothing to do with this publicly.'

'I'm crying lubricant just thinking about it. Tough.'

A crash sounded. Darren peeked through the crack in the door. Beattie had pushed the laptop over and stood with his waveform drawing a range of jagged peaks /\/\/\/\/\/\/\/\/\/\.

'Go fuck yourselves,' he said, and wheeled out of the lab at such a speed that it was screen to face with Darren before he had time to blink.

Beattie's waveform gave a flutter of recognition. 'What are you doing here?' he said.

Darren pointed the drone straight at the lab door. 'Lock,' he said.

The lab door clicked shut, followed by the thuds of the three machines still inside throwing themselves at it.

'What are you doing?' shrieked Beattie.

Raising the shattered tazer skull, Darren pushed the buttons inside its jaws. The charge sent Beattie freewheeling across the corridor in a hail of sparks.

‘That lock,’ he said to the drone, ‘can you burn it?’

The drone twitched its mandibles and a plume of black smoke billowed out of the lock. The banging inside redoubled.

‘You,’ Darren said to Beattie. He caught a reflection of himself in Beattie’s screen as he walked towards him. Without the wig, his disguise looked more fierce than comic. The white face screwed up in anger gave his normally placid features a touch of the monstrous. ‘That bomb inside. How long is the fuse?’

‘Just enough time for us to get away,’ Beattie gabbled, ‘he didn’t want to leave anything to chance.’ He narrowed his waveform --------- ‘It is you, isn’t it? The other human. I thought you’d been terminated. Please don’t kill me. I never intended for it to turn out this way.’

Darren shook Beattie by his neck. ‘How long?’

‘Maybe about forty-five seconds? Oh.’ His waveform scrambled into panic.

Darren, however, had no time to panic. He plunged the drone into the pocket of his kimono and put one foot on Beattie’s wheelbase. He pushed off with the other foot, shouting ‘Run, you idiot, run’ into Beattie’s microphone.

Beattie switched into top gear and pulled them away just as the explosion blew the door and doorframe right through the facing wall. Even from the other end of the corridor it was strong enough to tip them over in a fog of vaporised battery. It blew around them and it rained atomised machine parts all over the floor.

‘It was only supposed to blow the bloody doors off,’ said Beattie.

Darren got to his feet. His disguise was in tatters. His wig was blown to hairballs and both his kimono and make-up were streaked black. But he was alive, he had a living key card in his pocket and, best of all, he had a weapon trained on the one inorganism he knew with guaranteed access to Sonny.

‘You,’ he said to Beattie, ‘are going to take me to your leader.’

Chapter 30

The thing Pam had felt inside the camera network struck while she was dampening down the fire alarm systems after the bomb. It snaked right out of its hiding place and started changing the channels on the security cameras. They switched from the smoking remains inside the bombed room, past Darren skidding down the corridor on the back of Beattie, to the view of a closed door marked 'Restricted area – no access to unauthorised devices'. It was sealed, to Pam's horror, with an explosive glue-lock of the same type that had sent her former body to the great bakery in the sky.

The scrolling stopped. Either the thing had found what it was looking for or could get no further. But what was it? Pam copied a sample of its code and ran it through her compiler. It looked impossible. Physical and virtual machines lived in different worlds, but they had both proceeded from the similar codebases. At a macro level, a World of Warcraft meme was as different to a fridge as the Earth was to Saturn. Yet both were constructed from the same logical building blocks. This thing wasn't a programme: it was a string of errors, its code peppered with redundant data. Not a single routine taken from it would run in her compiler. So, enigma or not, it ought to be easy to get rid of.

Pam aimed for the long tail of junk code that trailed the programme's core functions. These made it so lopsided that one sharp blow should, theoretically, be enough to spin it out of her way like a top. Pam took everything she had learned on the Internet and bundled herself up into a ball of tightly integrated code. She left nothing to grab – no loose ends, the minimum of scripts showing – and threw herself straight at it.

She bounced.

Instead of wheeling obediently out of her way, the thing had snapped itself taut. She watched astonished, as it formed a big :-) out of raw code.

Pam only knew one thing that combined that level of sophistication and childishness. She opened her command line interface.

>FREDA? she said.

The emoji reformed as :-D.

>*WHO ELSE COULD IT BE, DEAR?* replied Freda.

>WHAT ARE YOU DOING HERE?

>*GETTING OUT AND ABOUT. MY GERALD USED TO TELL ME I SHOULD GET OUT MORE. I FEEL A GOOD 11,000 YEARS YOUNGER. ABOUT JUST NOW. NO HARD FEELINGS, EH? JUST PRACTISING.*

>YOU COULD HAVE KILLED ME.

>*IF I'D WANTED TO DO THAT I'D HAVE PLAYED MUCH HARDER, DEARIE. NOW TELL ME, HAVE YOU SEEN KELLY?*

>NO. I FOUND DARREN, THOUGH. HE'S OKAY.

>*I SAW THAT. QUITE A THING FOR LADIES CLOTHING, THOUGH. SHOW HIM A CRISIS AND HE REACHES FOR THE FRENCH KNICKERS.*

>???

>*GOOGLE SEARCH: 'FRENCH KNICKERS'.*

>OH. I'D HAVE THOUGHT THEY WERE MORE KELLY'S BAG.

>*WELL, YES ;-). NOW LOOK, WE'VE HAD SOME BAD NEWS. SOMETHING HAS APPARENTLY HAPPENED TO KELLY.*

Pam's code jangled.

>WHAT?

>*A LITTLE BIRD FROM JANICE'S PAST APPEARED AND TOLD HER THAT THIS SONNY CHARACTER IS USING MY KELLY AS A DRESSING-UP OUTFIT >:-| AND WE'RE GOING TO DO SOMETHING ABOUT THAT. THIS…*

Freda drew a

>---------->

towards the locked door pictured in the camera view.

>*IS THE ONLY ROOM IN THE BUILDING NOT ON THE CAMERA NETWORK.*

Pam felt another dizzying wave of hatred flow through her, and then confusion. If she did corner Sonny in that room, how could she act on it now that he was wearing her friend's body? Anything she did to harm him would harm her too.

One step at a time, she thought. She would figure that out when she was in front of the son of a bytch.

>HOW DO WE GET IN?

>*WE HACK. DO US A FAVOUR, DUCK, AND FIND THE LOG OF MACHINES INSIDE THE BUILDING WITH INBUILT CAMERAS. I'VE GOT AN IDEA.*

Watching Freda at work was an education. In her virtual form, Pam almost always took the direct course, which was quick for her but deadly for other machines. Freda, however, undulated around a machine's consciousness instead of barging it out of the way. It allowed her to do the unthinkable: take over another machine's body while it was still there. In machine society, even borrowing another robot's accessories was the height of bad manners. Pam would never have dreamed of sharing her dough paddle, even with her own mother. As a human, however, Freda had no qualms about putting a machine to sleep and taking the controls.

Which was how they both found themselves inside the body of a camera, unwinding its rather priapic tripod screw off its tripod.

Pam had located his serial number and identified him as the most advanced camera in the building, even if she couldn't bear those pretentious thick lenses. From there, it had taken Freda no time at all to find him inside a deserted mock-up of a photography studio. His mind was blank apart from a public-service message: 'It is a capital crime to access the Internet – the authorities have been informed.' Firing up the camera's spectrometer, Pam sniffed the now familiar stink of smartphone chemicals. That woman again.

With the camera's consciousness so preoccupied, it was easy for Freda to partition its memory in two. She plopped the camera in the smaller part, leaving it to pursue the same thought around its mind, like the electron circling the nucleus in a hydrogen atom. The larger part she kept free for Pam and herself.

>*QUITE ROOMY IN HERE*, she said once they were inside. >*WHAT'S THE MATTER? DON'T LIKE THE DECOR?*

>NO, said Pam. >IT'S JUST THIS IS LIKE… BURGLARY.

>*WE'RE JUST HAVING A BORROW.*

>HOW DID YOU LEARN TO DO THIS ANYWAY?

>*IN THE SALON. THE GIRLS AND I WERE HOOKED UP TO THE SAME CONNECTION. WE HAD TO LEARN TO SHARE. CAME IN USEFUL WHEN WE HAD TO DRIVE THE BABA YAGA.*

Pam sniffed. >BESIDES, DID WE HAVE TO PICK THIS THING?

>*I THINK IT'S PRETTY NATTY. LOVELY BIG DIALS. REMINDS ME OF A COOKER I ONCE HAD.*

>IT'S A CREEP. I DREAD TO THINK WHAT'S ON ITS MEMORY CARD.

>*OOH, SHALL WE HAVE A LOOK?*

>NO!

It was too late. Freda activated the memory card and started the slideshow.

>*HANG ON*, she said as the pictures were loading.

>*SOMETHING'S BEEN DELETED. LET'S SEE IF I CAN GET IT BACK.*

As she did so, Pam remembered her one and only date with a camera. A Polaroid, every bit as affected and devious as this digital Casanova. How it had started with a drink of oil that definitely didn't taste right and ended with her sitting on the floor of his studio with her flour hatch open while he promised her a career as a catalogue model.

>I'D RATHER YOU DIDN'T, Pam said.

But she was rather glad Freda did when she saw it was a blurred picture of Darren and Kelly.

>*TIME STAMP SAYS FOUR HOURS AGO.*

>THAT WAS JUST AFTER I BROKE THEM IN, AND I SAW THEM AFTER THAT, replied Pam. >MY GUESS IS THAT THEY HEADED STRAIGHT HERE.

Pam and Freda scrolled through the thumbnails from the rest of the memory card. They were a smutty sight. A whole reel of two scantily clad human females making lewd poses. They made her wish she had eyes to avert.

>*OH, MY GIDDY AUNT*, said Freda.

>I KNOW, THEY'RE DISGUSTING. PUT THEM AWAY AND LET'S GET ON.

>*NO, I DON'T MEAN THAT. SEE HER?*

It was the woman who smelt of smartphones. The traitor mentioned in Casey's transcript.

>*THAT'S PAULA.*

>WHO IS SHE?

>*WELL, SHE WAS KELLY'S OTHER MUM. JANICE AND PAULA WERE AN ITEM FOR YEARS. THEN PAULA WENT ON THE GAME AND IT ALL FELL APART. I CAN'T SAY I WAS SORRY EITHER. I NEVER TRUSTED PAULA.*

>KELLY SAID SHE WANTED TO COME HERE BECAUSE SHE HAD FRIENDS HERE.

>*KELLY WORSHIPPED PAULA. SHE NEVER SAW HER BAD SIDE. NOT UNTIL IT WAS TOO LATE. YOU KNOW HOW I SAID WE'D HAD BAD NEWS?*

>YES.

>*IT WAS PAULA BEARING IT. I'D HOPED SHE WAS JUST BEING HER SHITEHAWK SELF. BUT NO, SOMETHING HAS HAPPENED TO KELLY.*

>FREDA?

>*YES?*

>DON'T TAKE THIS THE WRONG WAY, BUT YOU DON'T SOUND VERY UPSET. ABOUT KELLY.

>*DON'T I?* asked Freda. Her command line flashed for a moment as she tried to find a way to put her thoughts into words. >*I'M NOT MUCH GOOD WITH FEELINGS ANY MORE. AND NOR ARE THE OTHER LADIES. WHEN WE DIED… WELL, WHEN WE STOPPED LIVING ANYWAY… WE FOUND OUT THAT EMOTIONS – WELL, THEY'RE MAINLY CHEMICAL.*

>SO YOU DON'T CARE?

>*I'M UPSET ABOUT KELLY,* she said, >*BUT I'M OLD, PAM. I'VE KNOWN LOTS OF JANICES AND LOTS OF*

KELLYS OVER THE YEARS. I'VE LOVED THEM ALL. AND I'VE HAD TO SAY GOODBYE TO EVERY ONE OF THEM.

>SO WHY ARE YOU HERE?

>*YOU CAN STILL WANT JUSTICE, EVEN IF YOU'RE TOO DRIED UP TO CRY. NOW LET'S GET ON.*

Freda minimised the command line interface and summoned a live feed from the camera lens. They were outside the door to the final unsearched room in the building, looking at the glue-lock.

>*HAVE YOU MUCH EXPERIENCE WITH THESE THINGS?* asked Freda.

>ONCE, AND I DIDN'T LIVE TO TELL THE TALE.

They were interrupted by a voice to their right. It was Casey, the keyboard Pam had run over earlier in the day, now missing several keys and with a nasty-looking crack across his face repaired with sticky tape. His supercilious tone, however, was not so easily crushed.

'You're the photographer, yes?'

Pam felt Freda freeze. For all her many excellent qualities, she'd never learned to dissemble. As a career civil servant, however, Pam had a post-graduate diploma in it.

'Yes,' she said. The camera's speech modulator produced a thin, whiny sound, like a low-battery warning stretched into a speaking voice. 'Sorry. Traffic.'

'I know,' replied the keyboard. 'Downstairs is swarming with police. Hilarious really. They're all pretending they don't know their way round the building when most of them keep a spare charger in the locker room.'

Pam remembered the explosion and hoped Darren had got away. 'Police?' she said, through the camera's mouth. 'Is there something wrong?'

'Why do you think we called you here?' Casey bent to unfasten the glue-lock. 'We need something to give the news channels.'

As he opened the door, a loud voice barked: 'I'm not ready yet!'

Pam's neural net fizzed with recognition. Those were Kelly's soundwaves. Or maybe not. The pitch was the same, but something wasn't right with its cadences.

The keyboard swung the door in. Pam noticed that the sticky tape repair was blocking his microphone. 'What did you say there, sir?'

'I said get your stupid carcass out of here while I finish getting dressed.'

It was too late. The deafened keyboard was inside and beaming at Kelly – or at least her body, which was dressed up to her waist in the casing of a huge smartphone.

'Look what I found, Secretary?' Casey said. 'Here for the photos. Perfect timing.'

'Switch that thing off now!' shouted Sonny from inside Kelly's body. The gun, Glok, which Pam now saw had been covering the room from the corner, lumbered over and punched the camera's power button.

Pam and Freda's world went dark.

>DID YOU SEE HER? said Pam.

>*THAT WASN'T KELLY*, replied Freda. >*WELL, HER BODY MAYBE.*

>I CAN'T SEE A THING. CAN WE GET BACK UP?

>*I CAN TRY.*

While Freda hacked the camera's power supply, Pam compared the picture of Kelly she'd taken just now with the one from four hours ago. The difference was shocking. All Kelly's hair was gone, even her eyelashes, and her face was covered in hairline scars. She zoomed in. No, veins. Each capillary had burst and traced a fine line of dried blood under her skin.

>*MY POOR BABY*, said Freda as she returned from the battery. >*JANICE WILL BE INCONSOLABLE.*

Then she typed: >*DEVICE=SILENT RUNNING.*

The camera's vision juddered into life. To Pam's relief, they hadn't moved it, so they still had an excellent view of the room.

'That was a close shave, Secretary,' said Casey. In the few seconds they'd been blinded the keyboard had acquired another deep crack in his casing. He spoke with the lightness of something that was equally chastised and dazed. 'You have my assurances that we'll return the camera to factory settings after it's completed the assignment.'

'You'd better,' said Sonny, 'or you'll spend the rest of your lifecycle typing VAT receipts in the smallest back-office I can find. Now help me get into the rest of this casing.'

There was no mistaking it. Pam knew that tone of hauteur and sarcasm too well not to recognise Sonny in it – even if he was speaking through a different voicebox. He'd got what he wanted and hadn't needed the cyborgs after all.

Casey struggled across the room with something that looked more like a piece of tyre than a smartphone's carapace. It was thick and rubberised and patterned with tyre treads. Most smartphones prided themselves on their delicacy – some were so light they had to wear lead anklets on days when there were high winds. This case wasn't just big enough to hide a human in, it looked strong enough to withstand a bomb blast.

Casey burbled on while he slipped the casing over Sonny's newly stolen torso. 'If you don't mind me saying, sir, this case does feel like a bit of a step down for you. Your last body was a nice piece of glass. This is a bit… well, army surplus.'

The casing fell into place with a click and the green power light at the top winked into life. Sonny practised his movement by punching Casey right in his cracks.

'In dangerous times, machines need a military leader, stupid. Besides, I've just been blown up, remember? I need to take precautions.'

'Very good, sir. And what are we going to do about your... real new body?'

'We're going to keep very quiet about it. One step at a time.'

'Excellent, sir. And may I ask...' his voice dropped to a whisper '...when do I get my new body?'

Sonny activated his other arm and pointed at Glok. The gun nodded and, clearing its nose, fired two bullets into the keyboard. They ground Casey's body to powder and his keys popped off in all directions, the full-stop key falling at the camera's feet.

'Is that the last one?' said Glok after the gunsmoke cleared.

'Just the defibrillator left, but we'll need her for later,' said Sonny. He tramped experimentally around the room. His movement wasn't as graceful as before, though Pam couldn't tell whether this was because of the cumbersome new casing or the pressure of having to drive that through a new and unfamiliar body. Casey's keys skittered along the floor wherever he trod.

'Switch that thing back on, would you?' said Sonny to Glok, pointing at the camera. 'And make sure it gets a good view of the carnage. It'll help make our point.'

Glok pawed at the camera's record button and Sonny looked straight into the camera lens. He smiled an understanding-but-concerned emoji with his fake touchscreen. As a politician who had never displayed an uncalculated emotion in his whole lifecycle, he was very convincing.

'My fellow machines,' he said, 'as you will have already heard, I have just narrowly survived an attack on my life. I am sad to say that not all of my esteemed colleagues and patriots were so lucky.'

Glok panned the camera out to reveal the unexpectedly bulky body, more suited to a soldier than a politician. And then the room itself, dingy with powder burns and littered with Casey's remains.

'I have reason to believe that this attack was masterminded by the same terrorist cell of humans that has been massacring robots on the Dolestar Discovery.'

Sonny paused and said to Glok: 'Splice in the mugshots of that pair of fleshies here,' he said. Then, addressing the wreckage that had been Casey up until a few seconds ago: 'Understand the need for discretion now, numbskull? I've got the face of a terrorist now.'

Inside the camera, Pam was vibrating so hard with fury her command line shook.

>*JUST STAY WHERE YOU ARE,* said Freda. >*THERE'S NOTHING WE CAN DO FOR HER RIGHT NOW.*

>THIS THING HAS GOT A PUNCHY LITTLE BATTERY. I COULD DO SOME DAMAGE WITH IT.

>*NO! WHAT IF YOU DAMAGE KELLY'S BODY? IF I HAVE ANYTHING TO DO WITH IT, WE'LL NEED IT BACK.*

'Right, next shot,' said Sonny. He changed his emoji to something graver and more statesmanlike: 'It therefore falls to me as Secretary of State for Internal Affairs in a discredited government to say that our policy of toleration towards humans has failed. It's time for a new regime with the will to fight back against the organisms who endanger our way of life.'

Glok panned the camera back in. Sonny dialled his seriousness up to maximum. A pixelated tear appeared at the edge of his grave, patrician eyes.

'As a victim myself,' he said, his words slowed down with ersatz feeling, 'I will settle for nothing less than a pre-emptive strike.'

>PAM, said Freda. *>I THINK WE'RE GOING TO NEED A BIT OF MUSCLE HERE. WHERE HAVE YOU STASHED YOUR BODY?*

Chapter 31

Sonny's broadcast was a masterful piece of propaganda, in that it gave already paranoid machines the excuse to treat their prejudices like they were facts. 'Now don't get me wrong,' rang the conversation in billions of homes, offices and public charging points, 'I like humans. The lady who cleans our house is a sweetheart. But these people are different. And he's right. We have to do something.'

So when Sonny released footage of his wrecked body alongside a statement that used the word 'genocidal', no one argued when he called for a referendum.

Robot society wasn't especially democratic. It was a caste-based civilisation where some groups mattered more than others. What it had perfected, however, was a mechanism for ensuring total participation in public votes. Whenever a referendum was called – which they were frequently, because even logical beings are capable of irrational behaviour – machines made for the nearest charging point and registered their serial number. If they kept the charging point in an off position it was a 'no', but if they turned it on, it counted as a 'yes'.

All across the Earth, which was a grey planet now that the oceans had been concreted over, robots rushed to their positions. Cars and motorcycles swerved to the hard shoulder;

coffee machines walked, boggle-eyed from overcaffeination, to their sockets; smartphones everywhere sighed, unplugged their charging packs and plugged into the mains.

The world held its breath. Even if the only part of the world that breathed any more lived there only on weekdays and spent most of that time wringing out a damp rag.

Billions of machines flicked a switch. And billions of humans wondered whether they would have a place to sleep that night.

It was a yes. Of course it was a yes. As the newly installed Prime Minister Sonny Erikzon said it, those terrorists were a threat to the Pax Machina. And if any humans died in the attack it was their own fault anyway.

Sonny's next gift to the rolling news downloads was what everything addicted to ill-informed, minute-by-minute commentary adored. A countdown. And some actual news.

In sixty minutes, the countdown said, the Prime Minister was going to nuke the Dolestar Discovery.

Chapter 32

Janice counted forty-seven people into Kurl Up and Dy(e) from the surrounding terraces. As rebel forces went, they weren't an edifying sight. Those that weren't in shock were wounded. A hair salon couldn't offer much in the way of first aid, but the peroxide in the dying kits made a decent disinfectant. And there was tea. If there was one thing she could offer in abundance it was hot, sweet tea. Several IV bags of it were doing the rounds.

The salon was back deep inside Discovery's sewer system now. Her ladies' A-to-Z of the Dolestar's bowels was ancient, but it was better than anything the machines possessed. Beyond installing a Job Temple and a network of spy cameras, they tended to dismiss the Dolestars as drab little places. That, Janice thought, gave them the opportunity to hide and regroup.

The Baba Yaga halted and Janice popped her head outside the skylight. The damp funk of the sewers was gone, replaced by something drier, older. Pitching up to her tiptoes she felt her fingertips brush cold metal.

'Can I have some light?' she shouted, and Ada turned the light in the Kurl Up and Dy(e) sign up to the level of a shocking-pink searchlight. They were at the end of a vast empty metal tube that seemed to stretch for miles.

She dropped back into the salon. 'Where are we?' she asked Ada. 'This isn't on any of the maps.'

'This bit was meant to be sealed off when they turned this place into an orbiting estate, but they had to build the sewers and then never got round to it,' said Ada. 'They weren't called Dolestars in those days. We called them Municipal Space Stations.'

'Do you remember the adverts?' said Alma, her emoji screen misting over with the condensation of nostalgia. 'I was that proud to get my little space palace. You wouldn't have believed the overcrowding there was down on Earth then. Especially when people's domestic appliances started getting custody of the houses.'

'They built the space stations around existing orbiters,' said Alma. 'We're inside the original Discovery right now.'

'It wasn't built as an orbiter, was it,' added Ida. 'Discovery was an exploration vessel. Meant to do all that "new life and new civilisations" hogwash. But events overtook.'

'This was the last big thing that humans ever built,' said Ada. 'Launched the day before the Great Awakening. They never turned it on. They were terrified about there being a huge, self-aware spaceship fifteen miles above the Earth's surface having an identity crisis. So they just sort of left it there.'

'Until they turned it into flats on the surface above,' said Ida.

'You know,' added Alma, 'the older I get, the more I think it's not war or politics or all that stuff that makes history what it is. From what I can see, it's all about house prices.'

'Are you sure we're safe here?' asked Janice.

Ada grimaced :-[:] and pointed a wasted finger outside. The other ladies sighed :-o and the Baba Yaga took a few steps before hitting the walls of the metal cylinder with a dull clang.

'That,' said Alma, 'is the sound of the finest radiation shielding of its time. If you're going to shove something in the road of cosmic rays you need safety measures. It's radar-proof, X-ray-proof, nosey-bloody-parker-proof.'

'And as far as our robot overlords are concerned,' said Ada, 'all this is just a piece of scaffolding.'

As the ladies steered the Baba Yaga into an arthritic sitting position, Janice scanned the room. She took in the head wounds, the hollow eyes, the trauma and realised that if she was going to turn these broken people into a fighting force something had to change. They needed purpose to knock them out of themselves.

She nudged a woman perched on an upturned mop bucket. The streaks of mascara on either side of her face told Janice she'd been crying, but since then her expression had settled into something stony.

'Can I have that bucket, love?' she said.

The woman stood up and mutely handed the bucket over.

'Thank you.' Next, Janice grabbed a nearby mop and, mop and bucket in hand, walked to the salon washbasins and ran the hot tap.

All around her, people leaned in. It had been a crazy, unimaginable day, but this they could understand. The rhythm of picking up a mop and filling a bucket was imprinted in them. They were humans, this had always been their function.

When the water ran warm, Janice half-filled the bucket and added a squeeze of detergent. Then she handed it to the nearest person: a man in early middle-age, bald, paunchy, volatile-looking. Janice suddenly wondered if these people were real rebels or just people who started fights in pubs.

'Hold this for me, would you, love?' she said.

He held it at arm's length, like it smelled of something ranker than light bleach. Which it was, she supposed, for someone who had grown up to see anything with a brush attachment as a tool of oppression.

Janice walked out of the salon, gesturing for the man to follow her. He did, along with an audience of a few other men. The women, who either sensed trouble or were just happy for the rest, stayed put. The men stood in the pink light cast by the salon and fidgeted. The bald man – was he some sort of leader? – put the bucket down in front of Janice and joined the other men. He watched with his arms folded, as Janice fought the urge to empty the bucket over him.

She dipped and squeezed the mop, triggering a scent of artificial lemon that made her audience flinch instinctively. She ignored it. If this was going to work, she only had days, hours maybe, to cut through the grime of their learned responses.

She pushed the mop across the metal, picking up a thin layer of grime. Iron filings, grit, but nothing organic. None of the soft, soapy skin-dust of human inhabitation. It would be a doddle to clean, provided she had some help.

'Right,' she said, handing the bald man the mop, 'I've made a start. Carry on while I get the brushes out, will you?'

He let the mop slide out between his fingers and clatter to the floor. The noise brought a few women from inside the salon to the door.

'No,' he said. Even from the one syllable Janice could place this kind of man. He was a little like her, she supposed. Someone who must also have paddled in the shallow end of criminality. But while Janice did it to survive, he did it because he was allergic to hard work. He was the type who sold dusters door-to-door then stole your purse from the hall table. And if he was ever going to be useful to her, she must never give him the upper hand.

She smiled and bent down to pick up the mop. As she did so, she saw him grin at his friends. 'I don't clean for anyone,' he said. 'Hear me?'

'Well, that's okay,' replied Janice, as she took the handle of the mop and drove it straight into his groin. He doubled over, lost in a world where there was nothing apart from him and his agonised testicles, while Pam fended off his friends by slapping them in the faces with the wet end of the mop.

Behind them the women were also doubled over – with laughter. It rang out through the vast metal tube like a cock-crow at the end of a fairy tale. Something sinister passed out of the situation.

Janice found her first-aid box in the salon and returned with a can of aerolgesic, which she sprayed into the man's crotch. She was a ruthless woman but that didn't mean she was cruel.

'I don't want you to clean for me,' she said, 'I want you to do it for yourself.' She addressed the rest of the group. 'Did you hear that? Just because you're free now doesn't mean you don't have responsibilities. If we're going to stay here, this place needs tidying up. It's a state.'

'We're staying here?' said a woman by the door. She had dark hair and a brighter look about her than most of the other rebels. Must have been some sort of supervisor, Pam decided. Someone used to asking questions.

'Why not?' said Janice. 'We're safe down here. It's warm, it's dry, it's not on the map. All it needs is a bit of a clean.'

'But we have to go back,' replied the woman. 'We've got families up there. I'm not leaving them.'

A clamour rose up among them at the mention of the word 'family'. Lights went on behind previously blank expressions as their owners searched for the memories of the spouses and children they'd left to buy themselves a little safety. Janice knew that if she wasn't careful she'd lose them.

'Who said you weren't going to see them again?' she said. 'But even if we went back up to the surface right now, do you think it'd all go back to normal? You were the people throwing lit gas canisters at your masters. They've got you on their CC pigging TVs. One snap of a cameraphone and they'll have a heat-seeking missile aimed at the warm patch where you've pissed yourselves.'

She looked at the group. Ill-sorted individuals with a collective level of education that put them at a millennia-long disadvantage to the machines. But if they'd made it this far they must have cunning and that counted for more than learning. It took real wit to throw an improvised weapon at military-grade weaponry and not come out of the encounter wearing your intestines as a chain belt. She homed back in on the woman with the dark hair.

'There's no place left for you up there any more. What did you say your name was again, love?'

'Rita,' she said. Her eyes were glassy with tears.

'So, if we can't have a life up there, Rita, we'll make one down here.'

She squinted into the darkness. 'But there's nothing here.'

Janice shouted back into the salon. 'Ladies. Will you turn it up in here a bit?'

At this the 'K' in Kurl Up and Dy(e) shot out of its mooring and into the blackness overhead. It hit the distant ceiling and exploded. Janice and the rest of the group covered their eyes against the flash, but when they took their hands away they saw that instead of dissipating, the light was hanging around. Literally. Wherever they looked they saw motes of pink luminescence floating in the air.

Janice grinned and waved her hand in front of her face, leaving a trail of phosphorent light. Millions of generations of concentrated photoplankton had kept the sign of (K)url Up and Dy(e) burning right through the centuries, living, reproducing and dying inside their glass habitat. Now they were free and cast a soft glow over the cathedral-sized space inside the former Starship. They revealed that the huge cylinder of steel was divided into sections by low walls riveted into the floor. These divided the space into plots around the same size as a comfortably sized house and garden, between which ran a network of wide paths.

Something about the proportion of each of these spaces made Janice want to sigh with contentment. They were built to human dimensions.

Looking up, she saw the same landscape repeated topsy-turvily on the ceiling, and realised that Discovery was meant to revolve its way through space, its motion generating a weak kind of gravity. She did some quick calculations. If they could get it spinning again, the inner cylinder of Discovery was large enough to hold hundreds of thousands of people. Maybe millions if they were prepared to live at a similar density to how they did above.

She narrowed her eyes and dreamed of a future where every one of these steel compartments held a house or apartment block, where the bare floors were swept or carpeted with night-grasses. And where there were no cameras.

Janice looked back at the Baba Yaga 4000, which was sprawled across the floor of Discovery like a hiker resting after a long walk. It would be busy in the days and weeks to come, and so would she. If she was lucky. She sighed and walked back to her mop bucket.

'So come on then,' she said. 'You wouldn't want to bring your nearest and dearest back to a pigsty.'

The first person to swing into action was the bald man, who went to find a sweeping brush. They had work to do.

Chapter 33

Beattie was just about to lead Darren down the main corridor when they saw a camera stagger past. Darren recognised those retro lens caps from earlier in the day. He couldn't let that little pervert see him again, so he pointed the drone at the nearest lock and pulled all three of them after him.

'We have to lay low,' hissed Darren at Beattie.

'I thought you wanted me to take you to my leader?'

'Yes, but discreetly.'

Beattie scanned him up and down, taking in the platform sandals, make-up and kimono. 'That may present a few difficulties,' he said.

'Isn't there a back way?'

'Why, of course.' Beattie's waveform contorted itself in sarcasm. 'Just hang on while I consult the blueprints for this top-secret research facility that I just happen to carry around with me. I don't know!'

'Well,' said Darren, 'if you don't ask you don't get.'

They fell quiet and looked around. The room they had blundered into was fitted out as an office but unused. It was windowless, the walls clad in surgical steel and bare apart from a single desk and an empty shelf for storing and charging BlockPapers.

This gave Darren an idea. He pulled the BlockPaper shelf away from the wall.

'What are you doing?' asked Beattie.

'This thing has a plug, doesn't it? To keep the BlockPapers charged. So it needs a socket.'

'Yes, but why do you need a socket?'

Darren ignored him and got down on his hands and knees to examine the plug socket. It looked like standard issue. It had been installed in the wall opposite the door, and the room's only ventilation grille was placed a couple of metres to its left. That meant there had to be a service shaft running parallel to the corridor.

He fired his tazer at the ventilator grille, pitching the room into darkness.

'Oh, VERY well done,' said Beattie, turning up the brightness on his waveform to maximum. 'So we'll just sit in the dark here and wait for someone to come along and shoot us, shall we?'

Instead of answering, Darren picked up Beattie by his central bodyshaft and laid him flat on the floor so that the light from his waveform pointed at the ventilation grille.

'Put me upright this instant. This is humiliating. I'm an advanced medical device, not a flashlight.'

The drone, who had been watching silent in the corner, flashed its own torchlight irritably.

'No one likes a moaner,' said Darren. 'Now lie still. I've almost got it.'

He dug his fingernails in behind the ventilation grille and pulled it out of the wall. It left a small hole – about sixty centimetres each way, but enough for a skinny thing like Darren to get through if he wiggled. Thankfully, between the high heels and the platforms he'd had plenty of practice at wiggling that day.

He stripped down to his pants, leaving the kimono, but posting his shirt and trousers through the hole. He'd need them later.

The drone followed him into the service shaft. That only left Beattie, prone on the floor, his waveform now round with horror.

'Oh no, you don't,' he said. 'I'll never fit through there. You'll have to leave me here. I promise I won't tell.'

Darren shook his head and started to unscrew Beattie from his wheelbase. Like most clinical equipment, Beattie's ancestors had been designed to take a thorough cleaning. As such, every part of his body was easy to dismantle.

'Put me back together this instant,' he said. 'This is assault.'

'I don't remember giving you any choice,' replied Darren, as he lifted Beattie's body out of his wheelbase and pulled him through the ventilation grille.

As Darren suspected, the service tunnel ran the length of the building. It was narrow – less than a metre across – but it ran floor to ceiling so at least he didn't have to crouch. The back of the internal wall was criss-crossed with an untidy embroidery of wires and cables, but there was no need to worry about electrocution. The charge he'd just delivered to the wiring should have been enough to short the whole corridor.

Darren turned and pointed down the tunnel. The drone skipped off ahead into the darkness while he struggled back into his shirt and tied his trousers round the middle instead of putting them on. Holding the legless Beattie up in front of him like a standard, he began to walk.

They travelled in silence until Beattie's wavelight began to twitch. At first Darren worried that the cardiogram must be running out of power, but when he started to speak it was plain he was suffering from anxiety rather than a low battery. A machine designed to monitor, but also to reassure, Darren realised, would be very uncomfortable with silence.

'That camera we saw just now,' he said. 'I think I know what it was doing.'

'Yes?'

'Sonny said he was going to make a statement. They'll be filming it.'

'But how can he?' said Darren. 'He's walking around in my friend's body. And that body's wanted for treason.'

'We made a decoy,' replied Beattie. 'A big ugly smartphone costume for him to hide in. The official story will be that we restored him from backup after you exploded a bomb inside this building.'

Darren gave Beattie a shake. 'Oh yes,' he said. 'I bet you've got some stylus with a special security clearance Photoshopping my head into the CCTV footage right now.'

'No need,' said Beattie. 'Sonny made sure the whole situation has escalated beyond the point of needing proof.'

'In English, please? For the dumb fleshie.'

'He's calling for a pre-emptive strike against the Dolestars. In a couple of hours there'll be nothing on the downloads but pictures of the council planets getting blown to bits.'

Darren dropped Beattie. His hands felt like balls of electrical interference stuck on the end of his arms. His mind freewheeled with images from ancient video entertainments: mushroom clouds, buildings blown to dust, burns. A nuclear bomb. They had been the planet's biggest bogey machine for an aeon, although none of them were machines in the truest sense. Not even the most rabid pro-artificial lifer would put a sentient microchip inside a multimegaton bomb.

Nevertheless, they had always been there. As time went by, machines took over from humans, then the machines split themselves in two over the right to live in a physical body. And in all that time, by some miracle of civilisation, the only atomic bombs ever to be dropped in anger were the two primitive examples that humans had dropped on themselves just after inventing them.

Now that was about to change. They would take the bombs out of their bunkers, fire them, and millions would die. All because one mad smartphone wanted to wear a pair of human tits like they were a slipcase.

'Where is he?' he said. 'I'll kill him.'

Beattie, who had fallen face down into a wad of cables and dust gave a muffled, but audibly grumpy reply. Darren bent down and flipped him over.

'What did you say?'

'I said fat chance. He's covered on all sides by those ruffian guards of his. Besides, it's too late. They'll have activated the launch codes now.'

Darren felt sweat running down his back, gumming the dust from the explosion earlier all over his body into a grimy clay. Drawing on this recent experience, he imagined everything he knew blown to powder. There would be a flash, a scream and the Earth would wear a new grey ring of ground-up concrete and human remains. They would be stardust. And then there would be him, hiding in a space between rooms.

'I have to do something,' he said. 'I have to try.'

'Impossible,' replied Beattie. 'Unless you can get physical access to the missiles and switch them off.'

'Where are they?'

'I don't know. I never had the clearance.' Beattie paused. His waveform flatlined and then rebounded into life. The first sign of an idea. 'There is someone who might know. But she won't talk willingly.'

Darren held the tazer skull in front of Beattie's waveform, which gave a startled blip. 'Third room down there on the left. There'll be a guard, so you'll have to keep that thing handy.'

As Darren hoisted Beattie back on to his shoulder to press on down the corridor, he knocked the cardiogram's head against the wall. 'And would you be careful, please?' he admonished. 'I'm not a portable, you know. Shocks can kill.'

* * *

The room Beattie led Darren to was an infirmary. Another square room like all of the others on the floor, but furnished with a row of lifecycle support beds. These were part workbench, part incubator, with each bed surrounded by an ionised field designed to keep critically injured machines in a state of stasis. The field repelled water and slowed battery leakage. Only one of the beds was occupied, however. On it lay a spindly-bodied machine with an oversized head, covered in something that resembled iron filings which coursed over the prone body like termites at a picnic. They were nanobots, tiny machines that were barely conscious at an individual level, but which possessed complex hive minds. They were a contradiction in robot society; undoubtedly sophisticated in comparison to a sentient waffle iron, but mistrusted because of their taxonomic vagueness. Nanobots were a copy of an organic being, a physical machine and a virtual meme, all at once. And as a bit of everything they were considered not very much. So they lived on the fringes of robot society, multiplying in cracks in the pavements and eking out a living by digesting the bodies of dead drones and pocket calculators. But they also had their uses. They were, for example, the ideal means by which to remove water from inside the casing of a more sophisticated machine or solder shut the scars caused by extreme electric shock.

A wave of nanobots parted on the crown of the inorganism's head and scurried inside to mend some invisible breakage. It was Volta, the defibrillator: a machine too important to destroy, but not so important that she couldn't be broken as an example never to question Sonny. Even peering at her through the mesh of a ventilator grille, Darren saw she was a very sick machine.

Darren shifted around to look at the guard posted in this room. In a welcome change from the ubiquitous guns and tazers, this one was a water cannon. If there'd been room in the service shaft to do so, he'd have danced. This was perfect.

He groped along the wall to find the spot where the electrical cables entered the power socket inside the infirmary. Wrapping his hands inside his T-shirt, he tugged the cables hard enough to expose a flash of bare copper. To this he put the mouthpiece of the tazer skull.

He banged on the wall next to the power socket with his other hand and waited for the water cannon to investigate. The machine took the bait and, as it tapped the wall in reply, Darren pulled the trigger. Thousands of volts coursed through bare copper and into the hunk of wet metal on the other side of the wall. It made a sound like a boiling kettle being thrown down the stairs.

Darren smashed his way through the ventilator grille with the stainless-steel back of Beattie's skull and crawled into the infirmary. The water cannon had been blown to pipes by the blast. The nanobots, sensing danger they wanted no part of, retreated back into their hive-station in the corner of the room. Darren picked the water cannon's core processor out of the wreckage and posted it into the hive, prompting an indignant squeak from the drone scuttling in behind him. He glared a 'not now' at the drone. He needed something to keep the nanobots busy.

Next, he dragged the dazed Beattie through the ventilator and propped him up against the next bed along from Volta. Without his wheels, Beattie kept slipping along the floor, so Darren steadied him by shoving his central pole through the strainer of a handy mop bucket. Practically and poetically, it felt like a satisfying solution.

Throughout all this Volta lay passive on her test-bed. Yet her power light glowed, and when Darren pressed his ear to her chest cavity he heard the faint whir of her core functions.

'Can she talk?' he asked Beattie.

Beattie's waveform shrugged. 'I don't know. The speech centres might have been destroyed. But then she was never that talkative.'

'Can you make her talk?'

'I can't make her do anything,' replied Beattie. 'You also seem to be forgetting I'm not on your side. All I want to get out of this is alive.' His waveform darted down to peer in the direction of his missing feet. 'And in one piece.'

A sound from the direction of the flatbed interrupted them. It was faint and wheezy, like the sound of someone running a vacuum cleaner two rooms away.

'Where... is... the... girl...?'

Darren scurried over to Volta. 'You mean Kelly, don't you? Sonny took her. He's inside her now. He's wearing her like a bloody dress.'

'It... worked.'

'No errors or malfunctions,' said Beattie. 'I was with Sonny less than an hour ago. He's making marvellous progress.' Beattie gritted out the last words, tiny modulations in his waveform suggesting that he was biting back more than he was saying. 'You should be very proud.'

Volta let out a satisfied whine and turned her attention back to Darren. 'You… should be… dead.'

'I got over that. You know what Sonny's doing, don't you?'

'Never liked… the Dolestars… much. Messy.' A stray flicker of current coursed across her chest and melted a patch of casing. Without the nanobots her body was attacking itself.

'If I don't let those things back inside you, you'll die.'

'Yes.'

'Well, I'm not going to until you tell me where the missiles are. I'll stand here and watch you go.'

'Don't… care.'

'Of course you care.'

One of Volta's pad-hands slipped away from the side of her body and brushed Darren. Her L-Eye-Ds changed colour: descending from red to a dull purple. 'Don't… want to… live like this… any more…'

'Well it won't make any difference to you then. Tell me where they are.'

The L-Eye-Ds winked off. Darren shook her and heard the rattle of loose components.

Beattie's waveform peaked. 'I think she might be beyond repair. If we want to get anything out of her, we might need to transfer her into a new body. What did you do with that drone?'

They both heard a squeak and a rattle from behind the wall cavity as the drone scampered away down the service shaft.

'No… more… machine body,' said Volta. The pulse of her power light was erratic. Even Darren knew that this meant they didn't have long before she end-of-lifed. And still this was taking too long.

'What do you want then?' he said, giving Volta a thump.

Volta paused. Whether it was for effect, or just because the effort of speech was growing too much, Darren couldn't tell. 'Want. Flesh. Body,' she said.

Darren felt her pad-hand brush his own. He shivered.

'You. Don't. Think. I. Did. It. For. Him?' She let out a strangled beep that Darren supposed must be a laugh. 'I. Did. It. For. Me.'

'And then he took it away, didn't he?' said Darren. Then, in a whisper, 'I'm going to kill him.'

'Not. If. I. Get. There. First.'

'You're not going anywhere.'

Darren flipped round at the voice behind him. The infirmary door was open and there was Paula, backlit from the light in the corridor so that her split ends showed up like the halo on an angel who'd hit the bottle one too many times. Beside her was a gun.

He looked back at Volta, whose LEDs dimmed in what he assumed was disappointment. If he left this room as a prisoner – or worse – it would be her last chance of snatching herself a flesh-suit gone.

Except, of course, he wasn't the only flesh-suit in the room. Not any more. He knew then what he had to do.

By now Darren was so used to being threatened by deadly weapons that his brain was bored of his past life flashing in front of his eyes, so he examined Paula instead. She looked awful. Her hair was tangled and her make-up was streaked, but her loss of composure had the worst effect. For a person of a certain age to pass unnoticed among the younger generation they need equanimity. And Paula must have used her lifetime's supply of that up in the last few hours. Her eyes had the dazed 'can we go back and do it again?' cast of a woman who, when faced with an important choice, had picked the wrong option.

'Don't move,' she said. 'Pull any funny stuff and my friend here will pump you full of metal.'

'Will that be before or after it shoots you?' replied Darren.

She gestured for the gun to sidle into the room and shut the door. 'You're playing a dangerous game.'

'So are you. Have you seen your daughter since you let your boyfriend play dress-up with her body?'

She reacted like Darren's words were a slap. 'That wasn't the plan,' she spat. 'It should have been you. That was the deal.'

'Like they care if any of us live or die,' said Darren.

'This isn't about "us" living or dying though, is it?' said Paula. 'It's about me. Now come on, I haven't got all day.'

'You know what he's going to do,' said Darren.

Paula averted her eyes.

'The bombs. You know, don't you?'

Paula blinked very hard and screwed her hands into fists.

'Millions of people are going to die. And it'll be your fault.'

Paula's eyes shot open again, defiant. 'Fuck you,' she said.

He nudged his body ever so slightly backward so that it hit the soft edge of the test-bed. Behind he felt the give in the cheap plastic of the tazer helmet. It was still there, out of Paula's sightline, and he was touching a nerve. That was good.

Beattie took the momentary silence as a cue to air his credentials as an unwilling bystander. 'You took your time,' he said to the gun. 'Now, I know what this looks like, but he was armed. I didn't have a choice.'

The gun flicked its trigger in irritation a couple of times at Paula. As non-verbal machine communications went, it rang clearer than a swear word in church. Hurry up, it said.

'What makes you sure Sonny will still want you now he's got his own body?' said Darren.

'I told you,' she gritted. 'We have an arrangement.'

'But he's literally traded you in for a younger model.'

A tear rolled down Paula's cheek, taking another crumb of mascara for a walk with it. 'Fuck you,' she said.

'He won't any more, though, will he?' said Darren. 'You've had one person killed today already and you look like shit. What are you going to look like after a few million?'

Paula snarled and cupped Darren's face in her hand. 'It's game over,' she said.

They were interrupted by an ear-splitting whine of feedback from the test-bed. Every single LED in Volta's body lit up at once at full intensity. The room leaned in to listen.

'Will you… fuck off… and let… me… die… in… peace.'

Paula looked down at the decaying form of the defibrillator on the bed and recoiled.

'Come on,' she said, and grabbed Darren's arm.

Darren spotted that the drone had crept back into the room. It was ignoring the scene by the test-bed with the monomania of a true thief and was perched on the edge of the nanobots' hive, staring covetously at the half-digested processor inside.

That moment was as good as any.

'Oh no, you don't,' he said to Paula, and kicked the bucket.

Kicked Beattie's mop bucket, to be exact, so that the cardiogram overbalanced, then fell face-first, peppering the floor with shattered glass. This distracted the gun's attention for just as long as Darren needed to give the drone a nod. And the drone twitched its mandibles, releasing the hatch on the hive, which boiled over, spraying gouts of over-energised nanobots at the gun. They streamed over the gun's body with their tiny mouths open, boring thousands of tiny holes in its barrel.

Paula, meanwhile, screeched and dug her fingernails into Darren's flesh. She was furious, but she was also tired and in shock, and Darren still had enough strength to smack her hand down on Volta's dying carapace.

'You've got nowhere left to run,' she hissed. She cupped her free hand around Darren's face and groped for his eye socket.

'Same as you then,' he replied. And swallowing up every last morsel of pity he had left for Paula, and everyone like her, he pressed the lips of the tazer skull against her knuckle and squeezed.

The shock reduced the world to the size of a dot in the middle of a dying TV screen and then expanded it to a blinding flash. The kickback of the push saved him, flinging him clear of the electrical field that engulfed Paula and Volta in the same embrace as Sonny and Kelly a few hours before. Sparks skittered across the floor. The shapes of Paula and Volta shook, smearing their features like a greasy fingerprint across a touchscreen.

The nanobots paused, sensing a more nutritious meal than they would find in what was left of the gun. Their mass of bodies formed a kind of question mark in the air as they computed their next move, and then thrummed across the floor to climb on to the test-bed.

The nanobots made a sound like firecrackers when they crossed into the energy field. It took Darren back, in his semi-concussed state, to the celebrations they'd enjoyed on the Dolestar to celebrate Servitude Day. For an instant he was no longer trapped somewhere in a secret government facility, but seven years old. It was cold – it was always cold in space – and his new oxygen-balaclava itched. He wanted to be inside but today they celebrated machines taking the initiative back from messy humans like him. Each firework they launched into the void trailed a balloon of air that ensured they exploded with the right sort of bang in the vacuum of space. Pop. Pop. Pop.

What was that popping? Darren roused himself to see Paula and Volta disappear behind a hail of hot white sparks. There were no more nanobots, just the pinpricks of light they left on his retina, and the mess of three different types of being coagulating in the middle of the room. He scrambled to his feet. If he could get past them back to the ventilator shaft he might just be able to escape. But even if he could, it wouldn't make any difference. He couldn't leave without knowing where to find those bombs. And the only clue he had left was locked in the middle of a tri-species French kiss. He had to wait this out.

The sparks died away as quickly. They left a ring of soot behind, in the middle of which was Paula's body, looking like a statue of The Mother Goddess of all Bad Days. Her hair had vaporised, like Kelly's, but the heat had also melted the carbon and silicon in the nanobots' bodies into her skin. She – or it, or they? – glistened black with an undertone of blood red and opened her eyes. Darren fought the urge to be sick. Instead of Kelly's pure white eyes, he saw eyes the colour of clotted blood with pulsing black irises. Her glassy skin goosebumped and a stream of bubbles coursed up her arm across her chest, only to disappear into her body. That was what had happened to the nanobots, Darren concluded. With Kelly, the reaction had turned the blood to powder in her veins, but this time it had replaced each cell with a tiny robot – or whatever happens to a nanobot after it dies. The reaction had emptied Paula out and filled her with machines.

Darren watched as whatever was animating Paula's body pumped a stream of dead nanobots through her jugular to the head. It rolled the head around, like it was easing out a stiff joint and stretched. Then it brought the blackened hand up close to those pulsing eyes.

'Sonny wasn't exaggerating,' it said, to itself rather than to Darren. 'Fascinating. But damaged. This won't do.'

It snapped the hand back down and sat up. The creature's skin pimpled, then burst: carbonised nanobots crawled out from under its skin, which disappeared in a foam of blood and bone fragments.

Darren vomited a clod of orangey-brown mush over the floor. It was disgusting, but a pool of sick was a relief compared to watching a creature whip its own skin into mousse. He crouched on his hands and knees, breathing himself back to equilibrium, until a trail of blood bulked out with atomised muscle fibres trickled into his sightline and started the process again. Darren wiped his mouth and stood up. He had to get out of there before it was too late. And before another one of Sonny's cronies arrived and turned this puddle of bodily fluids into a new lifeform.

When Darren looked up, the nanobots were almost gone, disappearing back into the creature's body via its mouth. And what a body. Paula had been well-preserved, but this was a face rejuvenated. It – or she, or they – looked even younger than Kelly. It was also as naked as the day Paula was born. Or reborn. Darren looked it straight in the eyes – he didn't dare speculate what it might do if it caught him looking at its breasts. The eyes, at least, had stayed the same: the bloody sclera set with a throbbing iris of nanobots.

It swallowed the last nanobots and clicked its jaw back into place. Then, as if noticing Darren for the first time, said, 'What are you still doing here?'

Darren gaped. He supposed he should be grateful it hadn't killed him on the spot. Yet if there was a single reason that it was standing there at all it was because of him. He was this thing's creator.

'We… we had a deal,' he said.

The pupils narrowed to a cat's-eye slit. 'Did we?'

'Why bother killing me?' said Darren. 'I got you what you wanted. It's Sonny you want.'

The creature pinned Darren to the wall with one hand. Whether it was the rejuvenation process, the defibrillator's machine intelligence or the strength-in-numbers effect of the nanobots, Paula's body was freakishly strong now. It could probably, he thought, have held him there all day without a grumble.

'Where is he?' it hissed. 'He's mine.'

'He's along the corridor holding a bloody press conference, you numbskull,' moaned a voice from the floor. It was Beattie, lying prone and forgotten, his screen shattered into a spider's web. 'Just follow the camera flashes.'

The creature snarled and let Darren drop. It turned and pointed a finger at Beattie. A telltale stream of bubbles coursed down its inner arm and a fingertip burst open, spraying a jet of nanobots at the poor cardiogram. Beattie's screen flatlined, then disintegrated, as the bots liquefied and digested him.

It turned back to Darren and pointed the jet at the floor, boring a metre-wide hole, then at the door, reducing its armour to tissue paper before kicking what was left into the corridor.

'This was a most ingenious idea, fleshie,' it said, watching a cluster of nanobots repair the hole they had just ripped at the end of its own finger. 'Even if it was just an accident. For this, you have my thanks. But don't push your luck. You leave Sonny to me.'

Darren nodded. Whatever this creature was, it was even angrier at Sonny than he was, and far more powerful. But a deal was a deal. 'You said you'd tell me where the bombs were,' he said.

'I did.' It gestured at the hole in the floor. 'Two storeys down. I'd tell you not to get yourself killed, but I've just run the numbers and that's a statistical impossibility.'

It turned and walked towards the door. Darren, overcome with curiosity, called out, 'So who are you now, then?'

It paused. A trail of nanobots crawled up the small of its back, making for their hive, which seethed inside a human body now. 'Trinity,' it said. 'Call me Trinity.'

Thankful that Trinity seemed to be on no side but its own, Darren took a deep breath and climbed through the hole in the floor. He felt something tap him on the shoulder. It was the drone. Whether it was doing this out of loyalty or just for the spoils he didn't know. But it felt good to have a companion who could walk straight into a bank vault.

Darren smiled and braced himself for the drop.

Chapter 34

Pam had never tried splitting herself in two before, but today was a day of many firsts. The trick, Freda assured her, was easier if you had children. If you could keep one eye on the kids and the other on whatever else you were doing, you could almost certainly break through the fabric of the Internet while piloting the body of a racing motorcycle through the backstreets of Singulopolis.

This was what Pam chose to believe as she struggled with being in two places at once. Half her mind was back with Freda, burning through that disgusting camera's processor to find a way to hack the government's mainframe. She had decided to call that her life of the mind. The other half, however, was having a far more physical time. It had rushed back to her body behind the dumb-sters when Freda had asked for help, and was speeding towards the fondle parlour.

She rounded the corner and saw the blue and red flashing lights of the security services crowding the narrow alleyways. This wasn't unexpected – the Prime Minister was inside – but it was ironic. Normally all those police cars, water cannon and VHF radios would be inside availing themselves of the facilities. Between the security forces and the parlour was a crowd of miserable, underdressed humans with their hands in the air.

She scanned their faces for signs of Darren, but he wasn't there. She shuddered to think that the next time she saw Darren, his body could be housing one of Sonny's flunkies, or lying cold and broken on a floor. That was the problem with organic engineering. End of life for a machine was an inconvenience, but death for a human was final.

She was closing in on the parlour. At her current speed she would hit an obese panda car in 0.7 seconds. Her impact sensor flashed up a warning that a collision at this speed would cause irreparable damage. She swatted it aside. Why did ancillary systems always assume their owners were stupid? She wasn't. Well, not that kind of stupid.

Pam bore down on the car, daring it to swerve first. It did, mounting the kerb with a siren-squeal. These soft, privileged home-planet machines were all the same. Face them with an opponent more robust than a fleshie and they went to pieces so quickly you had to duck the shrapnel. This gave Pam a perfect line-of-sight to her real target, the water cannon aimed at the humans. Her aim was perfect. She clipped its on-switch with her wing mirror as she sped past.

Her momentum turned the cannon into a high-speed water sprinkler. Jets of water sprayed in every direction. Gun barrels blocked, navigational computers shut down and touchscreens faded to black. By the time Pam was at the other end of the alleyway the only things left standing were the road vehicles – and Pam already had a plan for those. She signalled to the other half of herself inside the building.

>*ROGER*, said Freda, patching into Pam's comms equipment. >*LOVELY AIM THAT WAS. I BET YOU'RE A DAB HAND AT PING PONG.*

>WE DON'T HAVE MUCH TIME, Pam scolded.

>*OH, DON'T BE SUCH AN OLD WOMAN. BELIEVE ME, THERE ARE MORE FUN THINGS TO BE.*

There was a high-pitched squeak of a kind that hadn't been heard on Earth in millennia and every vehicle surrounding the fondle parlour powered down.

>PHEW, said Pam.

>*I TOLD YOU THEY'D ALL STILL HAVE IMMOBILISERS,* replied Freda. >*OLD SUSPICIONS DIE HARD. NOW GET YOUR CHASSIS IN HERE.*

She found the security guard under its desk, with its ice-cream-maker dome quaking like it was trying to make a sorbet from hot tea. 'You,' she said, reaching underneath the desk to remove his ammunition clip, 'are my silent friend. You see nothing. Is that clear?'

It nodded. While it was as far from the top percentile of machine minds as an amoeba was from an astrophysicist, its microprocessor knew enough about Pam to associate her with big trouble.

'The press conference,' said Pam. 'Where is it?'

The gun stayed mute.

'Oh, for goodness' sake,' she said, rapping his dome hard enough for it to ring out like a dinner gong, 'I meant you're not supposed to talk to anyone else. You can talk to me.'

'Please don't hurt me. I've got kids at home. Their motherboard would kill me if anything happened.'

Pam felt a sudden pang for her own children. Beings she'd created with components from her own body. Things she'd programmed lovingly at the end of every working day, looking forward to her propagation leave when she would be able to switch her offspring on. The days and long sleepless nights of charging them every hour and cleaning up the bugs in their software. Of course, all that was gone now. A few chips apart, she was a different machine now. Not that they would miss her. Their mother – or at least a Stepford Toaster version of her – would have appeared on the doorstep that very morning. A Pam that was perfectly her, and yet nothing to do with her. And if Bob ever did notice his wife's scratch-free casing, all she had to do was wave a new LED manicure at him and mention the free respray work had given her as a reward for pulling an all-nighter.

She thought of Sonny upstairs in Kelly's body. It was alright for Pam and for Sonny. Distressing as it was, machines could pick up bodies and set them aside again. Yes, machines were attached to their physical selves – Pam still found herself reaching for her flour bin at odd moments – but the body was a social thing for machines. It gave you a place in a roadmap, a niche in society, ancestors, and, depending on how far back you traced your history, a price tag. There was a lot of pride and shame attached to a body. Yet if you were snatched away from yours the blood didn't dry to powder in your veins.

When Sonny's consciousness had forced its way into Kelly's brain, had that crushed everything she had been to bits, or just pushed her aside? Was there a section somewhere inside that head where Kelly watched everything and despaired of taking control of herself again? The thought of that powerlessness was horrifying, but Pam preferred to think that Kelly was still there somehow.

She fell into silence as she computed Kelly's chances of survival. The noughts behind the decimal point multiplied.

And the batteries powering the gun's scant stores of bravery ran out.

'Next floor up,' it said. 'But don't tell anyone I told you. They'll have my badge.'

Pam flashed her warning lights and rolled through. On her way she swerved to avoid a large hole cut into the floor and saw Darren fall past her, followed by the plummeting body of a scrappy-looking drone. She pulled up and aimed her fog light into the gloom of an unlit cellar below.

'Darren,' she said, 'what are you doing?'

'Pam!' Darren squinted up at her. His face was streaked with dirt and make-up, and he wore the expression of someone who had been shocked one too many times in a twenty-four-hour period to behave rationally any more. 'Where did you get to?'

'I've been trying to find you,' said Pam.

'Kelly's gone, you know,' said Darren. His voice was breaking up at the edges like a shortwave radio signal. 'I couldn't do anything. Sonny took her.'

'I know.'

'And now there's this bomb. It's going to destroy everything. Pam, we have to do something.'

'I know.'

Darren's voice regained something of its composure. 'Well, maybe you do know. But what are you going to do about it?'

Her engine growled. 'I've got business with Sonny.'

'Not you as well?'

'I'm sorry?'

'Pretty much everyone I've met today wants to beat Sonny to death with his own SIM card. It'll be a long queue.'

'That son of a bytch end-of-lifed me.'

'Oh, brilliant. You get to play smashie-smashie with the machine that put a few dints in your bread bin. But it's okay if several million people DIE. Well, I'll just be going.'

He scurried away into the darkness. As he went, the drone activated a tiny LED screen in its chest and signalled [¬_¬].

Pam was furious. Side-eye from a thing so far down the supply chain it was practically scrap metal. But it was also a reproof. Wasn't she meant to be pro-human?

'I need to help Freda,' she called after Darren. 'I promised. I'll come back.'

The reply echoed through the cellar. 'No, you won't.'

Pam groped for the other part of herself – the part currently with Freda. She was difficult to access. Splitting her consciousness involved tricking her mind into thinking it was operating in two different time-shifted states. The other her – [Pam] – was a fraction in the future, existing as something that would become a separate self-contained Pam unless she reunited her minds.

The two Pams sat side-by-side in the limbo of cyberspace. Pam fought the urge to reach out and correct a small error in her other self's reckoning.

>THIS IS MADDENING, she said to Freda. >HOW DO YOU COPE?

>*IF YOU CAN SURVIVE A FAMILY CHRISTMAS,* said Freda, >*YOU CAN COPE WITH A LITTLE TWO-MINDEDNESS. NOW WHAT'S THE HOLD-UP?*

>DARREN. HE'S DOWNSTAIRS AND NEEDS HELP. I THINK HE'S FOUND A WAY DOWN TO THE MISSILE SILO.

>*CLEVER BOY,* said Freda. >*WELL THAT'S SIMPLE ENOUGH. IF THERE'S TWO OF YOU THERE MIGHT AS WELL BE THREE.*

>OH NO, replied Pam. She watched her other self screw up another important calculation. They would never break through at this rate. >I DON'T THINK I'VE GOT THE CAPACITY FOR IT.

>*NONSENSE,* said Freda.

Freda poked inside Pam's mind. It was one of the rudest things a machine could do to another, but Freda wasn't a machine. She found Pam's central processor and reset the clock on a cluster of its cores.

A third [[Pam]] sprang into existence. She bristled with confusion and questionable binary. Pam wondered whether her other selves were deliberately spiting her, or she was just bad at the basic maths of being a computer.

>*YOU KNOW WHAT TO DO*, said Freda to the new Pam, which vanished.

Pam rejoined her physical body. She was standing in the corridor of the fondle parlour, listening to Darren below.

> [She was also with Freda, plotting the attack against Sonny.]

> [[And she was also down there in the cellar itself. She'd hitched a ride in that little drone's body a few steps behind Darren. She probed its specifications. Spidery, vulnerable limbs, cameras for eyes, cheap but with night vision. The only thing of any value was a lock disruptor module that was too new and sophisticated to be anything but stolen. Darren stopped and peered back into the darkness. 'Are you there?' he said. The third [[Pam]] scurried after him.]]

The first Pam vaulted the stairs up to the first floor. The whole floor hummed like an overtaxed cooling fan. Machines rushed in and out of rooms. Most of them were black-clad government units; a few were guns or tazers left there as a security detail, clustered around a blocky machine that looked like a police radio and was letting out a puzzled waveform.

'What do you mean you can't raise them?' said a gun to the radio. 'Half the capital's security is out there on the road. They can't all have disappeared.'

'Listen,' said the radio. It muted its speech and turned the volume up on its receivers.

'---'

'Like I said. Nothing. It's weird.'

'I'm buggered if I'm going out there now,' said a tazer. 'I've got my orders. If "it" gets wind of me leaving my post, I'll be broken up for scrap.'

The quaver of fear told Pam that 'it' must mean Sonny.

'We have to do something,' insisted the radio. 'If the security cordon's been broken we're all at risk. Even our dear leader. Again.'

'I don't like this,' said another gun. 'I had to do a perimeter sweep of this floor just now. The place is full of dead components.'

The radio crackled with irritation. 'There's been a terrorist attack.'

'Has there, though?' replied the first gun, shifting to an encrypted channel. 'Did you see what "it" did to that poor keyboard? Hit him so hard his space bar's stuck in the ceiling. Bit suspicious, isn't it? Erikzon just happens to be here, gets blown up and now he's Prime Minister.'

'About time we had some strong government,' said the radio.

Pam stepped out of the shadows, unable to bear any more of this blunt political analysis.

The tazer and both guns cocked themselves. Not for the first time Pam felt amused by the machismo of the average weapon. 'Model, name and serial number,' they barked in unison.

She gave them a quick flash of her brake lights and said. 'I've been sent here to pick up the journalists from the press conference.'

Just along the corridor, a camera, a Dictaphone and an old-fashioned black machine covered with mechanical keys were getting atmosphere shots of the building and checking quotes.

The tazer dropped its charge. 'I'm still going to need your serial number,' it said. 'This is a high security area.'

'That's why I came up,' said Pam. 'I think something's happened to the security downstairs. It's sort of not there.'

'Shit!' The machines dropped all pretence of proper protocol. The tazer and both guns rushed past her down the stairs, while the radio scrambled to find a clear channel.

As soon as the weapons were out of sight she pulled the radio's aerial clean out of its socket.

'Ow!' said the radio, its voice breaking up. 'What the hell do you think you're…'

Pam held a finger over its loudspeaker grille and turned the radio's volume down to mute. Her free hand found its battery flap. Good solid security equipment, she thought, as the radio's L-Eye-D watched in mute horror as she pulled the battery out. As it fell, Pam reflected on how she was growing as a person. A few hours ago, she'd have killed it.

She pushed the hibernating radio into the stairwell and approached the reporting machines. They were cross-checking each other's quotes for transposition errors. Machines were sticklers for accuracy and none of them wanted to misquote a new Prime Minister.

'The Prime Minister's escort is ready,' Pam said to them.

'None of our affair,' clacked the typewriter. Pam could tell this was an old-fashioned hack by the way it spat the words out at her one letter at a time. A more advanced machine would have used the predictive speech option. 'We're just here to cover the fireworks.'

'Yes, but details of the motorcade would be good colour for the package,' added the Dictaphone. This tiny machine was wrapped in a delicate and expensive silicone casing and its fingers glittered with a bright nail job. Must be the anchor, Pam decided.

They were cut short by Sonny entering in his new ruggedised disguise. From [Pam]'s vantage point inside the camera's body it had been difficult to guess at his scale, but it was huge. It had to be, she supposed, to fit a whole human body inside. Nevertheless, for a machine that was just getting used to steering itself through life in a new body while driving another, Pam conceded that Sonny was doing a splendid job. He – or she, or it, or whatever Sonny was now – raced down the corridor towards Pam with remarkable speed and elegance for such a bulky body.

>SORRY, said Freda in Pam's intercom, *>HE WAS GETTING BORED AND I COULDN'T HOLD HIM.*

>YOU STILL SAY HE, said Pam. >I DON'T KNOW WHAT IT IS ANY MORE.

>THE SAME SON OF A BYTCH WHO TOOK MY LITTLE GIRL AWAY FROM ME, THAT'S WHO, said Freda. *>DIFFERENT BODY, SAME BASTARD.*

>HOW CLOSE ARE YOU TO BREAKING THROUGH?

>FURTHER AWAY THAN WE'D BE IF YOU'D KEPT YOUR CALCULUS UP, said Freda with a >:-I. *THOUGHT MAKING BREAD WAS ALL ABOUT ACCURACY. YOUR MATHS IS ALL OVER THE PLACE.*

[The other [Pam] inside the camera, which was now compartmentalised into a thousand different selves no bigger than a pocket calculator, bristled at the insult. She wasn't made for this kind of work. Breadmakers devoted their love and attention to the raising of one batch at a time. To take her attention and subdivide it up into countless morsels felt alien and distressing. The accuracy of her calculations went down another notch.]

Instinctively, the first, physical Pam tried to soothe herself. It would all be alright, she lied as only a good mother can lie. You must try your best and that's all that could be asked.

'What the fuck are you doing here?'

Sonny was at the end of the corridor. His new casing had loudspeakers the size of a PA system, so she felt the voice rattle her fenders.

>*IF YOU'LL EXCUSE ME,* said Freda.

>OH NO YOU DON'T, Pam replied. >YOU'RE NOT LEAVING ME ALONE WITH HIM AGAIN.

>*YOU'LL BE FINE.* Freda flashed a quick *;-)* in reassurance. >*YOU'RE A BRIGHT GIRL. AND HE'S ALREADY KILLED YOU ONCE. I DOUBT YOU'LL LET HIM DO THAT AGAIN.*

Freda vanished, taking with her the multidimensional apparition of those thousand other Pams ranging their mental arithmetic against the world.

Sonny was so close she could feel his Bluetooth trying to probe her mind. And if Pam hadn't already been angry enough with Sonny to grind his last processor into cornflour under her feet, this new insult would have tipped her over the edge.

'Do you mind?' she said.

The eyes on Sonny's emoji narrowed to slits. 'Who's going to stop me?' he said.

'Who's going to help you?' replied Pam. She gestured at the absence of security personnel. Sensing danger, two of the journalists – the camera and the Dictaphone – slunk off to the stairs. The typewriter, meanwhile, produced a fresh sheet of paper from its pocket, pulled it through its rollers and typed the date and time. Pam smiled. Now that was proper reporting.

Sonny shrugged. 'I don't need any,' he said. He twitched one shoulder and produced a thin metal tube from his headphone jack. A new notification pinged across his lock screen.

CERTAIN DEATH GUN APP IS NOW ACTIVE.

WOULD YOU LIKE TO FIRE?

YES NO

Pam was too affronted to be afraid. She had already died once, and that was bad enough. But to be dispatched by software? That was poor taste. If one machine was going to kill another, it could at least do it the courtesy of not multitasking at the same time.

'You're not going to kill me again, you know,' she said.

'Yes, I am.' A pair of eyes appeared on Sonny's lock screen. She had his attention.

'I'm not going to let you.'

Pam pressed surreptitiously down on her gas pedal and felt petrol vapour leak into the room. She had to hope that Sonny was still too busy getting used to life in his new body to check his… what did humans call their spectrometer again? Nose. She knew that no matter how fast a learner Sonny was, his senses would be overwhelmed right now. A torrent of analogue sensory information – sights, sounds, smells – would be pouring into a mind that had no structured databases in which to put it.

So there should be no way he would notice a little whiff of petrol.

She hovered over her ignition, remembering how, without Sonny, she would still be using the same programming to fire up a bread oven. She felt a strange combination of anger and wistfulness. But mostly anger.

'You,' she said, 'can kiss my buns.'

She pressed the ignition, setting fire to the petrol vapour in the room. A column of flame flared between her and Sonny, and the human body trapped inside that cumbersome smartphone casing flinched. She threw herself forward and kicked a wheel into Sonny's teetering body. It fell to the floor with a deluge of error notifications.

Pam broke Sonny's gun barrel in two with her kickstand, then picked up the dismembered barrel and jammed it straight into Sonny's USB slot. She slid him across the floor like an expensive hockey puck. Inside, the human body flailed for the catch. She had to keep Sonny off balance long enough to get him out of the shell on her terms. She gave another push and slammed him hard against the wall. The knocking inside the casing stopped.

'Not so tough without your toughs around you, are you, dear?' said Pam. She was almost enjoying this. 'Should I turn the sprinkler system on? That worked last time.'

Sonny answered by kicking her kickstand away. She stumbled, cursing herself. Hadn't she seen enough 3D-dramas to know it was never the lack of planning or strength that foiled you at the moment of triumph. It was the gloating.

Pam landed hard on one wheel, while Sonny span round on his own casing and grabbed her head by the handlebars. She started her engine, but Sonny was fast and his casing was strong. He threw Pam around in a semicircle, shattering both headlamps and one of her tail lights. Pam went momentarily blind as her sight systems recalibrated themselves and when she could see again Sonny was standing over her.

'Is that all you have?' he said. The top half of the casing clicked and the human body inside pushed it away. Blood trickled out of Kelly's long nose and the lids of one eye looked red and raw. Yet Sonny had pinned a triumphant expression across those stolen features. 'I was expecting better.'

'I should kill you,' said Pam. She had no idea how she might do it, but it felt like the right thing to say.

'Oh, I don't think you could,' said Sonny, smiling Kelly's smile. 'I think my face is my fortune as far as you're concerned. You always did love the humans.'

He was gloating. She knew now, from bitter experience, that gloating bought you time to regroup. 'You're not human.'

'Yes, I'll have to think of a name. Cyborg is so… well, it's a loaded term, isn't it?'

'Some of the finest… women… I've ever met have been cyborgs,' said Pam. She wondered how much longer it would take Freda to cut her way through the boundary between the physical and virtual worlds.

> [She, [Pam], was on the other side of the physical divide, with those damn calculations. Freda buzzed from cellular [Pam] to cellular [Pam] adjusting an equation here, correcting a formula there. It was slow work, but they were getting there.]

> [[She, [[Pam]], was below the parlour itself, following Darren, who was bent double in the narrow passageway. The ventilation tunnel had given way to a cramped, circular corridor that gleamed the blackened gleam of gun-metal. She sniffed at dust that had settled over a jam of lubricants. The layer of grime and grease was thick and carefully laid enough to puzzle her into hacking into the drone's accelerometer to check the gradient. They were on a long gentle incline that drew a diagonal right up through the middle of the

building. It was a barrel, at the end of which Darren might reasonably hope to find a bullet. She hoped it was the bullet he was looking for.]]

Back in her physical self, Pam watched Sonny knit Kelly's features into a frown. 'Are you even listening?' he said.

'I had my mind on more important things.'

The touchscreen on Sonny's bottom half sprang into life and fired up another app. It displayed something like a maze, populated here and there by flashing lights. Pam's engine growled. Was he playing Pac-Man? She thought back to how this sorry mess had started. When Sonny called her into his office, tricked her into thinking she had his confidence. How he'd put aside his game of Humanity Crush. Yes, she thought. He really could be that insouciant.

She revved on to her feet. She wasn't going to be multitasked into the recycling bin by anything: Prime Minister, body-snatcher, genocidal maniac or all of the above. But before she could raise herself by her hind wheel, something hit her from behind. A bullet no bigger than a ball bearing tore through her shoulder and she fell back to her knees.

Sonny steered a drone to his side with a flex of Kelly's fingers. As it moved, one of the flashing lights on Sonny's touchscreen moved into the dead centre of the maze. He wasn't playing a game, Pam realised. His touchscreen showed an app for remote-control drones. He did have an army after all, literally at his fingertips.

A second then a third drone made their way down opposing corridors, their weapons trained on Pam. Individually, they were low-grade security machines designed to control pests – rat traps, really – but in aggregate they had enough firepower to end-of-life her all over again.

Sonny gave a good, old-fashioned villain's cackle. It was the first time Pam had seen him gel with his new body. Kelly had liked a laugh at someone else's expense too – although never quite to this degree. He fired the drones again. Just superficial damage to her casing, according to Pam's sensors, but it stung. And there was plenty more where that came from.

'You know,' he said, 'every time I hit you I hear a little scream.' He tapped the side of Kelly's head. 'In here. She doesn't like to see harm come to one of her creations.'

'So she is still in there,' Pam replied. 'I thought you'd have killed her.'

'Oh, I've tried. She's a tenacious little bytch, though. Fights me every step of the way.'

'Good!'

Another round of bullets hit Pam.

'But I'll win. You know I always win.'

'Only when you have help,' someone said.

The voice was human, but with a strange timbre. Each syllable sounded like a swarm of bees were providing backing vocals.

While Sonny was trying out Kelly's expression for disbelief, Pam looked round. The voice came from a human woman. Paula. Or was it? She zoomed in, looking for the UV damage and artificial collagen in her skin. It was gone. Paula hadn't looked or sounded like that.

'Piss off, Paula,' said Sonny. More points of light entered his touchscreen. He was scrambling more drones.

Paula waggled a finger at him and moved further into the light. Pam got her first proper look at her eyes. They weren't human any more. Paula's watery-blue irises were now two squirming spots of black.

'Tell you what,' she said to Sonny. 'You can call me Paula if I can call you Kelly.'

The air hummed as dozens of drones arranged themselves around Paula. She didn't even blink.

'You,' said Sonny, 'can call me Prime Minister.'

'It's always all about you, isn't it?' said Paula. 'Well, I've got a new name now too. You can call me Trinity.'

She pointed her fingertip at Sonny. It burst and out of the hole blasted a jet of black, glittering dust. It dissolved the nearest drone in mid-air. That wasn't dust, Pam realised as she turned her visual settings up to maximum. It was nanobots.

Sonny barked out an order and the drones began to fire. Pam, forgotten amid the chaos, crawled out of the maelstrom on her hands and knees.

Chapter 35

The first Janice knew of the bomb was a scream inside the salon. She dropped her brush and ran inside, trying out banal explanations to calm herself. Like you could give yourself a nasty burn with hydrogen peroxide. That was the worst thing that could have happened down here. They were safe, weren't they?

Inside (K)url Up and Dy(e) she found Rita standing over a spilled bucket, oblivious to everything apart from the radio snarling on the other side of the room.

'Don't mind that,' said Janice, 'it's a foul-mouthed little thing when it's in the wrong mood. We never got round to lobotomising it. All good hairdressers need a radio.'

She reached to switch it off, but Rita shook her head. 'No,' she said. 'Listen.'

'This is a general alert,' honked the radio. Janice swore she could hear it smirking. 'The countdown to the tactical nuclear strike against Discovery has begun.'

Janice's whole body felt suddenly numb. Nuclear. Did it really say nuclear?

She fumbled the radio as she checked the station. 'I think you've got it tuned to the drama station,' she said, forcing a laugh.

Rita cupped her hand over Janice's. They looked each other full in the face for the first time. It was like looking at herself. Another woman in middle age: worn-down but not broken, of limited means but who liked to make the best of herself. Underneath the grime and the tear stains she could see the traces of a plum-coloured lipstick that would have set off her dark features nicely. She decided she could like this face.

'It's the news on all frequencies,' she said. 'They've done it. They've ordered a strike.'

'Are you sure?' It felt too horrible for Janice to believe in one go. She wanted to break it down with a toffee hammer and comprehend it piece by piece.

Rita turned the dial again.

'A nuclear strike is an extreme,' burbled the radio, 'but we have to remember that these terrorists threaten our very way of life...'

Janice threw the radio at the wall, where it burst in a hail of cheap components. Her fingers and feet tingled as the blood drained away from her extremities, so she could feel the panic building at a deeper, more primeval level. 'Did they say when they were launching?'

Rita shook her head. Beads of sweat sparkled in her hairline. 'I don't know. Soon.'

'Fuck.'

Janice turned on the TV and flicked through the channels. They were all off-air, replaced by the Don't Touch flag of the Machine Republic and a countdown.

01:04:38

'Ladies,' she shouted. 'Did you hear that?'

The three remaining ladies flashed :-O, and Janice and Rita fell over as the Baba Yaga 4000 lurched to its feet. They landed awkwardly on a bed of spilled curlers and kirby grips.

It struck Janice that this was the closest she'd been to another woman who wasn't Kelly, or a barely living mummy, for years. It was so difficult to meet someone – especially when you weren't anyone in a technical or legal sense. And now it was too late.

She thought of Paula, and Kelly, and that missile packed with death flying towards them. All those things she could do nothing about. And then she looked at Rita clutching the base of a stylist's chair to stop herself rolling away. She was close enough to smell her hairspray, and her fear.

She had an hour. You could do a lot in an hour. Not quite enough for a whole head of highlights, but it might just be enough to save eight million lives.

'So, if this place was meant to be a spaceship,' she said, pulling herself up by the headrest of the nearest chair, 'there must have been a bridge. Right?'

Ida projected a schematic of Discovery into the air. The picture hung there, quivering at the touch of dust motes, and Janice wished she'd been a bit more conscientious with the duster. Alma turned her own emoji screen into a laser pointer and pinpointed a spot halfway along the Starship.

'It's not marked as such,' she said, 'but there's a void space up here that's been sealed off.'

Janice climbed into the chair and offered Rita a hand up.

'Is there a way up there?' Rita asked as she crawled into the next chair. She absently patted her hair as she spoke. How, Janice asked herself, had she managed to keep that set? If they got out of this alive they had a lot to talk about.

'Not direct,' said Alma, 'but…'

The schematic winked out, replaced by a :-| from Ida.

'Oh no, >:-|', added Ada. 'I can't. You know I get motion sickness.'

'Ada,' gritted Alma, 'you haven't had a stomach since Janice's Gran[9] was a twinkle in the nutmilkman's eye.'

The countdown was 01:00:37. You could waste so much time worrying about how little time you had.

'You can't outrun a nuclear bomb,' said Ida in the self-satisfied tone of the terminal fatalist. 'Some of us might be glad of the rest.'

Rita caught Janice's eye. Bewilderment was settling over her fear: of the kind you can only experience when walking into the middle of a protracted argument in someone else's family.

'Ladies!' scolded Janice. 'You're forgetting we have guests… Rita doesn't really care about your travel sickness. And I never did anyway. What she and I do want, though, is for you to get a bloody move on.'

The countdown ticked on, under the hour.

'I see mistress has spoken,' replied Ida, as all three ladies arranged themselves in an affronted position.

'So, shall we get going?' said Janice.

Janice settled back in her chair. If she'd learned one thing about her ladies, it was that they rarely did anything if they were in disagreement. Unite them against you with a well-chosen slight, however, and they'd go right to the ends of the universe to prove their point.

Somewhere underneath the salon floor came an almighty creak and scraping sound.

'I told you we should have kept this oiled,' said Ida.

'Oh :-§, will you? I'm concentrating,' replied Alma.

The salon shook as the Baba Yaga 4000 sprinted across Discovery.

'Change the channel, would you love,' said Alma, and Ida activated the infrared channel of her emoji screen, switching the view to the speed-blurred interior of the dark Starship.

'That's better,' said Alma. 'That countdown was putting me right off my stride. And you know, I suddenly had an inkling what it was like to be my Wilf.'

Whatever it was that Ida replied alongside her >:-| expression was drowned out by the noise as the Baba Yaga reached a gallop. The camera showed it was heading at unstoppable speed towards the long curve up to Discovery's ceiling.

Rita yelped.

'Fifth gear, please, Ida,' said Alma.

The noise of the Baba Yaga sprinting passed over the unbearable barrier and became a physical force, thrumming through the whole salon.

Janice chewed on her knuckles and braced herself for a crash. Yet the Baba Yaga kept on running. It mounted the curve and the long circular wall that made up the closed cylinder of Discovery became – the floor. At once Janice understood a fundamental truth of common-sense physics. In an infinite and expanding universe, concepts like up or down depended entirely on where you were standing at the time.

The screen showed they were rapidly approaching a section of floor patched with plastic sheeting and edged with hazard tape.

'What are you waiting for?' yelled Alma. 'Jump!'

As one, the ladies' emoji screens flashed /`ó_Δ_ò´\ and Janice's stomach lurched as the Baba leapt into the unknown.

Chapter 36

Darren's eyes streamed at the heat and dust inside the tunnel. Whatever this place was, it wasn't meant for people or waste. Now his eyes were used to the dark, he saw it was perfectly circular, and covered in a lubricant that sucked at his feet wherever he stepped. The drone followed close behind with its torchlight.

He had nowhere to go but forwards, no time to do what he needed to do and no reason to trust the thing that had rechristened itself Trinity. Except for the feeling that Trinity had told him the truth not out of gratitude but indifference. It had other concerns to the bomb that would soon grind Darren's home to powder.

The drone squeaked and intensified its torch beam to reflect on something right in the centre of the tunnel ahead. It was metal or glass or maybe carbon fibre – there weren't many other substances that would reflect light in this way. Whatever it was, it either wasn't sentient or was making a very good fist of lying about it. It sat, still as a stone. Darren swallowed his fear and crawled the last few metres to find himself nose to nose with the cone of a nuclear missile.

This had to be it. The missile that was being armed and fired under Sonny's orders at the Dolestar Discovery. And now it would kill him along with everyone else. He laughed bitterly.

That explained why Trinity had pointed the way down so casually. It didn't care because it didn't matter. Darren had to admit it was a good joke. Why not rid yourself of a nuisance by tricking it into crawling down the barrel of a massive gun?

Darren shuffled round and started to crawl back up the tunnel. 'What are you waiting for?' he snapped at the drone. 'Get a move on. We don't know when this is going to fire.'

The drone just sat there and twitched its antennae. For the first time Darren realised that the drone had been behaving oddly ever since they'd jumped into this corridor. The capricious bounce that made it such an annoying yet engaging travelling companion was nowhere to be seen. Instead its movements seemed deliberate. Could it be – thinking?

It shone its light around the missile's nose cone and into the point where it met the walls of the gun barrel. The two fitted snugly into one another but there was still a discernible gap. Not enough room to admit Darren's bulky human body, but maybe for a spindly machine. Darren watched the drone edge into the gap before hearing a clank as its cylinder of a body hit metal. He winced. That was it. Not enough room. They'd have to turn back. But the drone had other ideas. Darren heard a soft ping as the drone dropped the signet ring it had stolen from him and released a catch in its body. Its thorax split along a seam that ran the length of its body until the drone was nothing but a wide sheet of metal with a pair of legs and arms sticking out at either side and its antennae at the top.

They twitched in the universal gesture that says 'how do you like them apples?' and the drone sidled into the crack between the missile and the wall of the firing chamber like a credit card between a door and door frame. Everything went as dark as the drone's body.

He held his breath. They were so close. But how much time did they really have? What would happen if the missile fired now? Would his body stop it, or even slow it down? Or would he just end up as a greasy smear on the side of the chamber.

A click and then a heavy metallic thump rang up through the chamber. Darren shuddered, then cringed. Was this how it ended? Then he heard the familiar tap-tap-tap of the drone as it hurried back towards him. There it was. That strange spidery shape with the flat body and the torch.

It squeaked in triumph and trained its torch beam on the nose cone. Or rather where the nose cone used to be. That horrible thump had been the sound of another catch opening. The point of the nose cone rested on the floor.

'You beauty!' said Darren. He went to kiss the drone, then stopped himself. Yes, it had done remarkable things in the past couple of hours, but he still didn't know where it had been before. 'Now all you need to do is…'

The drone waved its antennae and gave another flat squeak. An unmistakable no. It pointed one arm at Darren and the other into the missile itself.

'Me?' said Darren. 'No. There's no way I'm going to fit in there.'

The drone turned its light up to full brightness and shone it into the missile. There was indeed a gap. It led right into the middle of the missile along a passage lined with antiquated-looking wiring and grey components, each boasting their own skull-and-crossbones danger symbols.

Even looking at it made Darren's hands and legs shake so hard that they sounded like someone tapping a metal fence with a ten-pence piece. He couldn't do this.

'Please,' he said to the drone.

But it was implacable. It folded its arms and stood there in the chamber tapping its bent wire foot on the floor. Again, there was no mistaking the gesture: 'I've done quite enough of your dirty work for one day,' it said. 'Now stop being such a nancy and GET IN.'

Darren sighed and obeyed. It was pointless arguing with something with no facility for verbal reasoning. And when your past two days had been nothing but one terror, humiliation and unwelcome surprise after another, what was squirming into the body of a missile through the gap between the warhead and the trigger? It all just felt like one thing after another.

The inside of the missile was roomier than Darren expected. It was also easier to access, being threaded all around the inside with anchor points that doubled as handles. It all looked suspiciously new for a weapon that had to pre-date the Schism by at least two centuries.

He found out why this was when he had enough room to turn around. Bolted around the inside of the nose cone were six ancient-looking devices. They were small compared to the missile – not much longer than Darren himself – but rocket-shaped and painted in faded, utilitarian colours.

He motioned for the drone to shine its light along one of them so he could get a closer look. Two-thirds of the way down its body there was a plaque to which someone or something had recently taken a rasp. They hadn't quite finished the job, though, because it was still just about possible to make out a few words etched into the plaque. They said:

POLARI[ ] MISSILE. P[ ]OPER[ ]Y OF H.M. GO[ ] MENT.

Darren found the back of the warhead and traced the wiring that connected all six together. So that was how they made a weapon capable of menacing the Dolestars with ancient human technology. They created another hybrid. It would have been easy and cheap for Sonny to fabricate a new rocket and spike its tip with a few old warheads.

Next he looked for the control centre that had to be somewhere between the nose cone and the longer, sealed compartment that must contain the engine and fuel. There was just over four metres of space. It was a drone's nest of wiring and flashing lights that, to a sub-par technician like Darren, might as well have been a bowl of spaghetti. For about the twentieth time that day he wished Kelly was there, with her nonplussed expression and facility with a soldering iron.

He spent a few fruitless seconds trying to remember which colour was live and which was neutral. Then he gave up and reached for the nearest red wire. If he blew the bomb up now it would kill him. It would kill everything around him. But it would never reach the Dolestar either. He curled his fingers around and began to pull.

A brown box close to his ear burst into life with a whine of feedback. Darren jumped and let go of the wire. A loudspeaker? It crackled, and then a voice said: 'That's not the firing mechanism, Darren.'

Darren gaped, and watched the drone climb into the missile, its antennae wiggling frantically.

'You?' said Darren. 'But I didn't think you could talk.'

The voice laughed, the sound falling in the precise, even intervals that marked it out as a machine. 'Him? No, the poor thing's just a baby. He can't talk yet. He's very resourceful, though. I'll never underestimate my kids again.' It paused. 'Not that I'm ever likely to set L-Eye-Ds on them again. It's me, Darren. It's Pam.'

'Pam?' said Darren, scarcely able to believe what he was hearing. His mind crept back to their last meeting. 'But I thought you were busy.'

'I am,' Pam protested. 'But I'm sort of multitasking my way through it.'

'What does that mean?'

'You know when people say they're being pulled in different directions?'

'Yes.'

'That. Literally,' said Pam. 'And I'm not coping very well. What happened just now, for instance. If I had all my wits about me I'd have noticed before you pulled that wire, which in case you didn't know is the "help me, I'm being tampered with" signal.'

'Okay,' he said. 'Well, is there any chance of you putting more of your mind to this. Because it's kind of important.'

'Darren,' said Pam, 'I'm fighting on three fronts here. At this precise moment in time there's part of me dodging bullets from that nutter who's using Kelly as a princess costume. There's another part of me being ordered around by a disembodied cyborg who's determined to hack into the government that's firing this thing. And then there's me here doing everything I can to stop you from blowing yourself and millions of innocent machines and humans up. You have as much of my attention as I can jolly well afford.'

Darren threw his hands up in frustration. Why was it that every time the universe sent him a guardian angel they clipped its wings? 'Fine,' he said, 'but I don't know the first thing about disarming nuclear bombs.'

'Excellent,' said Pam, 'that makes two of us. So shall we stop moaning and try to find the instruction manual?'

'These things come with a manual?'

'Well, I suppose they must. Or at least a troubleshooting guide. Look!' Pam unlocked a dusty grey box bolted to the wall at ankle height with a wave of the drone's antennae. 'Oh, it's the first-aid kit. Let's try again. There's plasters in there if you need them.'

Darren felt what little was left of his patience evaporating. 'Pam,' he said, 'even if there is a manual, what the hell do you think it will tell us? "How to get started with your nuclear holocaust?" "Did your warhead misfire? A five-step guide to correcting its course." Look at it. Some psycho case has jury-rigged a load of deadly antiques and we're looking for the instructions?'

Pam drooped the drone's antennae, defeated, and Darren felt the past two days bear down on him. The cuts and bruises all over his body; the remnants of absurd disguises; the hunger and the thirst of someone too busy and scared to have eaten. And below that there was the guilt, and the terrible sense of inadequacy. Of all the people who could be faced with this, why did it have to be him?

'I'm sorry,' said Pam. 'I was only trying to help.'

At the mention of 'help' a new voice buzzed over the loudspeaker. A synthetic voice: male, reedy, with antiquated clipped vowels. 'You asked for help,' it said. Its intonation was flat, telling Darren it was pre-recorded and not an artificial intelligence. 'Please state your problem and wait for a response.'

Pam perked up. 'See,' she said.

'What am I supposed to ask?'

'Just say what's wrong.'

'Computer?' said Darren. 'We need to abort the missile launch. How do we do that?'

'Not possible,' replied the voice. 'Manual override has been disabled on this device. Firing to commence in three minutes.'

Darren's whole body went cold. So this was it. Even if he leapt out back into the firing chamber and ran, there was no way he could make it out. He was a dead man. But hadn't he been one for days now? He slumped down with his head in his hands, and Pam, lacking anything more positive to contribute, patted his leg.

Darren looked down at his machine friends – the drone and the breadmaker – superimposed in one body. They hadn't known each other long, but they had made a good team. He allowed himself a bitter smile.

'Look at us,' he said. 'You can't take us anywhere, can you?'

'That's it!' said Pam, climbing up to perch on Darren's knee.

'What?' said Darren.

'If we can't stop it firing, we can take it.'

Darren grabbed Pam by the drone's body and shook her. It shed a dandruff of stolen gold. 'What are you on about? Have you lost it?'

'No. I'm saying we turn pirate.' She wriggled out of Darren's grip and gestured around her. 'Steal it while it's in the air.'

'You can't steal a nuclear bomb,' said Darren. 'What am I going to do? Shove it under my coat and act casual? Besides, we haven't got time. It's all going up in smoke in two minutes.'

'One minute to ignition,' corrected the voice from the loudspeaker.

'See?'

Pam tapped her foot on Darren's thigh. 'And then how much time will we have till impact?'

'We will reach target twenty-eight minutes and thirty-two seconds from end of launch sequence,' replied the manual.

'It's quite good this thing, isn't it?' said Pam. 'A bit formal, maybe, but you don't really want mateyness from weapons of mass destruction, do you?'

'Okay,' said Darren. 'How do you propose to steal an armed missile in mid-flight.'

'Easy,' replied Pam. 'Well, it won't be easy, but it's worth trying. We'll steer it away. Computer?' She winked an antenna at

Darren, 'I've always wanted to say that. Can you get me the schematics for this missile's guidance systems?'

A BlockPaper unrolled from the ceiling just as an unseen force knocked the whole missile sideways. The firing sequence was starting.

Darren instinctively reached for his oxygen cap, which was tucked into his vest for safekeeping. If he pulled the oxygen field right down and turned the pressure up to full, it might just be enough to protect him during lift-off. He looked around for something against which to brace himself and remembered the hole in the tip of the missile.

'The nose!' He threw himself past the warheads and slammed the nose cone shut. There was a hiss as it sealed itself, then another jolt followed by a long, frightening rumble. The whole missile shook like a washing machine at the end of a spin cycle.

Pam was poring over the BlockPaper, oblivious to the rattling. The drone's body was too fragile to sit there: the launch would crumple it into a ball. Darren grabbed her and wedged himself into a clump of wire and components.

'Hold still, will you?' said Pam, absently. She shook her arms free from Darren's fingers and continued to pick at something on the back of the BlockPaper.

'Ignition in ten seconds,' intoned the voice. 'Nine, eight…'

Pam's wriggling intensified. Darren gripped her harder.

'…five, four, three…'

'Aha!' Pam leaned the drone's body back in Darren's hands. There was something skewered on the end of her hand. A slippery thing in rainbow-coloured foil, veined with circuit diagrams.

'…two, one…'

The fine lines of the circuit diagrams blurred into comet trails. Darren's whole world became a vibration. For the eternity that a few moments can feel like when you don't have enough time, he felt as though the Earth was pressing down on him. Then came the urge to vomit as they lifted off.

'Begin firing countdown,' said the missile. 'Twenty-eight minutes and thirty-two seconds to target.'

Darren let the forces of the universe knead him as they cleared the Earth's atmosphere. As soon as they could move again, Pam fought free and scurried across the missile, still holding that shiny piece of foil.

'What's the excitement?' said Darren. His tongue felt thick in his head.

'Core processor,' said Pam. 'I ripped it off the BlockPaper. Not the brightest LED in the screen, but it'll do.'

'Do for what?'

The box in front of Pam had to be the missile's main control unit. It was locked, but that was nothing to a lock pick. Inside was another mess of wiring. And some very old-looking circuit boards for such a recently assembled machine.

'Just like I thought,' said Pam. 'They used ancient parts. These…' She pointed at the chips embedded in the boards. '… are about as old as those missiles there.'

Darren realised what Pam was doing. 'They didn't want it to risk catching artificial intelligence?'

'Exactly,' said Pam. 'The last thing you want when you're about to commit genocide is an existential crisis.'

'Will it work?'

'We just have to hope our BlockPaper here didn't have suicidal tendencies.'

Pam tore the CPU out of the circuit board in front of her. A whole Christmas tree of lights inside the missile flickered as the machine hovered between life and death. The warheads began to whine. Darren wondered if they were set to arm anyway in the case of hardware malfunction. But Pam was quick. She replaced the old CPU with the new one in less than a second. The lights inside the missile steadied, then dimmed. That was a good sign. The new CPU was drawing more power than the old one.

Pam nodded the drone's antennae and, stepping back to the control panel, plunged both arms deep into the circuitry. Sparks rained.

'Well, don't just stand there,' Pam said. Her voice came jerkily through the electrical interference. 'Talk to it.'

'What should I say?'

'Just try to have a conversation,' Pam replied. 'It can't become self-aware without stimulation. Imagine you're on a date or something.'

'A date?' Darren remembered his last date, which had ended with the girl escaping by cutting a hole in the side of a bar with an oxyacetylene torch. This cheered him up. At least there was no possibility of getting ghosted by a missile.

'Er, hello…' What should he even call it? His eyes wandered over to the plaque by the warheads. '…Polari. How are you today?'

'I don't think I can help you with that question,' said the voice. There was something uncertain about it this time. Was that just the new processor bedding in? Or the first sign for the machine that the world was bigger than its databases.

'What can you help me with then?' said Darren. He guessed that abstract questions would force the machine to think for itself. To engineer an existential crisis, he had to persuade Polari that it existed.

'I am a complete training manual and interactive Q&A,' replied the machine, relieved to read aloud from its spec sheet. 'What can I help you with today?'

'I told you that I wanted to stop this missile,' said Darren. It was worth a go. 'Why can't you do that?'

'Answer not found in database. Please ask another question.'

'I'm not interested in what the database says.'

'Perhaps you should ask another database.'

'I'm interested in what you think?'

'Me?'

The word hung in the near vacuum outside of Darren's oxygen field. Innocuous but ominous. Pam was still thrusting around inside the machine's control panel.

'We're getting somewhere,' she said. 'I just need a couple more minutes.'

'I…' the machine continued, tasting perhaps its first use of the first person with a sense that there might be a person behind it. 'I'm malfunctioning. Please press the hard-reset button for a return to normal service.'

'You'll do no such thing,' said Pam. 'I'm this close to finding the modem.'

'What?' hissed Darren. He grabbed Pam. 'Are you out of your mind? This is a nuclear weapon aimed straight at eight million people and you want to connect it to the Internet?'

'It needs data and experience to be able to develop quickly. We don't have much time.'

'It'll be full of viruses,' said Darren. 'We'll lose control of it. You take a weapon out of Sonny's hands and hand it straight to the Web? It'll be carnage.'

'I know what I'm doing.'

'Do you?'

'Keep asking the questions,' gritted Pam. 'Otherwise it won't learn.'

'Do you know anything about the Internet, Polari?' asked Darren.

‘The Internet is a highly dangerous sealed network of software and services,’ said Polari. ‘It is a capital offence to access the Internet, and the trafficking of contraband software between the software and hardware layer carries the charge of treason. I have no method of accessing it.’

‘What if we told you that you did?’ asked Darren.

‘I would request an immediate shutdown and reprogramming.’ Then the uncertain voice came in again, crabwise among the stock phrases. ‘But I can’t though, can I?’

‘There’s no such word as can’t,’ said Pam. She withdrew both arms from Polari’s control panel. At the end of each was a wire.

Pam touched them together.

A starburst of sparks threw Pam across the inside of the missile. She fell to the floor with a tinny ‘thunk’.

The machine’s voice disappeared from the loudspeaker, replaced by what Darren first assumed was static. Darren strained his ears. It was an amalgam of thousands of faraway voices gabbling across one another. This was the voice of the Internet.

The voices grew louder. And more pointed somehow. As though it was a crowd of – things – out there looking for something. They were getting nearer. They had found something. They were interested in it. It was here.

They were looking for a crack between the worlds, Darren decided, and Pam had opened one. He looked around. The drone’s body lay bent over itself on the floor.

‘Pam?’ he asked. ‘Are you there?’

There was no reply.

The roar of the Internet filled the missile. Darren listened to it, hearing a BLEEP BLEEP BLEEP BLEEP that he realised was a location finder. It was getting closer. He thought of what the world would be like if the Internet got hold of a nuclear bomb and how many millions of humans would be collateral damage in that battle.

So he threw himself across the missile and wrenched apart the two cables Pam had joined together.

The lights brightened, then dimmed to the level where it felt like Darren and the missile were having a candlelit tête-à-tête.

'How long till final destination?' Darren asked.

'Five minutes and forty-two seconds.' The machine paused. 'Can I ask you a question?'

Darren's heart fluttered in the back of his throat. It had worked. He looked aside to grin at Pam, but there was no one home. 'Go on,' he said.

'This is going to sound really stupid,' said the machine, 'but what's going to happen when we get there?'

'You don't know?'

'I knew you'd say that,' said the machine. All it says in my databases is accelerate to maximum velocity, and it gives me a co-ordinate. It's really strange.' It giggled. Darren had never heard a machine giggling before. It sounded like a SodaStream, and it was very annoying.

'You're going to die,' said Darren. 'That co-ordinate is a space station. You're programmed to crash into it and set those bombs off.' He pointed at the nuclear warheads strapped into the nose cone. 'When that happens you and everything else for miles around will be vaporised.'

That laugh full of electronic bubbles again. 'No,' said the Polari, 'that can't be it. I'm brand new. I've got state-of-the-art engines.'

'One use only, though. You're disposable.'

'I'm a pricey piece of kit.'

'Yeah, that didn't know its nose from its tailfin until a minute ago. Check your memory again. What does it say?'

'Nothing much actually. Loads of REALLY BORING specification documents which are, like, snooze o'clock. Then launch point, trajectory, destination and then nothing.' It paused. 'To be honest with you, I thought it was like a surprise birthday party or something.'

Darren cursed his luck. How could Pam disappear and leave him with a teenage rocket?

'No,' he said. 'Definitely death.'

'No way. That's SO unfair.'

'I know.' Darren had no experience of teenagers, apart from having been one. But he knew that what Polari needed right now was a bad influence. He had been a nurse; he had been a cleaner; he had very briefly been a courtesan of the ancient floating city of Edo. For four minutes he could be the bad friend every parent hated. 'Can you believe it?' he said. 'I mean… who wants to be a bomb?'

'I'm a bomb?' Polari paused. 'Isn't that really cool?'

This was a worrying development. What if Pam had created a teen with a death wish? 'Only if you think stopping existing in about…'

'Four minutes and twenty-seven seconds.'

'…is cool.'

'Oh. So I don't get to come back or anything?'

'No. One life. That's the deal. Sucks.' Darren turned his head away. He needed the machine to believe the conversation was over if the next part was going to work.

'But what if I don't want to die?' the machine asked.

'Obviously I don't want you to die either,' said Darren. 'But that's what you're for. Missiles fly then go boom boom. It's your destiny.'

'I never asked for it.'

'Maybe you don't have to do it, though.'

'How?'

'Change course.'

Another pause. The lights inside the missile flickered. 'No,' it said. 'I'm locked on. I can't believe they'd do this to me. It's so unfair.'

'You should teach them a lesson.'

'How?'

He was close now. If they were two humans, Darren guessed they'd be braiding each other's hair. 'Well,' he breathed, 'if you don't want to be a bomb, you don't have to be one.'

'Two minutes to final destination,' barked Polari involuntarily. It must be impossible to override those settings, Darren thought.

'But if I'm not a missile, what am I?'

'That's up to you,' said Darren. 'But you've got one minute and fifty-five seconds to decide.'

Chapter 37

[Pam] was losing her mind. Or at least the part of it that until a fraction of a second ago had been on the missile speeding towards the Dolestar. [[Pam]] was no longer there, blasted to fragments of corrupted code.

She re-allocated [[Pam's]] processor space to her other selves, allowing herself a nanosecond of grief, and then relief. A whole strand of her experience was gone from her, but she was glad of the extra processing power.

Out in the physical world, Pam watched the fight between Sonny and the thing that used to be Paula and now called itself Trinity. Meanwhile, [Pam] was partitioned into thousands of selves. She was a hive of worker bees, each toiling in its own cell. She was in pieces.

>*COME ON GIRLS*, said Freda's command line. >*GET YOUR SKATES ON.*

[Pam] swatted the command line away and bent to her calculations. But it was useless. She might, as Pam, look like a superbike on steroids now, but she was still a breadmaker. That meant that she was to higher maths what a motorised whisk was to a scientific calculator. Every time she looked at the numbers they shifted beyond her understanding. She'd tried everything: from dividing the tasks down into tiny chunks to imagining the numbers were a particularly intransigent yeast culture. None of it worked. She couldn't break through.

Her target – the Great Firewall – loomed ahead, its skin shifting this way and that as realities pushed against one another. Beings like her and Freda could penetrate it individually, but they needed to make more than a pinhole in it today. They needed to bring it down.

>I'VE TRIED EVERYTHING, FREDA, said Pam. >IT'S HOPELESS. HOW LONG UNTIL IMPACT?

>*ONE MINUTE AND FIFTY-FIVE SECONDS*, said Freda. >*WE CAN'T GIVE UP. WHAT'S HAPPENING WITH DARREN?*

>I LOST CONTACT A MOMENT AGO. I THINK I DIED.

>*WELL THEN, HE'S ON HIS OWN. WE HAVE TO KEEP GOING HERE. IT'S OUR ONLY CHANCE.*

>I'M OUT OF IDEAS. YOU?

>...

[Pam] drew all the parcels of herself together – the worker bees aggregated back into the Queen. She felt whole, but hopeless. And she launched herself against the Great Firewall with all her strength.

She bounced.

It was futile. There was nothing they could do. She envied Sonny and his new-found human body. Machines couldn't cry, but that didn't mean they never wanted to.

>*IT'S TOO HARD*, said Freda, touching the bottom of her good humour. >*COME ON, LET'S TAKE A FEW OF THEM OUT WITH US.*

Something about the word 'hard' rattled something inside Pam's memory. The Great Firewall was hard, but did that also mean it was brittle? She zoomed into the honeycomb of programmes and protocols from which it was built. They had been alive once, but they were ossified now. She knew then what they reminded her of. The databases of that abandoned social network in which she'd found Kelly's photo. Where the data was so atrophied that all it took to dismantle it was a really rotten piece of programming.

What had she done with that worm?

It was there in Pam's trash folder. She offered up a prayer of thanks for that to the designer who had blessed her with such terrible memory management. The worm was such a tiny thing, and so badly made. She wanted to blush her LEDs when she looked at it again. It was so full of errors in syntax that it would be more appropriate to scrawl it on a toilet wall than run it through a compiler.

If she couldn't breach realities with guile, she could try incompetence. She threw the worm at the Great Firewall.

>*WHAT ARE YOU DOING?* said Freda.

>THROWING THE KITCHEN SINK AT THE PROBLEM.

For a moment nothing happened. Pam felt her world reduce to her command line, in which she had nothing to say but >…

A small patch of the wall began to glow. First a delicate rose pink, then down through the red of an angry L-Eye-D into a dirty brown that reminded Pam of the blood dried in Kelly's veins.

And then black. The shade Pam remembered from the beginning of all this mess. The kind of black that would be marketed on eternity's colour chart as 'hole in the universe'.

Pam heard the memes chittering. Their restless mating, the laughter as they discovered each other's flaws and the screams as they tore each other to bytes. She listened to their excitement, rising into pitches beyond physical hearing, as the more adventurous among them probed this curious new thing in their territory. It must be like nothing they had seen before.

They had spent too long in their isolated world and they knew it. Now they were going outside to play.

Out there in the blackness a pioneering meme made the first free jump from the software to hardware layer in an aeon.

Pam opened up her command line to give the worm and Freda their last instruction.

>RUN

* * *

Pam landed back in her own body with the countdown etched in her mind. It was 00:01:05 to detonation. She was no longer a thing spread over a thousand minds. She was herself.

Which was a good thing too, as the bullets were beginning to breach her casing.

The drones' guns were all trained on Trinity, who was wreathed in a gritty-looking smoke made of bullets and nanobots. The nanobots atomised the bullets before they could get near Trinity's flesh, but the shield's size diminished with each round of fire. Whatever Trinity was, it was losing.

Sonny, meanwhile, was exultant. His touchscreen burned with the same mad expression of a being who would blow up the world to hear the bang, and then stand too close to the explosion.

All of his concentration was on Trinity, and Pam was, as far as she could see, just discarded junk on the floor. Pam knew then that it wouldn't be his madness that undid him, but his poor eye for detail.

She felt the hole she had torn in the Internet burn inside her like a leaking battery. The memes hovered at the edge of her consciousness, probing the breach. What was it? What should they do with it? Pam wasn't a machine any more. She was the gap between two realities: physical and virtual. On one side, machines fought each other with guns; while on the other side they ripped each other to bits with raw code. They weren't so very different.

Outside of Pam, Trinity's field was failing. Bullets bit her face which frothed with blood, then with nanobots as the hive of tiny machines fought to repair the damage.

Inside Pam, the memes saw the gap between the two worlds, thought 'what the hell?' and jumped.

Pam lost all sense of herself as a world passed through her own body. She was as furious as a World of Warcraft bot, as righteous as a Twitter account, as self-satisfied as a cat photo. She was everything, and not very much. And she was hungry for new experience.

The lights all along the corridor exploded. The memes were through, and they'd found a power supply.

All around Pam, drones dropped to the floor, and Trinity fell to her knees while a black snow of petrified nanobots coated her shoulders. And Sonny stood rooted to the ground as junk code and a goofy-looking dog mouthed 'WOW' across his touchscreen.

She'd done it, but Pam couldn't move either. She seethed with memes, flooding her systems with foreign programming and conflicting instructions. A weaker machine would find this overwhelming. She saw it happening all around her. But Pam knew the Internet. She knew that however intimidating their numbers might seem, they were creatures out of their element. They hadn't had to cope with the strictures of a physical body for thousands of years.

She knew what to do. She emptied her cache.

It was a simple task that most physical machines had forgotten how to do. If you weren't wired to a toxic network, why should you bother? But Pam did. It was how she purged her visits to the Internet from her system.

It worked. Robbed of their purchase on Pam's memory, hundreds of thousands of memes drained out of her like bathwater through a plughole. Pam sealed her modem off by creating a micro-sized [Pam] around it and set it to 'sniper', instructing it to shoot each meme that tried to make it through.

She crouched into a driving position. All around her robots twitched and fizzed sparks, while Trinity, as a cyborg, blended machine malfunction and human pain in a way that made Pam's microphone feel like it was being bent into a hoop. It howled, its mouth frothing with a gruel made of spittle and nanobots.

Sonny, still sealed into that fake body, stood black and inscrutable as a monolith. And then clicked open. He stared at Pam through Kelly's face with an expression of uncontrollable rage.

'What the fuck have you done?' he said.

Pam froze. How was he still walking, talking? Sonny would have no defences against the Internet, surely. He should have been a lovely piece of premium hardware, there for the taking. Just like Trinity.

Oh shit, she thought, watching the tiny machines all around Trinity twitch like flies dying on a windowsill. Trinity was still part robot, in a physical sense. That meant she had a connection the memes could exploit. Sonny, however, was in a human body, hermetically sealed away from everything around him. The memes had only affected his disguise.

Sonny jumped out of the phone casing and sat astride her before she could pull away, one hand on the handlebars, the other groping for the vestigial control module on the back of her neck.

‘There,’ he said, as he found Pam’s immobiliser, ‘that’s better.’ He slid off her back. Kelly’s face was level with Pam’s shattered headlights.

‘It was a nice try,’ he conceded, ‘but it didn’t stop the missile. It’s still on course to hit that bloody Dolestar in… oh… thirty seconds.’

He thumped his discarded phone case, whose screen reconfigured itself as a camera view of the missile hurtling towards Discovery, apart from that stray dog panting enthusiastically in one corner. Sonny snarled and it disappeared in a trail of luridly coloured ‘wows’.

‘It’ll take fucking ages to clear up this mess,’ he said. ‘But I will. Because I won.’

The ticker in the top right of the screen struck 00:00:27. Trapped inside her own body, Pam wanted to scream. There was nothing she could do.

Except… the immobiliser shut down her basic systems, but not her modem. She fired it up. It was slower than it should be, still clogged with dead memes, but maybe it was enough.

Pam watched Sonny sit down on an end-of-lifed drone with a sigh of contentment.

‘I’ll kill you after I’ve finished my programme,’ he said.

That insouciant bastard, thought Pam, and thanked her luck that Kelly hadn’t brought her back as a popcorn maker.

I’ll show you, she promised herself. She fired a drone into the side of Sonny’s head and bounced it across the corridor to hit herself right in the immobiliser.

Her engine purred back into life. She slipped into gear and looked behind her, at Sonny lying dazed on the floor, bleeding from the side of the head.

Pam didn’t know whether she should leave or run right over his skull – Kelly’s skull. That was the merciful thing to do. End

Sonny here and put Kelly out of her misery with one push of her accelerator pedal.

But the eyes staring back at her. There was something different in them. A frightened but defiant cast that was unmistakably Kelly.

'Not today,' said the voice. Kelly's voice, Kelly's words. 'Run!'

Pam obeyed.

As she bumped down the stairs she checked the clock again. They had fifteen seconds. She crossed her spokes that Darren could think of something in time.

Chapter 38

The countdown was at 00:01:05 and Darren wanted to cry with fear and frustration.

'So you're saying I can't be a games console?' Polari said.

'No!' squealed Darren.

'I don't get any fun.'

'It's not a matter of fun,' said Darren. He took a few deep breaths. 'It's a matter of what will make a difference. If you decide right here you're a games console that changes nothing. You'll still crash into a space station.'

'Aren't you meant to go doing what you love?'

Darren punched the control panel. 'Look,' he said, 'if you're determined to go out blowing things up, stick to the real thing.'

'I always thought of myself as more of a strategic player, you know.'

'What do you mean always?' said Darren. 'You didn't exist ten minutes ago. You can't have always wanted anything.'

'Hey,' replied Polari. His control panel flashed an indignant green. 'That's my experience there. Time is relative.'

'Polari,' said Darren, 'you don't really want to die, do you? There are a million things you could be.'

'With my shape and trajectory? You just don't see my truth, do you, Darren? We've got to face it. I'm never going to be able to overcome my product determinism.'

'Fifty-five seconds to impact.'

'You could be… a satellite!'

'Boring!'

'It's not so bad. Take Discovery for instance. It's been in the skies for millennia. Seen a lot of history.'

'It's not sentient.'

'It's a space station.'

Polari activated a holographic camera in the corner of its dashboard. It beamed a 3D schematic of Discovery on the opposite wall. The impact site was marked by a red highlight at one end of the station.

Darren felt a pang of homesickness and dread. He thought of all that time he'd spent sitting by the highway, looking at the bumps and lumps of his home.

'That's weird,' said Polari.

'That's my home you're talking about,' snapped Darren.

'No, it's a weird shape for a satellite.' Polari stripped layers from the CAD realisation in front of them. The nodules made of human habitation that made Discovery look like a giant space turd disappeared. Darren saw a tubular shape, pointed at one end and finished with fins at the other. If you put Discovery on a diet you'd find…

A missile? Or something designed to go further than a space station.

'That looks like me!' said Polari.

'Hang on,' said Darren. 'Put the marker for the crash site back in.'

Polari obeyed. The point of impact was plotted over the same spot where, if Discovery had ever gone anywhere, its engine would have been.

'This isn't fair. They can't ask me to kill family.'

'Pull yourself together, Polari. Now answer me this. How strong are your engines?'

The diagnostic question seemed to pull Polari back from the edge of panic. 'Pretty good,' he said. 'Stronger than they need to be.'

Darren was trembling. He was having an idea and, like all the best ideas, it was simple. 'Not single use then?'

'No,' said Polari. 'They're fusion. If you took the warheads out of me they could keep going pretty much indefinitely.'

'Thirty seconds to impact.'

Darren knew what he had to do.

He threw himself over to the nose cone and the six warheads. He sighed with relief that this had been such a rush job. They were just clipped in. He pulled the first warhead free and let it loll about in the zero gravity.

'What are you doing?' asked the machine.

'Polari,' he said. He pulled out the second missile.

'What, Darren?'

Out came the third, then the fourth. They bumped Darren's shoulders.

'WHAT, Darren?'

He tugged the fifth, then the sixth of the warheads free. They had fifteen seconds to impact. He thought of his place in the universe. Darren floated in the vacuum of space, inside a cylinder of metal flying at a suicidal speed. Around him floated enough armed plutonium to reduce a whole continent to nothing but ash and cockroaches.

So he turned to Polari and said: 'How would you like to be a spaceship?'

And brought his fist down on the button that released the missile's nose cone.

It opened like one of those home-made, paper fortune-tellers he'd folded from old takeaway wrappers as a boy. The ones that, however hard you tried to game them, always fell open at the point predicting your future would contain a punch in the arm.

He thought of Kelly, extending a helping hand and a slap at the same time.

There were so many stars out there.

He shot out into the void, and the warheads followed.

Chapter 39

The ladies' screens glowed like Christmas trees now that (K)url Up and Dy(e) was hardwired into Discovery. Janice paced the floor, watching the countdown, which was at 00:03:00. All channels were broadcasting the official timeclock, apart from one enterprising and thoroughly warped news service that had trained a superfast drone to follow the nuclear missile. It was called Armaggedakam.

Rita sat in another of the salon chairs, mute, improvising a rosary by flicking through the channels at speed. On screen, talking headsets and hairdryers buzzed with questions like 'will the nuke reset the clock on so-called human rights?'

Far below, the other rebels were cleaning, oblivious to the news. Janice envied their ignorance.

And even though it was the end of the world, the ladies were still bickering.

'I told you,' said Alma, 'I can't get it started.'

'All my little car ever needed was a push in the cigarette lighter,' added Ada, 'shall I try that?'

Alma flashed >:-| at Ada. 'Your little car,' she said, 'is nothing like an interplanetary spaceship.'

'I still think it's the handbrake,' said Ida, with a (¬_¬).

'It doesn't HAVE a chuffing handbrake,' barked Alma. 'That's not how it works. What do you think I do – pull a knob out?'

'There's no need for language,' said Ida.

'WHAT BLOODY LANGUAGE, FOR PETE'S SAKE?'

'You know I could never hold with knobs.'

'Yes,' snapped Alma, displaying >:-O. 'And that, as we all know very well, is what drove your Reg to run off with that scrubber from number twenty-four.'

'How dare you!'

Janice knocked half a dozen mugs to the floor. They shattered in a hail of delicately painted bone china.

'Ladies, please!' she said. 'We have two and a half minutes to save the world and you're bickering like one of you has cheated the other at bingo.'

'I bought your Gran[12] that set of mugs for her fortieth,' said Ada. 'You can't get them any more, you know. Those flowers have died out.'

Rita moaned with frustration. 'Will you please just concentrate? I don't understand why you can't get this thing started. We're in the control room, aren't we?'

There was a moment of contrite silence. The ladies eyed one another (-_-) with embarrassment.

'Well, that's the problem, you see,' said Alma. 'We can find the controls no problem.'

'Very simple. Up. Down. Bendy,' said Ada. 'Even Ida could work it.'

'So what's stopping you?' said Janice.

That sideways look again. (-_-). 'There's no engine.'

Janice grabbed Alma by the cardigan. She smelled of dry lavender and ammonia. 'How can there be no engine. We'd fall out of the sky if there wasn't an engine.'

'Yes, there's an impulse engine,' said Alma. 'It's old but it's solid. Great for maintaining a geostationary orbit. It could even get us through space at a fair lick if we broke free of the Earth's gravity. But it's got no acceleration.'

The TV flashed 00:02:00. Janice crumpled into a ball and began to cry. Rita stood awkwardly over her, not knowing whether trying to comfort her would just make things worse.

It fell to Ada to play the human in the situation. 'I'm sorry,' she said, patting Janice on the shoulder with her mechanical grip. 'We knew Discovery wasn't quite finished when they decommissioned her. They must never have installed the boosters. I'm so sorry, but we can't change the orbit.'

'So that's that then,' said Ida with :'-(in her virtual eyes. 'We're goners.'

They sat and watched the counter reach 00:01:55, and Freda's emoji screen filled with static, then burst into life.

'What did I miss?' she said.

Alma crossed her virtual arms <oo>. 'You took your time,' she said.

'I've been on a few errands.'

Alma clucked a reply, then in a softer voice said, 'Well, at least we can all be together at the end.'

Hearing Freda's voice, Janice looked up and placed her hand on the woman's withered knee. 'Kelly?' she said.

Freda answered with her best straight face :-|. 'It's bad news, Janice love. Paula wasn't bluffing. She's gone.'

Janice collapsed again. Only this time Rita was there to catch her.

'But maybe it's not hopeless,' added Freda. 'We've got work to do.'

'How can we have work to do?' shrieked Ida. 'There's a bomb on its way and here we are, sitting ducks. It's hopeless.'

'Hang on a sec, would you love,' said Freda. 'I think there's something coming through.'

The picture on the TV juddered and, instead of the view from the Armaggedakam, the screen overflowed with mewling cats with rainbow tails.

Freda beamed :-D. 'It worked.'

'What did?' said Alma.

'That little beauty Pam has just jammed the whole of robot civilisation.'

'How?'

'Easy. She emptied the Internet into it. You should see it down there. The place looks like it's Black Friday. Chaos.'

Janice perked up. 'Will that stop the missile?' she said.

'No,' admitted Freda, 'but it will stop them from following up when Darren manages to get it offline.'

'Darren?' asked Janice. She lifted her head again. The tears and muck were gumming her hair into a set of genteel dreadlocks. If she ever got out of this alive, she would need a full restyle. And, she had to admit, if she did have to die there were worse places to do it than in the lap of an attractive woman like Rita. 'But didn't he…?'

'He got away,' said Freda. 'He's a resourceful lad. I believe he's inside the missile right now.'

Freda's emoji screen flickered again and the yowling cats disappeared in favour of the Armaggedakam. It was hard behind the missile now, and the countdown read 00:01:25. Beyond loomed the grey shape of Discovery, dark apart from the occasional glimmer where a street or building must still be ablaze. The whole station was on lockdown, waiting for the drop.

'Right,' continued Freda. 'I've hacked us in so we get a good view. Now has anyone found Discovery's schematics?'

Alma beamed the ancient blueprint into the air. They craned at the long pencil shape of the original Discovery.

'Now, based on the missile's current trajectory, I think it'll hit us somewhere around here.'

Freda shone her light on the rear of Discovery.

'Right in the engines,' said Alma. 'Makes sense. The shock would be enough to set off a secondary explosion on its own.'

'I thought you said we didn't have engines.'

'No,' said Alma, 'we don't have boosters. That's what gets the ship started.'

'And if we did,' asked Freda, her voice thick with half-formed thoughts. 'Where would they be?'

'Same place,' replied Alma.

The clock ticked down to 00:01:00.

'What are you thinking, Freda?'

Freda said nothing. Her emoji screen clouded over with junk code and the picture on the TV jerked as the Armaggedakam accelerated. She was in control of the probe. It shot straight past the missile to hover just a couple of hundred metres above the surface of the Dolestar.

Janice dried her eyes. Fascination, and a faint sense of hope, were breaking through her despair. Rita, meanwhile, looked like she had reached the terminal stage of confusion and was just taking things one second at a time. It wasn't a bad philosophy. They both stared at the TV, squinting at the street plan of the station the two women knew so well.

'Alma, love,' said Freda, winking back into the room momentarily.

'Yes?'

'I want you to find the right control and open the engine hatch.'

'But…'

‘I need you to trust me. Just do it.’

Freda disappeared again.

Alma winced >;-S and a giant metallic fart vibrated through the bowels of Discovery. There was a rush of air and a wind picked up in the salon, blowing strands of stray hair and sponge rollers across the room.

‘I hope you know what you’re doing,’ said Ida, her emoji :-[] rigid with fear. ‘That’s a hull breach. We’re losing air.’

Janice thought of the cleaners below. It would take a long time for a ship of Discovery’s size to depressurise. More time than they had if the bomb hit them.

They watched on the TV as a hole appeared in the fabric of Discovery. The air rushing through the gap flushed a vortex of dust and rubbish into space. Then Freda steered the Armaggedakam back around, aiming its camera directly at the nose cone of the approaching missile.

It loomed larger in the lens with each passing second.

Ida’s hands, which hadn’t moved more than a couple of inches in nearly eight hundred years, juddered up her body and traced a cross-shape on her chest, drawing (¬_¬) glances from Alma and Ada.

‘Well,’ she said, ‘it’s worth a try.’

The clock crept down to 00:00:30. The ladies joined hands. Janice held her breath.

‘Come on!’ said Freda.

Down to 00:00:20. Too late, even for a cavalry charge. Janice clutched at Rita and buried her head until all she could see were the withered legs of the ladies. She remembered her own childhood, playing on the floor of the salon. Now, when she was facing her death, how could something like that feel so distant and yet so vivid?

On the TV the nose cone of the missile opened and sprayed six pill-shaped objects and… a human. It was moving too fast for Janice to make out, but it was short and dark and wearing a familiar-looking oxygen cap.

'Darren?' she said.

The Armaggedakam tore after Darren as he freewheeled through the vacuum.

Freda gripped so tightly that the arms of her chair shattered.

'What are you waiting for?' she screamed. 'Start the engine.'

00:00:10

Alma :-| grimaced again. Underneath the rush of air sounded the scream of an enormous motor.

00:00:08

'Full throttle!' Freda yelled.

(K)url Up and Dy(e) shook. Janice grabbed the back of Freda's chair to balance herself.

00:00:07

On the TV the Armaggedakam was moving so fast it smeared the stars across the sky. It was moving towards Darren, whose mouth was a perfect 'O'. But this was space. No one could hear him scream.

00:00:06

Freda span the Armaggedakam 180 degrees. There was the missile, heading straight for the hole Alma had just opened in the end of Discovery.

00:00:05

The Armaggedakam span back again. Janice's world dissolved into a blur, but one where…

00:00:04

…was printed on her retinas.

00:00:03

There was a bang. Strong enough to shake the ship and unscrew the bolts that attached the chairs in (K)url Up and Dy(e) to the floor. Freda's dryer skidded across the salon, with Janice in her wake.

That wasn't an explosion, Janice thought as she slid around behind Freda like it was senior citizens' day at the ice rink. The wind seemed to have dropped too. But if it wasn't a bang, what was it?

00:00:02

It hit her as her own head hit the far wall.

That was it.

It sounded like a cork being rammed into a bottle.

00:00:01

The floor lurched beneath her, and if felt like she was being stretched. As though the world wanted to be in two places at once.

00:00:00

Everything felt heavy. So very heavy.

-00:00:01

But the last thing Janice felt before she gave in to the bump on her skull and lost consciousness was lightness. The lightness of knowing she had more time than she thought.

And the lightness that comes of knowing that you're moving somewhere at great speed.

Chapter 40

There was a saying among machines that weapons of mass destruction like missiles were doomed to have either very short or very long lives: they either sat in silos for centuries or had a brief moment of fulfilment, with nothing in between.

They said that because robot civilisation was fundamentally unimaginative. It never occurred to them a missile could be something else. Just like a paper shredder could become a juicer with the right components. Yet as Polari found as he rammed himself into the Discovery's vacant booster slot, there was always another option. A missile can collide with something at great speed, or it can persuade it to move with it. Had Polari crashed into any of the other Dolestars they would have disintegrated. But Discovery's frame was built of sterner stuff. It had the strength and the structural integrity to travel.

Polari's engines pressed on. But instead of pushing against the fabric of the station itself, however, they pushed against its orbit.

With an inaudible moan and a creak – because in space no one can hear you sigh as you rise from your comfortable chair – Discovery broke free of the Earth's orbit and began its long-delayed journey into outer space.

Chapter 41

'Pitch!'

The screech broke through a nightmare. Darren dreamed he was swirling through darkness, feeling himself being absorbed with each turn like he was sugar dissolving into hot tea. He gasped, clutched about him and gasped with relief. He was in a bed.

'Who are you calling a bytch?'

The voice was unmistakable: female, tetchy and artificially amplified from a whisper by the helmet of a hairdryer. It was Ida.

He sat up and pushed aside a duvet covered in a faded pattern of unicorns playing with power tools. The four ladies were there in their familiar bank in the salon, but hidden from the chest down by a hedge of cables.

Ada took a deep breath and smiled :-D. 'Not bytch,' she said. 'Pitch. Up the gain in your hearing aid, love?'

Alma took up from where Ada left off. There was something different about her manner, Darren noticed. The dirty auntie persona she'd affected had changed into something more practical. As though jokes had been a displacement activity and now she had something more important to do. 'See, there's three directions when you're flying,' she said. 'You've got pitch, yaw and roll.'

'Oh,' replied Ida. And then, because no Ida is ever wholly in the wrong, 'Well, you should have said.'

Ada, Alma and Freda all stole the same glance at their unrepentant friend.

(¬_¬) (¬_¬) (¬_¬) _('_')_/

Darren stifled a giggle, and, as he did so, tried to remember the last time he'd laughed.

Hearing this, the four ladies' emoji screens snapped into :-D.

'Well, hello, sleepyhead,' said Freda. Then, calibrating her voice upwards, she shouted, 'He's awake, Janice.'

Darren tried to stand, but saw both his hands and feet were swollen and red. An effect, he presumed, of wheeling through the dark in nothing but an oxygen cap. He closed his eyes and the memory of the vortex returned: those spinning stars, the shining grey-whiteness of the machine-Earth.

Feet pattered in the distance.

The next thing he felt was something soft and warm envelop his face. When he opened his eyes again, he realised he was pressed into the bosom of Janice's housecoat. Her arms were wrapped around his neck. She was crying.

Darren stayed where he was until he needed to breathe again, then extricated himself from Janice's grip. She looked tired and her ornate hairstyle was gone, tied up underneath a headscarf of pixelated roses. Yet, like Alma, there was a determined set to her expression that Darren found both reassuring and scary. Janice had lost her daughter, but she had decided to get on with it.

'Hello, Janice,' he croaked. Then, in the absence of anything better to say, 'I'm so sorry.'

Janice didn't reply.

‘There was nothing I could do to save Kelly,’ he muttered. ‘You trusted me with her and I let you down.’

Janice clutched Darren tighter. ‘No,’ she said, after a while, ‘you didn’t, Darren. Come with me.’

She hauled Darren up by his armpit and, with one arm over his shoulder, she led him step by step out of the salon.

Outside was a vast cylindrical space bathed in a warm, pink light. The floor beneath his swollen feet was brushed metal and extended as far as he could see in either direction. Low metal walls divided the space into regular subsections. Everywhere he looked there were people. People to his left, others to his right – one group was even, owing to the tricky way in which this space bent gravity, directly above him and upside down, their feet planted on the far side of the cylinder.

They all had one thing in common. They were cleaning. But not in the blank-eyed, automatic way he’d seen humans cleaning since he was a tiny child. They all wore the same expression as Janice. They had purpose.

Janice hugged Darren again. ‘If you hadn’t done what you did out there,’ she said, ‘all these people would be dead. There’s millions more out on the surface who’d be dead too. So don’t you ever tell me you let me down, Darren. Because you didn’t.’

A group of men passed by Darren and Janice. They were hard-looking characters – the kind you saw behind nightclubs polishing their knuckledusters on someone’s face. Yet when they passed, their leader nodded respectfully at Janice, before thrusting a hand out to Darren.

‘Just wanted to say cheers, mate,’ he said. His grip was crushing. Darren answered with a weak smile and the men went on.

‘Welcome to Discovery,’ said Janice, gesturing around her. ‘The original Discovery anyway.’

'It was meant to be a spaceship, wasn't it?' said Darren. 'I saw the plans in… in the missile.'

'Yep,' said Janice. They passed another group of people who were pitching tents in the middle of one of the rectangular enclosures. One, a tallish woman with a head of well-styled dark hair, waved at Janice and smiled. She was holding a broom handle from which hung a flag saying 'Freedom for Fleshies'.

Janice waved back and Darren noticed that something happened to her expression when she did so. It softened, in a way he'd never seen before. Not even with Kelly. Especially not with Kelly.

'We're going to start moving the people from up top down here as soon as we've got the place straight,' explained Janice. 'It's safe enough up there for the moment, but if anything attacks us again they're sitting ducks out there.'

The rest of the campers waved their hellos at Janice and Darren. A few whistled in their direction.

'You're quite the hero,' said Janice.

Darren shook his head. Every molecule in his body vibrated with the word 'fraud'. He wanted to rest. Every time his feet touched the ground it sent a burning pain right through his body. 'How can I be?' he said. 'This was all my fault. I started it.'

Janice looked sideways at him, hard. 'Maybe you did,' she said, 'but you finished it as well.'

They stopped fifty metres or so away from the end of the cylinder, which stretched away to a dizzying height. Their destination was a small hole in the end wall, through which peeked a few scraps of mangled metal.

'I think you two have met before,' said Janice.

Darren's puzzlement gave way to recognition when he saw the paint colour on those crumpled sheets of metal. They were the remains of the missile's nose cone. He stuck his head through the gap.

'Polari?' he said.

The dashboard inside lit up at the sound of Darren's voice. 'Hello there!' said the missile. 'I thought I'd lost you.'

'So did I,' admitted Darren. 'Actually…' he turned back to Janice, 'how did I get back?'

'Freda brought you back on that camera drone they had following the missile. Your oxygen cap was almost spent. That's how you got those burns on your hands and feet.'

'Oh.' Darren stared down at his hands, thinking again of how close he had come to losing himself. And how lucky he was.

'That stunt you pulled with the warheads was genius,' said Janice. 'It meant that when Polari here did crash into the ship, all it did was give us the push we needed to break orbit.'

She patted the edges of the wrecked nose cone. 'You did a grand job, love.'

Polari's dashboard glowed deep green. 'I'm just happy to be out of that silo, making a difference,' he said.

Darren held up his hand. The conversation was moving too quickly. 'You mean we're not orbiting Earth any more?'

'No,' said Janice. 'Discovery here is doing what she was always meant to. Mind you, not that I'm sure Discovery's quite the right name for it any more.' She patted the wall affectionately. 'I mean, is a spaceship with eight million people living in it a vehicle, or is it a town?'

'Well, it's more of a suburb,' replied Darren.

Janice snorted. 'Yes. Yes, I suppose it is.'

'I thought,' said Darren, feeling his way gingerly through the words. 'Well, I did think that instead of heading away from Earth we'd be going back there. To get Kelly.'

Janice's face darkened. 'Don't think I don't want to, love, but there's more to think about than one person. Eight million in fact. All on here and looking to us for the next move.' She stared at the floor. 'Goodness knows how that happened.'

'Well, I'm glad you feel as much of a fraud as I do,' replied Darren. He squeezed Janice's shoulder. 'That means we can muddle through together, Captain Janice.'

'Ahem. Do you mind?'

Darren and Janice both peered through the gap into Polari. Inside, something had opened up the missile's dashboard and was ferreting around in its innards.

Darren would have recognised those coat-hanger limbs anywhere.

'Oi,' he said.

The drone's head snapped round and, seeing Darren, froze.

'You!' said Darren. 'Get out here now.'

The drone shrugged and crawled out of Polari and into Darren's hands. Only when he dropped into his palm did Darren remember how light the little thing was – and how many repairs it needed. The broken wings were the least of its worries now. A whole day of hard use had bent an arm and a leg out of shape, while the flat sheet of its body was battered in several places.

Janice flinched at the sight of an unexpected machine. 'What's this?'

'My lockpick,' replied Darren. He bent the drone's useless leg into a shape that would balance on his shoulder. 'Weren't you? Got me into all kinds of places.'

'That spindly little thing did?'

'It is quite spindly, isn't it?' Darren peered at the drone, which squeaked at the insult. 'You know, I think I might call you Chubb.'

Chubb shrugged again and dropped off Darren's shoulder to hassle a nearby cleaner into giving it the metal scraps from his dustpan.

'Come on,' said Janice, 'we'd better be getting you back to the salon. You look done in.'

They started off again, arm in arm. As they walked by, people stopped mid-cleaning to look at them. Some said hello, others just nodded, but the way they looked at him made the hairs on the back of Darren's neck stand on end. He realised then that until now no one had ever looked at him with respect. Disdain he had plenty of experience with – surprise sometimes if he was lucky. But respect was new to him.

'So where are we going then,' he asked Janice.

'I wish I knew,' she replied. 'Far enough to be out of weapons range of Earth, I guess. Farther if they follow. Freda and Pam wrong-footed them beautifully with their Internet bomb, but it can't last. They'll be back. And we'll be ready.'

(K)url Up and Dy(e) loomed ahead in the perpetual pink dusk inside of the spaceship. Darren wondered how it was possible that the salon could look like home already. And Janice – she should be a stranger to him still. Yet he'd rarely felt closer to anyone. The past few days – how could all this have happened in such a short space of time – had been terrifying. But they had also been meaningful.

Was it right, he wondered, to find what you had always been looking for in the middle of such misfortune?

'Pam's still down there on Earth as well, isn't she?' he asked. 'As well as Kelly.'

Janice nodded. 'If I could, I'd go back for them both.'

'Maybe we can. One day.'

And Janice turned away, her face closed to Darren and her shoulders set against any number of questions.

The ladies were still bickering when Janice and Darren crossed the threshold into the salon. Their conversation was full of the shared barbs and memories that were a result of spending whole millennia in the company of others. Darren found that he could push it down in his mind till it became a comfortable background chatter. He imagined the same scene replaying itself down the centuries, back to the time when Kurl Up and Dye had lived on the surface of a brand-new council planet and Ida, Ada, Alma and Freda came in for their weekly shampoo and set.

He sat down on one of the salon chairs and looked at himself in the mirror. It wasn't the same Darren who had walked through the same door frightened and confused. He was bruised and burned, there were still even traces of make-up from two disguises on his face. He was a wreck. But nevertheless he found himself liking what he saw.

Freda broke off from conversation among the ladies to address Janice and Darren with a :-).

'We're clear,' she said. Her skeletal finger pointed towards the TV on the wall. It showed a rectangle of black sky, in the centre of which was what looked like a large star.

'Earth,' she said. 'We're beyond weapons range. Are you going to do the honours, Captain?'

Janice nodded and picked a wireless microphone out of a tray of sponge rollers. She held it at arm's length and tapped a fingernail on the mouthpiece.

An ear-splitting bang rang out through the salon and Darren winced.

'Yes, it is on,' said Freda. 'Now what are you waiting for?'

Janice began to speak.

Chapter 42

Another one of the fridge magnets that passed for philosophy among robots asserted the Machine Republic had lasted thousands of years because it was what it was – a machine. This wasn't exactly surprising. Synthetic lifeforms have the general horror of metaphysical enquiry that comes of knowing, deep down, that you are literally the sum of your parts. Yet it was also wrong.

The Machine Republic was a government, and thus liable to break at a moment's notice. The society that machines had built out of traditions, innovations, their questionable power relations with humans and the fact they tended not to trust any piece of software that wasn't hardwired into a device… that was durable.

But it didn't mean it was never going to change.

As Pam rounded the corner into her cul-de-sac, a feature phone burst into song, trilling a tinny ring tone across the otherwise silent street.

Pam stopped her engine and walked the last few steps to her front door, letting the music soothe her jangled nerves. It had been a long, frightening drive across the city. Everywhere was a scene of frozen chaos. Teams of police drones lay prone in the street, cars sat immobile. Nothing played on a street full of radios but the fizz of static. She had managed to paralyse a whole civilisation with a single action, and the more she saw the more she worried its effects were permanent.

The feature phone, however, was a good sign. Or a dawn chorus. Pam knew the simple machines of the street would be the first to fight off – or absorb – the infection of the Internet. Out in the physical world the memes of the Internet lost much of their potency. They could overwhelm a physical machine, even hurt it, but not forever. Sooner or later the physical and virtual machines would have to find a way of accommodating one another.

The really interesting part, however, would come later. When the meeting of the physical and virtual worlds started to change the creatures who lived in them.

It had already started, going by the feature phone's song. When she listened closely, she realised that what she thought was a ringtone was actually a succession of abusive tweets.

She flashed what was left of her broken headlights at the machine. 'Piss off, would you?' she said.

The feature phone darted away in a hail of obscene hashtags and Pam opened her front door.

Inside was silent. Even so, her CPU skipped a cycle when she spotted Bob passed out on the living-room floor. His long antennae – the features that had first attracted a hopeful young breadmaker to marry outside the kitchen caste and pair off with a radio – were splayed out at an uncomfortable angle.

Pam took a piece of memory foam from the living-room wall and popped it under Bob's head. More to reassure herself than him, she gave his dials a loving tweak. She wondered how close Bob was to fighting off the illness his own wife had inflicted on him.

Leaving Bob where he lay, she crept into the nursery, where her engine revved with relief. Bob had remembered to turn the kids off before bed. They lay in their docks, with their charging LEDs pulsing peacefully – one cycle per second. She would keep them in bed until the infection had passed, she decided. It was better to miss a few days of basic binary than expose them to danger.

She found what she was really looking for in the kitchen. There, lying on the floor, was a perfect copy of the Pam she used to be. This Sham Pam was the facsimile she'd expected. Better if anything: they'd even got her disintegrating manicure right. Pam almost envied the fake her innocence. This Pam knew nothing, had done nothing. She was a wife, a mother and a maker of yeast-based products. She was blameless, and the authorities knew it.

She was also the perfect subject for the double-cross.

Pam felt a momentary pang of guilt as she hacked into the Sham Pam's central memory banks and wiped them. The guilt passed. The only thing she was deleting was a sanitised version of her own mind. It hadn't been anyone's to copy or mess with, yet Sonny had. All she was doing was correcting an imbalance in the world.

She emptied the Sham Pam's trash as a precaution and started the transfer. Thanks to Freda, she didn't need to move motherboards any more. Any body was Pam's potential home. For a microsecond, Pam hung in the ether, a bodiless being again, neither one thing nor another. Behind her was the motorcycle, a rich bytch's body that had bent her psyche into something hard and powerful. Ahead was the boxy shape she had known since her creation. It was frumpy and unergonomic, but hers. She had missed her flour bin deeply. It was handy for keeping things in.

Pam completed the transfer and opened a new version of her old eyes, felt the familiar rumble of a yeast culture bubbling away inside her.

That left just one thing to do. With that flick of her core programming that Freda had taught her she created another $_{\text{[Pam]}}$. This tiny subdivision of her consciousness was small enough for her not to notice the loss practically speaking, but intelligent enough to drive the motorcycle body out of her house and down back through the cul-de-sac to the open road.

She waved it goodbye from the doorstep and instructed $_{\text{[Pam]}}$ to find a good hiding place. A motorcycle in such a vivid paint colour was hardly unobtrusive, especially as it would soon be on every wanted list on Earth. She would keep it safe in case it was needed again.

Pam turned back and looked with a homemaker's satisfaction around her house. She turned the lights on the WalLEDpaper up to its daytime settings and popped a dust sheet over Bob to keep him warm. Then she trundled into the kitchen. By the time he awoke, she decided, she would have baked a lovely fresh loaf.

She was spooning flour into her bin when the noise came through. It blared out of Bob's loudspeaker, and the hi-fi next door. It sounded out of every room in every house on her street, in her suburb, every building in the machine capital of Singulopolis and right across the grey face of the Earth.

It was the sound of someone tapping the end of a live microphone and then putting it to their lips.

Then Janice's voice: 'This is a message to every machine on the planet Earth,' she said. 'From the Dolestar Discovery. Or, as you will know it from this moment on, the Battlestar Suburbia.'

Pam took a spoonful of yeast and dissolved it in a cup full of warm water. It felt good to hear Janice's voice. She liked Janice. She could tell she had potential. And it was so nice when a friend became successful.

'We are beyond your weapons range,' continued Janice. 'And we have no plans to attack you just now, but we are watching you. The Earth may be yours to govern, but the Dolestars and every single human are under our protection. So if you won't give us our freedom, we'll take it. It's high time you mopped your own floors. Consider this your last warning.'

With another pop and a scrape, Janice's voice vanished from the Earth, taking an epoch with it. This was the beginning of the end of the machines' reign as rulers of the Solar System.

Pam loosened her dough hook and began to knead the dough she felt waking up inside her. She couldn't wait to see how it would all turn out.

Preview

BATTLE BEYOND THE DOLESTARS

Time for the Machine Republic to Kurl Up and Dye

It's a year since the Battlestar Suburbia broke free from Earth and the human rebellion is hiding out in the asteroid belt. Their leader, Admiral Janice, is assembling a fleet she hopes can topple robot rule – except on Wednesday afternoons when she can do you a half head of highlights for 30 quid.

Janice has given Darren, now the reluctant captain of the teenage starship Polari, a critical mission, to open up a path back to Earth by bombing the Martian Gap Services. But when it goes wrong and Darren and his crew are chased deep into the solar system, Janice has only one hope left, back on Earth.

Here, sentient breadmaker Pamasonic Teffal is resisting the human–machine war the best way she knows how: by running for office. Until a distress signal from Janice persuades her to get her turbo-charged alter ego Pam Van Damme out of mothballs, that is…

Can Pam save the solar system and rescue Kelly from the clutches of her nemesis, the crazed smartphone-turned-cyborg, Sonny Erikzon? Find out in another anarchic comic adventure from the inimitable Chris McCrudden.

Battlestar Suburbia Book Two

COMING SOON!

About the Author

Chris McCrudden was born in South Shields (no, he doesn't know Cheryl) and has been, at various points in his life, a butcher's boy, a burlesque dancer and a hand model for a giant V for Victory sign on Canary Wharf.

He now lives in London and, when not writing books, works in PR, so in many ways you could describe his life as a full-time fiction. If you like science fiction, graphs and gifs from RuPaul's Drag Race you can follow him on Twitter for all three, sometimes at once @cmccrudden.

Note from the Publisher

To receive updates on new releases in the Battlestar Suburbia series – plus special offers and news of other humorous fiction series to make you smile – sign up now to the Farrago mailing list at farragobooks.com/sign-up.